YVONNE PAYNE enjoys a duel l
Kritsa, a village in Crete, G
Human Resources (HR) cont
sun that inspired her to write
letters.

Secondary school strean
classes did not feature on Yvonne's timetable, despite her
being an avid reader, and author of eagerly awaited, hand
written, serialised stories for classmates. Leaving school at
sixteen Yvonne worked in retail – a move that eventually led
to her writing company newsletters and training materials,
which subsequently launched her successful HR career.

As a regular contributor to Crete related forums, which
included sharing children's stories based on observations of
Cretan village life, Yvonne finally decided that the time was
right to tackle a novel. With bins full of crumpled paper,
Yvonne realised the adage: 'Write what you know' was the
answer. So she started to research the true story of a Kritsa
lass who, in 1823, participated in a fierce battle against
Ottoman oppression. Research into tales of Kritsotopoula
(Girl of Kritsa), plus firsthand experience of Cretan food,
customs, mountain hiking, and donkey trekking, delivered
the inspiration for Yvonne's first novel: *Kritsotopoula –
Girl of Kritsa.*

PRAISE FOR *KRITSOTOPOULA*

Yvonne has to be commended for the amount of research she has undertaken to give authenticity to life in a Cretan village in the 1820's and under Turkish rule. Unfortunately the acts of barbarism that Yvonne attributes to the Turks are true.

Her vivid descriptions of village life and the battles, along with her sensitive portrayal of the innermost thoughts of her central character are both moving and believable.

Rodanthe is depicted as a young and innocent girl until the atrocities she witnesses by the Turks both hurt and harden her.

As relatives and friends lose their lives her desire for revenge and freedom from the Turkish yoke knows no bounds. Masquerading as a young boy, she joins the rebels and moves across the area of Lassithi with them, sharing in their rough life and exploits.

She plays a leading role as a spy and decoy as well as taking a stand beside the men in battle.

Rodanthe was a real person and is acclaimed a heroine in Kritsa. Yvonne has made a very plausible story of her life and this is a very readable book.

BERYL DARBY, AUTHOR OF *YANNIS*

Kritsotopoula
Girl of Kritsa

YVONNE PAYNE

SilverWood

Published in 2015 by SilverWood Books

SilverWood Books Ltd
30 Queen Charlotte Street, Bristol, BS1 4HJ
www.silverwoodbooks.co.uk

ISBN 978-1-78132-265-9 (paperback)
ISBN 978-1-78132-266-6 (ebook)

British Library Cataloguing in Publication Data
A CIP catalogue record for this book is available from
the British Library

Set in Sabon and Trajan Pro by SilverWood Books
Printed on responsibly sourced paper

To all Κριτσοτεσ (Kritsa folk) past, present and future

Key Locations in this Story

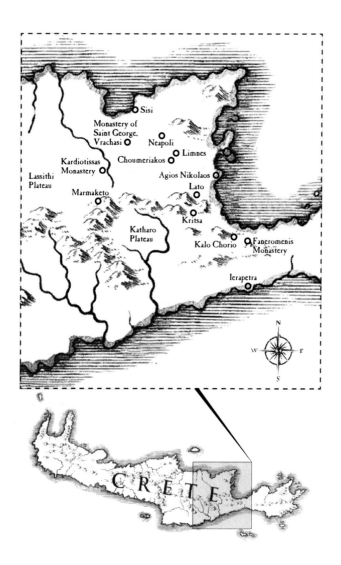

PART 1

RODANTHE

1

LOST!

Am I dead? No; if I were, I'd not suffer this agony: bright red lights of pain piercing absolute blackness. I'll be dead soon. I'd open my eyes but the effort is too much. I'll sleep. I must be awake but it's barely light. Oh, the pain, how can I bear it? How odd, I'm in a chapel. Perhaps I am dead. The Panagia has such a kind face. Ah, if I'm face to face with the mother of God I must be dead. I can't be, the pain is too real.

'Panagia Mou, Mother of God, help me!'

Ferocious barking across the forest clearing brought Thea to the low arched rock entrance of her cave in time to see a lone rider race through driving rain. With practised care, Thea hid herself. Despite the steep gradient, the horse bolted, its hooves slipping in thick mud. It seemed the man was unused to riding for he grasped his mount awkwardly around its neck, not realising the trailing reins bumping its flank encouraged it onwards. When the rider fell, landing heavily like a sack of olives dropped from a cart, the horse didn't alter its stride. Thea waited, fighting her instinct to offer aid. The inquisitive dog reached the prone body to sniff urgently without provoking a reaction. Still cautious, the woman crept to the body and pushed her dog away.

'Good girl, let me see. Let's hope he's dead, it will be less trouble.'

Apart from the pelting rain, the forest glade was quiet as Thea timidly reached across the slight man to haul him on his back. Her action opened his cloak to expose green woollen britches, a fine white cotton blouse with a traditional second blouse peeking through, and an amazing yellow silk waistcoat. With a gasp, Thea sat back on her heels, amazed to see a young woman, her long hair trailing in a muddy puddle.

'Well, well, you are a surprise, my pretty goldfinch. Who are you running from I wonder?'

The nearest place to hide the girl was the chapel just a few paces away, so Thea dragged her to the entrance. Due to excessive rain, the wooden door was swollen and stiff on its hinges. After resting the girl on the ground, Thea forced the door wide enough to pull her unwieldy load into the dry chapel. Instead of tending the girl, Thea abandoned her in a muddy heap, picked up her twig broom, and returned to the indented blood-streaked mud where the girl had fallen. She scratched over the viscous surface, and then dragged the broom behind her as she walked backwards to the chapel to erase the incriminating trail. Once inside the tiny, bare chapel, the only place to give shelter was behind the iconostasis at the rear. Glancing up at the icon just inside the door, Thea spoke to it from habit.

'Panagia, I need you to watch over Goldfinch. We've heard some dreadful stories in our time, but never had a delivery like this. Oh, listen to that dog, she sounds distressed. Please guard the girl and give me courage, Panagia.'

Instead of leaving the chapel via its door, Thea wriggled through a low gap in the rocks next to where the mysterious girl lay, and then dropped into a cavern below the chapel. Using a well-worn route, she dashed through the cave complex, passing a storage area to enter her vaulted living chamber. Her dog crouched in the cave entrance, growling with its hackles raised, watching a mud splattered mare walk slowly into the clearing to drink from the pool. Keen to keep the dog away from the horse, Thea picked up a worn rope fixed to a rusty hook lodged in the cave wall, and made a loop to slip over the dog's head. This action woke two puppies sleeping by the fire, and, as they scampered to suckle their dam, Thea touched the dog's head lightly to reassure it, then nervously walked to the horse.

Swallowing hard, Thea picked up the trailing reins and led the mare to the far side of the clearing, where she worked quickly to remove the saddle, saddlebags, and a long-barrelled rifle. With her heart pounding, Thea dashed to drop her haul in the cave entrance. It disappointed Thea that the horse had not run off, so she flapped her apron at it while making hissing noises, not realising the unperturbed beast had trained for the din of battle. Now drenched to the skin, Thea took the mare's reins in one hand and led her downhill until she rounded a bend. With her free hand, Thea searched her apron pocket for the stones she kept there to aim at goat heels when they needed to move along a track. Thea dropped the reins to let the horse pass, giving it a hard slap on the rump. It trotted away, not galloping until the hail of well-aimed stones stung its rear.

Confident the torrential rain would wash away telltale hoofprints, Thea hurried back to pass a rocky overhang where a solitary hen fed on easy pickings from the sodden ground. With a reluctant sigh Thea called the tame bird to her, and with expert hands snapped its neck without noticing two feathers flutter into the mud. After stomping over the embers of her fire, Thea couldn't think of anything else she could do to hide her presence, so with a whispered prayer that her goats would stay out of sight, she went back through the tunnels.

'Someone has treated you cruelly, little Goldfinch. My Panagia has donated a couple of precious wax candles to give us the best possible light. You'll need to give thanks that the saturated ground cushioned your fall. If the mud were sun baked, you'd undoubtedly have worse injuries than a few broken ribs. You could have done without that horse's kick to your head. I'll have to stitch that gash.' Maintaining her soothing chatter, Thea discovered bruises on the girl's arms, a badly swollen ankle, chaffed wrists, probably from tight bindings, and a nasty ragged cut that narrowly missed the artery in her left wrist. Thea decided her priorities were the girl's head and her cut wrist.

To create suitable thread for sutures, Thea made a nick in the hem of the bright waistcoat and drew out lengths of silk to use in her single precious needle, left as an offering to the Panagia years ago. Before stitching the head wound, Thea cut away a patch of hair for a clearer view. To tend broken ribs, Thea removed the girl's clothing and created a bundle, leaving the extremely long cummerbund to one side. When she struggled to remove the girl's swollen foot from its boot, her action brought forth pitiful cries of pain. Her ministrations complete, Thea spoke directly to the icon.

'Keep watch again, Panagia, I need to go back.' Then she scooped up the discarded clothes. 'I'll hide these, Panagia. Shame I can't make use of them, they look so warm. I'll take the boots later.'

Had the girl been conscious she'd have marvelled at how the woman apparently disappeared into the rocks without trace. Once in her storage area, Thea opened the cedar trunk to remove a length of soft cotton, last used as swaddling when she was a babe. It was clean, despite its musty smell.

On her return, Thea called, 'I'm back, Goldfinch', and then addressed the icon. 'Now, Panagia, please keep her from waking, as I'm bound to cause hurt. Do you see how this swaddling makes excellent binding for broken ribs?' Leaning back to admire her handiwork, Thea noticed the discarded silk waistcoat. 'Here, Goldfinch, have your bright plumage. I'll rest it across your shoulders to stop the cloak chaffing.'

The girl snarled, 'Touch me again and I'll kill you!'

Thea recoiled in shock, then realised the aggressive girl spoke while unconscious, so she soothed her with, 'Hush, you're safe with the Panagia.'

None of the eight men whipping horses along the track from the pasha's stronghold at Choumeriakos had previously used this route towards the mountains, so they had no knowledge of the small stone chapel in the clearing where paths diverged. If by chance they'd heard tales of miracles performed by the worn icon of the Panagia resting on her niche just inside the chapel door, they'd not have given the superstitious Christian nonsense a second thought. However, they would have been interested to know a terrified woman watched their approach.

Each man was so keen to prove worthy of a place in the entourage of their new pasha, who commanded Crete on behalf of the sultan in Constantinople, that they disregarded all personal risk to gallop uphill through treacly mud, following close behind their furious leader. A crossroads caused the party to halt where plane and walnut trees gave way to sparse shrubs. The animals' foaming mouths and heaving flanks gave the watching woman evidence of their exertion, while raised voices and conflicting arm gestures illustrated disagreement among the group of riders.

Despite her rain blurred vision and the hooded cloaks covering each rider, the woman knew they were Turks; no one else had such fine beasts. She guessed their quarry, and weighed up what to do. Should she let events play out, or walk into the clearing to share what she knew? Fate took over when her three goats sprang down the cliff, and her dog dashed out to take up a snarling, defensive stance. Two geldings reared. They pranced backwards to jostle a mare; its rider fell. Two men dropped from their mounts and dragged their fallen comrade clear of flailing hooves, and another caught the agitated horse. One Turk rode at the dog, and swung his long curved sabre in a low arc to sever its head. With a jubilant shout, as if he'd outwitted a great foe, he used his bloodied blade to flick the head into bushes. In horror the woman gagged, then chewed her knuckles to swallow her scream. Three uphill riders stopped in their tracks, and one raised his hand to signal that they should not rush back. Once satisfied that this was not a rebel ambush, he reluctantly returned.

On one side of the clearing, water seeped from a rocky overhang to form a pool, and, in some distant time, someone had dragged stone blocks to form seats around it. With a flash of inspiration, the woman realised that it was an obvious place to take the injured man, and once there the Turks were far less likely to notice the chapel. It was time to take control, so she adjusted her hood over her face, leant on her stick, and stepped forward.

'What a dreadful tumble, My Lord. I heard your shoulder break. Come to the pool, and I'll bind you to ease your pain.'

As two men lifted the injured one and followed her, the woman masked her sigh of relief. 'That's right, My Lords, gently now. Let him rest here.' The men accepted a woman taking control of an injured man without question. This woman took a small, rusty blade from her belt and cut a strip from her muddy skirt, made of discarded sacks, to make a rough sling. Satisfied she could do no more, she then pointed downhill and tried to tell the injured man he should return to the garrison to find a physician.

Two men walked away from the group to hold a whispered discussion, then one approached the woman and surprised her by speaking in the local dialect. 'Thank you, Grandma. My friend, Jerez, is fortunate that you were here. Is this where you live?'

'Oh no, My Lord. Those three goats sheltering in the cave entrance are mine. I just follow them as they graze, and they generally find somewhere we can shelter. I've slept there for three nights now. When the rain clears, I'll move on.' The man found it difficult to understand all he heard. It was as if the woman's mouth didn't fully open, but he caught enough to interpret for the others.

A man a few paces away thumbed his moustache and spoke. When the woman failed to respond to him, he grabbed her close and yanked her head cruelly backwards. Her hood fell away. The man recoiled in revulsion and flung her down. Instinctively, she pulled her hood over her dreadful, scarred non-human face, and then curled up to expose the least possible amount of her body to the anticipated angry kicks.

'I'm not a leper, My Lord. My face was burnt.' With one side of her face squashed in the mud, the woman saw the two small chicken feathers within her reach and hid them in her muddied palm. Without noticing her sleight of hand, her tormentor strode away, leaving her in a trembling heap. Astonished that the pasha had left her, his men gladly responded to his command to follow him.

This left the kinder man, who prodded the woman with his foot, perhaps not quite trusting that she was clean. 'Sorry, Grandma, our pasha's treatment is poor thanks for your aid.' He opened his woollen rucksack, and, ignoring the rain dripping from his hood, used a gentle, cajoling tone.

'Here, I have a barley rusk. Join me, sit on these rocks.' The woman shuffled over to sit a respectful distance from him. She was grateful for the opportunity to dip her hand in the pool to clean away some mud, and with it the feathers. As the man sorted through his traditional Cretan rucksack to find the rusk, the woman's single eye followed his hand in hungry anticipation.

'Here, take this. Who passed by in these rainy days?' He recognised the hunched silent woman didn't trust him, not even when he pushed a rusk towards her. 'Come now, you've seen how hot headed my pasha can be. We must find a young girl before she comes to harm. He's worried sick. Please tell me, have you seen a girl? She's probably frightened, lost, and alone.'

After a pause, the woman answered, 'She wasn't alone.'

With a frown, the man turned to the now mounted pasha, and passed on the information to earn a barked reply. He turned back to Thea. 'My pasha is very worried. It sounds like rebels have her. How many did you see?'

Enveloped by her hood, the crone's querulous voice stated, 'I saw an onion.'

'Take it, and this apple too. Now, tell me about the girl.'

'Who is she?'

'The pasha took her as his bride. When he became ill, she disappeared. She'll be terrified.'

'She didn't seem frightened, just wet. A large man rode a donkey and a younger man a decrepit horse.'

'What else?' The man tried to keep the impatience out of his voice. 'Did you notice anything else?'

'The younger man had a beautiful waistcoat the bright colour of a goldfinch's flash. The girl sat behind him, and clung tightly. I thought it strange that she should laugh when getting so wet. Perhaps it was her sweetheart.'

The man didn't want to be the messenger of such news;

the girl's escape had disgraced the troop, and for it to have been accomplished by only two rebels was unpardonable. Inspired, he said to the pasha, 'You were right, she has passed here. She's with a band of brigands. At least six, all armed with guns and one carrying a scimitar. This woman says one of them wore a yellow waistcoat. They headed to the mountains. Shall we?'

Irritated at the news, the pasha shook his head. 'This rain has washed all traces away, so we'll not track them. Besides, we can't be sure how many days lead they have.' In a loud, sneering voice, designed to instil fear in his subordinates, he continued, 'Your failed commander will never rest in paradise. He should have listened to the words of the Prophet Muhammad, peace be upon Him. He reminded us of the perils of strong drink and lust. Now I'm pasha I'll administer devoutly, as Allah wills.' His warning delivered, he turned his horse downhill.

As if part of the rock, the woman waited until she reckoned the troop must be half way to their garrison. Then, with the knot of fear still in her stomach, she rushed to the chapel to find the swollen door so wedged that she needed to barge against it. At her third attempt, the ancient wood split in two. One piece fell inside with a clatter and almost knocked the icon from its ledge. Kneeling on the plank, Thea thanked the Panagia for safe delivery.

The Panagia is beside me. How does She leave the icon? I must be behind the iconostasis, so the Turks must have left me here to spite the pappas. Argh, why do they drag me? My ribs are on fire, I cannot breathe. Each bump is torture. I must die.

As Thea tended her patient, she kept up her routine chatter with the Panagia. 'It's too risky to leave our Goldfinch behind the iconostasis, in case women pass by to leave their offerings to you, Panagia. See how this poor child writhes in pain and screams in fear. She confuses me with whoever did her harm. She's taken some sedative, Panagia, so now I'll sit by you in the doorway and try to rid my knee of its large splinter. It must have got there when I knelt on the broken chapel door to pray. Ah, that's better, I can see the splinter. I'll dig it out with my needle. At least this piece of door provides a warmer seat than the stone floor. Now, Panagia, I must hide Goldfinch. Do you have any ideas? Although there's no way I can get her through the drop behind the iconostasis, my cave is certainly the safest place for her. Ouch! Oh, now I've dropped my needle.'

Thea lifted the plank to search for her needle. Inexplicably, the icon fell with a clatter.

'Argh! Oh, it's you, Panagia. What a fright! I'm just going to fetch my rope to drag this plank away. Did you want a ride?' As Thea returned the icon to its ledge she had a grin on her twisted face, not realising what a hard task she'd accepted.

It took Thea all morning to move the unconscious girl to the small cavern beneath the chapel. She'd used the long cummerbund to bind Goldfinch to the plank, and then dragged her out of the chapel, up to the cave, and through the tunnels to rest directly below the iconostasis. Now Goldfinch slept on a mattress of hessian sacks stuffed with last year's dried leaves, herbs, and grasses. Distressed at the girl's agony, Thea spooned a herbal sedative into the resisting mouth, an action that brought an angry, 'No! I'll not taste your damned Turk food.'

'Hush. Don't fight me, Goldfinch, it's to heal you.'

The girl spat. 'I'll die before I taste it, and kill you if you force me.'

With a weary smile, Thea wiped sweat from Goldfinch's

brow, and reflected on the marked difference between the girl's fevered rambling in the rough dialect of peasants and her rich clothes of rank. Aware that there would be no resolution to the mystery until the broken body healed, Thea warily resumed spooning sedative into the girl's resistant mouth.

What is this place? I've not been afraid of the dark since schoolboys locked me in the cupboard. They soon let me out when Brother Dimitris threatened them with a long mulberry stick. Argh, such agony. Panagia Mou, how shall I bear it?

The next morning, as Thea swept the chapel, she heard Goldfinch's fevered ramblings from below, and realised that any chapel visitor would also overhear. 'Listen, Panagia. She sounds like a tortured soul in Hades. I hope my draught soothes her before she scares benefactors away. What do you make of those strange swirls on her hands and feet? I can't wipe them off. There she goes again. I'll try to distract her with chicken broth. I killed my hen to hide signs of domesticity, otherwise the Turks might have guessed it was a good place to hide our girl.' Confident her voice would carry through rock fissures, Thea called, 'I'm coming, Goldfinch. Don't be alarmed, the Panagia watches you.'

With her clogs tapping out her progress through the cave complex, and closely followed by two boisterous puppies, Thea carried a bowl of steaming broth and two precious tin spoons. 'Are you awake, Goldfinch?' The girl groaned at Thea's light touch. 'Good, your fever is down.'

'Where am I? Who are you?'

'My name is Thea. I've been taking care of you since you fell from your horse.'

Obviously confused, the girl asked, 'Why was I on a horse? How long have I been here?'

'Four days. Don't worry, the men think you are far away. What's your name?'

'Men? My name is…Oh, I don't remember.'

'Never mind, I call you Goldfinch.' Her guest slipped unconscious, leaving Thea to eat alone.

Has Papa found Mama? It was my fault she was murdered. Will God forgive me? That evil man found a rose with stronger barbs than he imagined. Now I must kill that bastard, Omar.

With a rush of compassion Thea leant forward to kiss Goldfinch, and then crooned a long forgotten lullaby.

No singing! Sorry, Roula, you were right. My singing was arrogant. I was angry. Who are they to stop us singing? Now it's as if I murdered Mama with a song.

The next time Thea checked on her patient, the girl stirred, and tried unsuccessfully to rise.

'Will you release me?'

With a chuckle, Thea replied, 'You're not captive. You've broken ribs so I bound your chest with swaddling bands. I wound your cummerbund around you and a plank to keep you still. I'll remove it now.'

'Where are my clothes?'

'They had to come off. I needed to see your wounds. Mud brushed off your cloak, which acted as your blanket. Everything else was so mired they'll need a wash. Here, to prove you're no captive, take your silver knife. It was tucked in your cummerbund.'

The girl's hand trembled as she took the blade. 'This is

odd. I'm sat in the near dark with a hooded figure, but I feel safe. Thank you, and I'm sorry for taking your bed.'

'You haven't. I sleep on a ledge by the fire near the front of the cave. We need to be quiet, sound travels up to the chapel.' As she listened, the girl tentatively touched her bristly scalp, and Thea answered the unasked question. 'Sorry, I cut a patch of hair to see your wound. It needed stitches, like your wrist.'

The girl hardly glanced at her cut wrist, and, as if to divert attention, said, 'When can I leave?'

'Oh, not for weeks. Your ribs will heal in their own time. Rest now, and I'll prepare supper.'

After a fragrant pot of thin chicken broth with dry rusks of bread, Thea encouraged the two boisterous puppies to stay in the bedchamber as a distraction for her patient. Three days later, Thea stooped to clean up after an 'accident' that triggered a thought.

'Goldfinch, I've just realised you've not moved your bowels all the time you've been here. I'll find green figs to make you a laxative, and if that doesn't work I'll visit a quarry to beg some explosive black powder.' Instantly slack jawed, the girl gawped at Thea. Full of concern, Thea asked, 'Why does that alarm you?'

Goldfinch laughed so hard it hurt her broken ribs. An attempt to speak through hysterical laughter brought the excited puppies to jump up playfully. Each time the girl tried to explain the cause, laughter took over until tears streamed down her face and hiccoughs left her gasping. Eventually, the girl fell back exhausted. Once she regained her breath, she explained.

'Black powder reminds me of childhood. Before I was born, Turks took most churches for mosques or stables, although they left the one near our house where my papa is the pappas. One of my earliest memories is of Papa being distraught when the *aga* demanded his church bell because Turks needed metal. Papa thought it was just another way of demoralising Christians a week before Easter, but Turks hadn't reckoned on the ingenuity of Grandpa and his friends! They used stolen black powder in the hills above the village to tell God we'd not forgotten Easter.'

Intrigued, Thea sat next to the girl. 'Go on.'

'Covert whispers alerted us to an Easter Sunday miracle due at dusk. Mama took me to our flat roof and held me close, then pointed out a puff of smoke blossoming from the cliffs. Seconds later a boom, louder than thunder, made us scream. With the blast echoing around the hillside, shock waves moved the ground beneath our feet like an earthquake. By the time the second explosion rang out everyone in Kritsa was watching. Loud cheers welcomed each of the next six clouds of smoke, then fell silent in anticipation of the explosion.

'It was fun. The Turks thought themselves under attack. The *aga*, our local ruler who'd been with one of his wives, ran into the street wearing only a sheet. It was over before any officer mustered a force, so Christian folk shouted, "Christ has risen!" and hurried home. Embarrassed, Turks just melted away. The best joke is that it has happened every Easter Sunday evening since then. Although troops try to catch them, the culprits choose a different site each year.'

Thea stroked the girl's face. 'Perhaps more memories will return. Now I must go out. We've no rusks left, so I hope to have snared a hare in one of my traps.'

'You're so generous, Thea. A Turk would say I ate the camel and all it carried!'

'Camel?'

With a rare smile, the girl said, 'It's a giant pack animal, used by Turks in other lands. I heard that saying as a child, but it wasn't until I went to school that I saw a picture of one.'

Over their meal of boiled greens with snails but no hare, Thea asked, 'Does your scowl indicate pain, or are your thoughts far away?'

Still frowning, the girl said, 'At home, I started each breakfast by saying the saint's day. I've lost track now. It must be late January. It was a point of honour to get it right, but some annual festivals move in line with moon phases so I can remember crying in frustration when I got it wrong. It helped me at school though.'

Delighted to learn more of her unusual visitor, Thea asked, 'Does your papa still have a church?'

'Yes, it's dedicated to Afentis Christos, the Transfiguration. Our bishop once paid a rare visit for our saints day service on the 6 August. I was inside polishing his special chair with beeswax when I heard him comment that the small church dominates the north of Kritsa. Well, the bishop echoed the words Papa used when proudly telling anyone with time to listen about the church, so I mistakenly thought Papa would be pleased with me. I stood and made a small curtsey, then, in the piping, self-confident voice of a ten-year-old, said, "Good morning, Your Eminence. This has been a parish church since Venetian rule." Oblivious to Papa's horror, I drew the bishop's attention to the bright frescoes, and my favourite one that Papa had told me was a portrait of the man who'd commissioned the wonderful work. With enthusiasm, I pointed out our icons – one of Saint George, and, of course, one of Christ at the highest point in the church. Without a pause for breath, I explained how Papa would like the evangelists too, but until each Christian had enough to eat, any spare coins were for communion bread. Papa made an exploding sound when I added, "Mama thinks it's the promise of a hunk of bread that gets people to the services." Under Papa's mortified stare, I felt my cheeks burn. The bishop smiled, and said,

"If this minx helps you in the parish I see why you still get a good congregation, despite the efforts of your Turk neighbours." Then I felt my papa's shame, and ran.'

Hopeful that the girl would keep talking, Thea said, 'Did you enjoy school?'

'Oh yes, especially mathematics. I remember one day Papa had made the long trek to the hilltop monastery housing our secret night school. If he'd come to bring news from home I'd have been so happy, but his purpose, as always, was to spend time with the abbot. My mentor, Brother Dimitris, lightly touched Papa's arm to stop him from walking past me. Now, I must admit to the sin of pride, because I enjoyed hearing Brother Dimitris tell Papa that I could calculate Easter dates, a feat beyond most boys. Full of anticipation, I hoped for a word of praise. Instead, Papa called over his shoulder, "Well, as long as she's not a disruption I'll be much obliged if you can keep her a while longer."

'When Brother Dimitris realised that I'd run off in tears it didn't take him long to find me. From my bed in the cramped space above the classroom, I heard the heavy door open. My tiny nook flooded with light for a few seconds until he closed the door. I sniffled quietly into my sleeve, and listened to his lesson preparations. At last he opened the door, and I shrank away from the shaft of bright sunlight. The monk spoke without turning. "Your papa is proud of you, even though he finds it hard to show it. I think it's because he carries the cares of the community on his shoulders." Behind the shut door I raged with childish anger, and shouted into the black silence, "Oh yes, the good pappas of Kritsa loves everyone but me!"'

Wary of the girl's emotion, Thea brought her back to the present. 'Let's free you from that board and I'll judge how your ribs are healing. Raise your arms, and I'll unwind the swaddling. Oh, the bruising is dreadful, but I can't feel any protruding ribs. Let me bind you again without the wooden support.' Ignoring the lack of response, Thea continued, 'Good job you're not a well endowed girl, I've squashed you flat. I've brought you a new white smock a woman once left as an offering to the Panagia. You will be warm enough if you wear your cloak on top. Now get comfortable and go to sleep. I'll stay with you.'

A hand clamped across Goldfinch's mouth to wake her. Thea breathed, 'Quiet!' Time froze. Sounds came through unseen rock channels. Someone, or something, was up there. Then, Thea realised what she heard. She squeezed Goldfinch's hand for reassurance. A woman groaned, as if stiffly rising from the floor, and then struck a tinderbox to light a candle.

'Oh Panagia Mou, what shall I do? Would you still watch for me if I bowed down? I don't have the stamina to go on.'

As anguished sobs resonated through the rocks, Thea pictured the woman prostrate in front of the icon. She relinquished her clutch on the girl's hand, and moved to sit against the rock wall, next to the shaft that led directly to the chapel. In her odd voice, Thea said, 'My Child, start from the beginning.'

First a low gasp and then a small cough, the sound someone makes when preparing to speak. 'Oh, Panagia Mou, shall I bow down and marry Abdul? I cook, I clean, and he relieves his needs with me. I sell my vegetables at market so cost him nothing. After the pasha's murder, the new man instructed their imam to insist on fundamental principles, so I must leave or marry Abdul. It would only be on the outside, I'd keep faith privately. This pasha has ordered the garrison to move to Neapoli, so if don't go with Abdul I'll need to move to Limnes, by the lakes with banished Christians.

'Panagia, small things can make a big difference. If only Jorgiakis had stout boots, my decision would be easy. Although my son is almost grown, his mind is still that of a child. He is good at working the land and carries our vegetables to market. Now he's outgrown his boots he stays barefoot, and keeps his boots on a thong around his waist. Abdul made him wooden clogs, but he refuses to wear them.'

'Give me his old boots.'

At Thea's odd command there were two shocked gasps, one above ground and one below, then silence. Thea sensed the woman gazing at the icon with devotion and hope, whereas Goldfinch thought she'd gone mad, even when the woman went outside to call her son and Thea risked a brief 'Trust me, stay quiet'.

'Here we are, Jorgiakis. That's right, kiss the Panagia. Now will you give those boots to the Panagia so she will hear your special prayers? You could tie them to the iconostasis. Come, I'll help you...Oh, Panagia Mou, how can I thank you? This is truly a miracle. Look, son, new boots...'

'Too big, Mama.'

'Let me test. No, they'll be fine, you're still growing.' The covert listeners recognised a ripping sound. 'Here, stuff the toes. My skirt was too long anyway.' The sound of satisfied stomping gave evidence of the boy's pleasure. 'Thank you, Panagia. I can't imagine how you did this. I'll never bow down. I'm sorry for even thinking of it. We have left you his old boots, and half of my basket contents of rusks, eggs, onions, and cabbage. Oh, Jorgiakis is off to test his new boots, so I'd better catch up with him. Goodbye, Panagia.'

When Thea was certain the woman had gone, she explained, 'I panicked when I heard her up there. After all I'd done to hide you, I was annoyed that I'd left your boots in sight. The Panagia must have sent us that boy.'

Sincerely, the girl said, 'You are like the Panagia herself to me, Thea, and such a quick thinker. Do many women come this way?'

'Not as many as in the past when women moved more freely. We used to have plenty to live on when offerings included candles, oil, wine, bread, eggs, and herbs. Sometimes women left clothing that Dora altered to fit us.' With a throaty chuckle, Thea added, 'I developed good speed, dashing to extinguish a candle before it burnt low. We even liked the smoky taste of rusks dipped in lamp oil.'

Being the daughter of the highly regarded first pappas of Kritsa coloured the girl's thinking, and she thought stealing offerings a terrible thing to do. Reading the judgement on the girl's face, Thea responded defensively.

'It's the thought behind an offering that is important. By the time I snuffed their candle or ate their rusk, God had already accepted the sacrifice.'

The girl might have found a counter argument but for her burning curiosity. 'Who's Dora?'

'My dear mama, who died years ago. Rest now. I'll go to collect our latest offerings, and then check my snares.'

When Thea triumphantly returned with a hare, she found Goldfinch sitting at the front of the cave. 'It's good to be in daylight again, you'll have to drag me from this seat. Can you tell me where I am?'

Sweeping her hand around, Thea said, 'This clearing must have formed generations ago.' Then she pointed. 'That is where you came from, up the track from Choumeriakos, and that herd path winds up to Lassithi, a plateau in the mountains.'

This brought another rare smile from the girl as she said, 'Grandpa takes his flock to Kathero Plateau, and can look down to Lassithi from there. What about that cobbled path?'

'It goes to Vrisses, a hamlet clinging to the cliff below the Krematon Monastery, named locally as the Hanging Monastery due its precarious position. Stay there, Goldfinch, and I'll sort this hare out before I join you by the fire.'

They sat together companionably, watching the flames, sipping herb tea, and listening to the stew's gentle bubbling. Eventually the girl initiated conversation. 'While underground I imagined I was dead. I wanted to be dead. This daylight makes me realise I must face up to living. You're good to me, Thea. Who are you?'

'I'll never know. As a babe, I suffered boiling water over my head. Someone brought me to die beneath the icon of the Panagia. Dora was an outcast, a tiny twisted form of a woman who nurtured the myth of the Panagia. From the cave beneath the chapel she heard a wounded animal.'

'But it was you?'

'Yes. She found me screaming in a reed basket, wrapped in soiled swaddling with only the remains of my head exposed. Dora didn't expect me to last the night, so every day after that she told me she loved me. I grew up with constant pain in the scar tissue. Much of my childhood is a sedated blur.'

'That sounds dreadful, Thea. How long have you been alone?'

In her odd mumble, Thea replied, 'Six summers. Sometimes I wish for death because I'm so lonely. Perhaps you'll stay?'

She looked quizzically at Goldfinch, but failed to get the desired response when the girl said, 'Let's decide when I'm well. How did Dora get here?'

'I'll always regret that I never asked. She didn't give birth to me, but in all ways she was my mama.'

'We all take our mamas for granted, until it's too late.' This statement was so full of fresh pain that Thea hoped to hear more. Instead, Goldfinch clenched her eyelids tight to trap her tears. 'I won't make the same mistake with you, Thea. Please know that I'm grateful for all you've done.' To accentuate her thanks she hugged Thea, then accidently knocked the woman's hood. The girl's hand flew to her mouth to stop her cry of revulsion, while Thea stared back, devastated. The remains of Thea's crushed face was a mass of livid scars and odd white lumps, as if someone had tipped molten candle wax over it. She was bald apart from the few wiry strands curled around a perfectly formed ear on the same side of the head as a perfect eye. In place of the other eye there was a swelling, half the size of a walnut, surrounded by an almost perfect circle of short hair, perhaps once an eyebrow.

Then Goldfinch did the most amazing thing: she kissed the repulsive face. 'You tended me as if you were my mama. I love you for it.'

The stunned woman touched where the girl had kissed her, and murmured, 'You kissed me. I love you for that.'

As if embarrassed, Goldfinch took a kindling stick to stir the pot, releasing the aroma of hare stew, and then asked, 'How did I get here?'

At the end of her proud account, Thea said, 'I managed to convince those Turks that phantom rescuers took you away. They'd curse to learn my Goldfinch was so close all the time.'

After bestowing another kiss, the girl smiled and said, 'Rodanthe. My name is Rodanthe.'

Not caring that her hood fell askew, Thea embraced the girl. 'I'm pleased to greet you, Rodanthe. We can relax while our supper cooks, so take your time, tell me your story. Start at a happy place.'

'I lifted his head high to expose the vital part of his throat. Then, I stuck my knife behind his jaw. In a continuous movement I drew my blade out through his throat to sever his jugular vein. Throughout my task I held my breath, and risked a covert glance at the man next to me. He pretended not to watch, but I felt his concentration. I knew his blade would flash if I made a mistake. The heart continued a few beats, pushing blood through the wound with a spurt. I was ready for it, and didn't flinch. The body slumped forward. The wound ceased to bleed, it was a swift and tidy kill. "Bravo Rodanthe," said Grandpa. I noted his smile, and the proud tone in his voice as he passed me his kerchief to mop my face. I tried hard to appear nonchalant – well, as nonchalant as a nearly eight-year-old can be when basking in glory. Grandpa took the warm body to place with all the others. Then he turned to my eight-year-old cousin, Manos. "Now it is your turn. Grab the lamb as I have shown you."'

A few seconds passed before Thea snorted with laughter. 'You had me there, Rodanthe. I hope all your stories are as good. What happened next?'

'Despite Grandpa's encouragement, Manos screamed in rage and vowed never to kill an animal. Disappointment showed on Grandpa's face, so he shrugged and sent us to find Grandma. We went to the women skinning a huge pile of lambs and goat kids. It was a revolting sight, and the bloody metallic tang in the air had attracted colossal numbers of flies. Through his tears, Manos explained the smell reminded him of the recent bloody Easter. It made him feel unwell, so I sat him by a tree and went to find Grandma, full of concern that he might be ill for a more sinister reason as there was an epidemic of bloody flux in the village. His ma, my aunt, was busy nursing her orphaned grandson Nikos, and my mama was tending Papa. This left our grandparents to care for us and assist the slaughter.

'Grandma found me, and before I could explain about Manos she grabbed hold of me, wrenched my head back, and demanded, "Did Grandpa let you use a knife?" I loved Grandpa. I trusted him absolutely, and knew without doubt that he adored me, so I lied, but the dried blood on my face gave us away. As Grandma roughly washed my head under a stream she direly stated it was time for me to spend more time with women rather than Grandpa and boys.'

When her laughter subsided, Thea commented, 'What a strange time to slaughter.'

'There were terrible events that Easter. Turks demanded a crushing levy, including spring lambs and goats.'

Keen to hear more, Thea said, 'Despite such things, I'd have loved a real family. Tell me about village life, and Manos. You smiled broadly at his name.'

2

INNOCENCE

Manos and I were like twins. Despite our very different natures, we were inseparable – well, except when we were on different sides of the donkey!

Dove was a beautiful grey beast, with long, soft ears that wriggled and twitched to show how much he enjoyed us giving the patch between them a good scratch. On top of a once colourful handwoven woollen rug sat a hard wooden saddle that Great Grandma never rode. Hung from either side of the saddle, tied on with stout ropes, were two long panniers almost touching the ground. Grandpa had made these huge baskets the way his pa had taught him, using strong, young olive sticks for the frame, woven with whip-like branches of mulberry.

Every morning, Great Grandma brought Dove down the narrow street, just wide enough for him and his panniers. She'd tap on the grille of the unglazed window of the house next door, and then repeat the action at our house, calling, 'Free rides to Rabbitsville.' Then we'd rush out of our respective doors, each wiping a milk moustache from our top lip with the back of our hand as we ran, vying to be the first to get a kiss as she swung us high into a pannier. What a way to view our world.

A feat of Great Grandma's was an ability to name every Christian in the village, so no matter which way she took us it was always slower than it might have been as she continuously stopped to say 'Hello'. Women fetched and carried all manner of things, like laundry, firewood, vegetables, or dishes of food with tantalising aromas, so they were always glad of an excuse to stop. Yet they chattered about boring things: weather, food, rabbits, dogs, husbands, children and Turks. They used strange theatrical whispers for their juiciest gossip, and we soon recognised when that was due. Both women would peer up and down the road, pat the top of their black kerchief, and then one would give a little cough. 'I'm not one to talk behind someone's back, but let me tell you about...'

The second woman would search in her apron to find us an apple, fig, carrot, rusk, or, if we were really lucky, cake. Then, pinching our cheeks, or worse still kissing them, to pretend she was only interested in us, she would say, 'Really?' Then they'd launch into a full description of the scandal. It was as if they thought us deaf once our mouths were full, as we knew about adulterous husbands, the three widows making a few immoral coins per week, the girls who were no better than they ought to be, and the latest family to bow down, although we didn't know what these terms meant.

It was such a struggle not to laugh as Manos mimed along to the gossiping women, moving his mouth and eyebrows in exaggerated shapes. Each woman wore a kerchief wound tightly around her head, across her nose, then tied in a knot at the back, leaving only her eyes peeping out. Despite their hidden faces, and the fact that they all dressed in black from head to toe in perpetual mourning, we immediately knew our own mama, aunt, or grandma.

Dove often took us on the 'Green Road', worn in the grass between trees as it meandered towards the hamlet of Pergiolikia at the top of Kritsa. This route meant leaving our long street of houses, each owned by a member of our family, to pass Papa's church. We swayed and jolted with each donkey step, laughing, chattering, and waving at everyone we passed. Dove took dainty steps down a narrow path to reach a lush meadow that overlooked the foot of the gorge, with a stand of carob trees along one edge. Here he knew his own mind and headed for shade, ignoring our indignant squeals when he took us too far into the branches. The tiny yellow flowers of carob released a cloying, heady scent, attracting bees in such number that I was frightened to pass beneath the buzzing boughs. Each summer the trees dripped green pods resembling bunches of long beans, but it was when they turned a rich brown colour, with a texture as hard as horn, we became interested in them. As teething babies, we'd chewed and sucked on them for hours to ease hot, sore gums, enjoying their sweet, rich taste. I took some home for Papa once, and he told me that some people called the pods locust beans, or Saint John's bread because they were all that sustained that holy man during forty long days and nights.

Sometimes Dove took the perilous steep track down to the cobbled road, and I longed to continue the journey on that winding road right down to the fishing port of Agios Nikolaos. Encased in our basket cocoon, this was a most painful route, and we soon knew to brace our knees against the sides to prevent bruised faces. Luckily, Dove knew to turn on to a dirt track to the church of Panagia Kera as soon as possible.

Most exciting was when Great Grandma turned right down our street and into the village. Dove ignored any cats, dogs, or chickens going about their particular business in the street as if they did not exist, and expertly stepped around rather than through heaped refuse. He never paused at the spring at the end of our street; instead, he plodded on at a steady pace downhill. We rode past the last Christian homes and businesses where we waved to all the grandmas queuing to put trays of food into the baker's oven, and marvelled at the knife maker with exciting blue sparks flashing from a knife held against his grinding wheel. Next was the cheerful carpenter, standing knee deep in piles of curvy wood shavings giving off the fresh scent of pine. I always wondered why he was so happy as he busily hammered nails into coffins. On the main road through the Turk quarter, we fell silent in awe. Here, big square homes with wooden balconies allowed men to stand outside their windows, as if walking on air. Beneath these balconies, traders shouted encouragements to enter at passers-by. Two waiters, each with clean aprons and fine tassels swinging from their fezzes, bowed then smiled their welcome, gesturing entrance to their rival coffee houses. Next was a butcher's, where a carcass swung from a hook in the ceiling, diligently watched by a cat willing the meat to fall. Then there were several shops selling all manner of things from soap to leather boots, and finally we passed the barber wielding his razor at a frothy face.

Depending on which side of the donkey we rode, we either saluted the guard outside of the aga's house, a long, low grey stone building taking up much of the main street, or waved to ducks on a pond, the centrepiece of his elaborate garden. Two of the aga's guards stood rigidly to attention outside of his front door, both resplendent in green pantaloons topped by a bright red jacket edged with gold braid, gold buttons, and a shiny green cummerbund excitingly stuffed with two silver handled guns. If the aga wished to sit in the shade of his ornate garden, a slave walked ahead of him to brush the path clean. Once in the garden, scented by roses and shaded by plane trees, he sat on a magnificent throne often chatting to the imam, or the *kardi*, the local administrator. Sometimes the overweight aga fed bread to ornamental ducks clustered noisily about his feet, unaware that he looked absurd in his flowing silk gown. Often Manos saved a crust just in case he had an opportunity to feed the ducks. Of course, Christian children were not permitted entry, so Great Grandma halted Dove as close to the garden gate as possible. Then, even if Manos's lob was not accurate, the ducks saw his action and jostled after the crumbs, squabbling loudly.

To avoid a large Turkish *kafenion* full of loud, brash off-duty troopers, Dove took an alley to the side of the garden, and when he clip-clopped down this passage the sound echoed under a small bridge. Where the alley and street met at the market place, we waved up at the harem. Even though the women were invisible to us, their voices drifted down from behind ornate latticework. Like beautiful caged birds, these women saw the world through grilles. Their restricted view took in the street where so many people bustled about, it matched Grandpa's description of the far off city called Megalo Kastro. Here in Kritsa, tradesmen carried their goods under the windows of the harem, with competitive shouts to describe their wares and encourage women of the household to send a servant or slave down to buy. The cries of the hawkers were so exciting. Sweet sellers offered rose flavoured *loukoumia*, crisp *halva* with pistachios, and baklava, a nutty honey-drenched pastry. Haberdashers had sheets our female cousins longed to add to their trousseau, and tinkers tunelessly rang their approach, their pots clinking as they walked.

Occasionally a more exotic merchant set out his stall of dyes, aromatic oils, and spices from the orient. He used tiny gold scales, so fine that they judged the worth of a single peppercorn, and to complete the transaction he used a flimsy twist of paper to encase the treasure. His elaborate flowing costume, woven with golden threads that shimmered despite the constant dust of travel, and his theatrical hand gestures drew lingering gazes to fingers bejewelled with rubies, emeralds, lapis lazuli, and turquoise. For crowning glory, his black silk turban sported three long blue and green feathers, set bobbing by his slightest movement, ensuring the wonderful 'eye' on the end of each one winked at the world. I coveted his silk slippers, the bright colour of new grass. Their long, pointed toes curled up towards his shins, then bounced like coiled springs. A giant towered over the merchant to guard the precious stock, his vigilance obvious. His pantaloons hid the bulk of his legs, while the sheer green fabric of his top blouse emphasised huge biceps. This goliath nonchalantly tapped his hand against the scabbard of his long, pointed sword, a subtle menace. Behind the merchant stood his grandson, a miniature replica of the guard, who used long fronds of palm to fan cool air over the trader, ensuring a constant tantalising aroma filled the air.

When Dove finally cleared the brash metropolitan rush, he turned right through a stand of eucalyptus trees, anxious for a taste of the clear water that had rushed down from the Katharo Plateau to fill the complex cisterns of the Kavousi Spring. One hot day as Dove drank, tipping us forward at an uncomfortable angle, I saw my papa walk past. I shouted 'Hello' and asked him to lift us out of the panniers so that we could drink. Deep in conversation with his deacon, Papa ignored us and walked along the path to the Church of Saint George by Kavousi, his long grey cassock sweeping the path behind him. This was so unlike the times when we met Manos's papa. He'd pick us up, one under each arm, and tickle our faces with his bristly moustache as he gave us both a loud kiss. To hide my disappointment, I teased my cousin that the clerics were off to feed a dragon kept behind the iconostasis in that church. I evilly told him it would eat one small boy called Manos every day until Saint George got to Kritsa to kill it, then laughed at the flash of alarm on his face.

One time, as we waited on the donkey for Great Grandma

to reach us at Kavousi Spring, there was a loud explosion from the fields below Kritsa that made Dove jittery. To calm the donkey, Manos used a soothing voice to tell the animal, with an authority passed on from his brother, the troops were practising with new grenades. Dove wiggled his ears as if interested, so Manos explained how each soldier flung a lit grenade, then ran in the opposite direction to take cover before it exploded. Another two explosions in quick succession were too much for the startled creature – he set off, fast. We bounced helplessly in the panniers as Dove sped along a cobbled track. I grinned at Manos in excitement, then laughed at his pale, terrified face.

High walls on either side of the track ended at a sentry box. Six soldiers sprawled under shady mulberry trees instead of being alert to unauthorised entry or exit to the village. Eventually the steep uphill gradient caused Dove to slow, and then he headed for a strip of inviting shade by a tiny chapel. When Dove disturbed a man and woman wrestling on a rug, the frightened animal shied and brayed. I thought the woman would be cross because the man tore her blouse then jumped up and dashed away. Instead, she directed her shrill anger towards Dove, until she saw us.

'What a joyous delivery for the Chapel of Saint Yorgos!' I gazed in awe, hypnotised by the deep blue eyes of a tall, beautiful angel. Her long golden hair shone like a halo, just like those around the heads of angels on icons, and it rippled down her back to hide her wings. Hot jealousy coursed through me as she stroked Manos on the cheek, then I laughed when she called him a pretty girl to bring a fast 'I'm a boy!' To my amazement, the angel lifted me out of my pannier and held me against her bare bosom, as if I were a baby. I stared into her angel face, enchanted by red shiny lips, and hoped she'd kiss me.

She cried, 'Delightful, twin boys, like peas in a pod.'

When Manos shouted, 'No, she's a girl!' my angel strangely commented, 'Even better, one of each will suit more customers.' Thrilled, I received her dainty kiss, enjoying how those delicious lips cast the scent of freesias and roses with no comparison to the loud, wet kisses planted by hairy-lipped aunts and grandmas!

Our magical interlude ended with Great Grandma's arrival. She gasped for breath, wiped her red, sweaty face on her apron, and then pushed stringy grey strands of hair under her skewed kerchief. She totally ignored my protests and wrenched me from my angel's arms to drop me in a pannier, accompanied by an incomprehensible tirade. Disturbed by Great Grandma's shouts, another angel appeared in the chapel doorway to call out at a young man who was bolting uphill. When Manos piped, 'Hello, Cousin Lukas' the youth didn't even wave. While Great Grandma led Dove downhill, Manos pulled unnecessary faces to indicate she was angry. I knew it would be a long morning if she remained irritated so I composed my first mantinade: a two-line poem that villagers create without second thought to express emotion. Triumphantly I sang:

'Up at Saint Yorgos an angel kissed my face,
And Cousin Lukas ran off at fast pace.'

Great Grandma made a strange 'harrumph' noise, followed by 'Fallen angel!' A few paces later, she sang:

'Keep your angel secret to earn a treat,
On this donkey you shall have a seat.'

Our route home was always steeply uphill, and with no room in the panniers we usually trudged behind Dove's rear as it swayed from side to side under its heavy load. One day, Manos had whispered, 'Look at those strange bushes waddling uphill, they ate Dove and Great Grandma.' We giggled and dropped our token amount, not that it mattered much since we habitually abandoned our load. Inquisitive, Manos would stoop to investigate the rustle of a lizard, a mewling nest of kittens, or an injured bird, and, of course, whatever he did, I did too. 'Angel Day' was so different. I felt like a queen riding aloft, spoilt only by Manos sitting rigidly behind me with sweaty hands tight on my waist.

*

Thea proved an excellent audience, and her questions enabled Rodanthe to relish long forgotten memories.

'Oh Rodanthe, I can picture the scene. Pass me that rag – look, I'm crying with laughter. Tell me, what did you collect when you were out with your great grandma?'

'We always took grass for the rabbits and greens for dinner. If we had been near Panagia Kera church, we also had olive twigs for goats, yucky cabbages, and, in the right season, almonds for biscuits. A trip to Kavousi Spring meant oranges and lemons for Grandma to make into refreshing juice, salted lemons for cooking, or delicious spoon sweets for the twelve days of Christmas.'

As Rodanthe drifted into a private reverie, Thea checked the stew and declared it ready to eat. Afterwards, Thea suggested they take a brief walk, and although Rodanthe leant on her friend's stick, the pain in her ankle soon had them back by the fire. With the prospect of a long evening, Thea was keen to hear more.

'Give me a glimpse of a really happy Christmas.'

3

TWELVE DAYS OF CHRISTMAS

The week before Christmas I was always on my best behaviour, and cheerfully completed tasks at home just in case impish goblins took up residence in our chimney early. Mama said goblins arrived at midnight on Christmas Eve, while we were all in church, and stayed until twelfth night. They are naughty, ugly creatures, anxious for an opportunity to spoil food and make a mess. They recognised a similar impishness in children, so if we behaved well the mischievous goblins copied us. It was important to keep a mid-winter fire in our grate, because if goblins were warm they didn't move about to cause trouble, so I happily fetched wood from Grandpa's store. Although I did try to be good, I trusted that the strange, hairy creatures would get the blame for any small misdemeanours so that I still had a faultless record when Saint Basil paid a visit on New Year's Eve.

In the run up to the food-filled holiday, all grandmas were busy cooking. They made *melomakarona* biscuits for Christmas day, with semolina, cinnamon, and cloves served drenched in honey, and *kourabiede* biscuits for New Year, scented with rosewater and sprinkled with powdered sugar. The delicious smells were tantalising, especially as we were only eating approved fasting foods, but no matter how we pestered the treats remained intact for the special days.

Just past our house there was a patch of flat land, worn hard and bare over the years, where our extended family

41

ate and socialised in warm weather. On that wonderful Christmas morning two pigs, each on their own spit over separate trench fires, already dripped fat to cause smoky sizzles. Our male relatives grouped around to make sure the pork cooked to perfection. I learnt each man needed a *raki* before turning a spit handle for the length of time it took the next man to quaff a drink, then, after a rest for another *raki*, he would feed wood into the fire, a task that required yet another drop of the potent colourless spirit. Papa sat forlornly at the edge of the group with an untouched *raki* in his hand, at odds with the festive atmosphere that buoyed the other men.

I joined my cousins to go carol singing, all enthusiastically banging triangles of metal to accompany our efforts. Although most women impatiently shooed us away with floury hands, men usually joined our reedy voices and then found us a coin. Of course, we squabbled about everything, from what to sing to where to go, and even whose turn it was to hold the money box, but at the final share out we had enough for all of us to anticipate a visit to the sweet seller.

On my return, a magical scene greeted me. Men had carried tables outside for older girls to cover with the best crochet or embroidered linen available. Every household produced plates, cups, spoons, jugs, pots, and tins to make sure that, today at least, no one needed to share. Each carefully set table had pots of wild flowers, and mounds of salads made from cabbage, greens, mallow flowers, plus fragrant herbs. Beside piles of bread, there were dishes of cucumber, garlic and mint dip, creamy goat's milk butter, jugs of orange juice, water, and wine. My mouth literally watered at the sight. A few cats hid under tables in clever anticipation of dropped scraps, but there were no women.

Confused I took the few steps to our house, where Mama greeted me cheerily. 'I was hoping you'd be back soon. Go and wash at the spring. When you get back you'll have a surprise.' That was all the bidding I needed. I ran, then halted in dismay at the long queue of children with similar instructions to wash. Some big girls were in charge, and, determined to do a thorough job, they used coarse cloths to rub us each in turn, bringing a bright rosiness to our cheeks and protests to our lips.

I ran through our doorway at full speed, then stopped mid-stride to gaze at my beautiful mama. She wore her fine wedding clothes, now kept for only special occasions. A white smock fell past her knees to cover her white cotton ankle-length pantaloons. At the back, red silk swathed her smock from her waist down, and a white apron, handwoven with red and black threads in a complex geometric pattern, covered the front. Her black jacket had delicate flower motifs traced in gold threads, evidence of her embroidery skills, and small splits set in the fabric at her wrists allowed the edge of the smock's long sleeves to create a frill. A black silk kerchief, edged with tiny coins from her dowry, was tied less severely than usual, allowing more of her face and a little of her glossy black hair to show. A wide red cummerbund and a necklace of coins gave the outfit a flourish. I was spellbound.

Pleased with my stunned admiration, Mama explained, 'Grandma commented on the unseasonably warm day and suggested we wear our finery', then she grabbed me unexpectedly. I squirmed to wriggle away as she made a fuss to check that I was indeed clean. 'Well, you're squeaky clean, so take a peek on my bed.' Imagine my delight to find a miniature replica of her outfit. Then, with Mama's hand in mine, I strutted proudly in the only complete set of new clothes I've ever owned. We walked self-consciously to the festivities, and although we noticed the men and boys with damp hair and clean shirts, we pretended to disdain their appreciative whistles.

Someone had sensibly decided that we'd sit in family groups, with each grandma making room on the table for her special *Christopsomo* – Christ's bread – made with flour, olive oil, eggs, fruits, and nuts, marked with a cross and then baked in a communal oven. The natural deference to the church meant we sat at the top table, and although the head of each family would bless their own bread before handing out slices liberally doused with honey, my papa was to say Grace, then bless and break our bread to signal the start of the meal.

Mama anxiously mouthed, 'Where's your papa?'

At first, his absence went unnoticed as each family group noisily greeted each other with lots of kisses that we children tried to avoid. As new arrivals sat down, women of their party poured drink, offered *mezes*, or moved seats to what they thought a more appropriate position. An expectant hush fell to make Mama's discomfort palpable as everyone's gaze turned to Papa's vacant seat. Various women came to whisper to Mama that their vegetables and pies were ready. Mama assured them he'd arrive soon. Finally, Manos's Grandpa Babis came to say huge trays were overflowing with fragrant pork so it would be a good idea to start serving. In the end, they agreed to wait five minutes.

A child noticed them first. 'Listen, I hear God singing.' It was Papa, of course. He proudly carried the large crucifix aloft and passionately sang out Christmas carols, followed by a rag tag ensemble of the six least desirable citizens of Kritsa. He smiled broadly at the assembly. 'I thought that, with the risk of having food left over, it would be a good idea to extend a Merry Christmas to these hungry people.' Put like that there was no brave dissenter, although the faces of those around me told tale that this was one Christian notion too far. Papa delegated four lads to collect the small table from the back of the church, and asked if there were any spare seats. He received two chairs, passed over a row of heads, then went to the woodpile to select four pieces to use as stools, and finally walked to his place.

Murmurs quickly replaced the stunned silence. 'Whore', 'Drunkard', and 'bloody Turk' reached my ears, and my experience of women eagerly sharing whispered news told me this gathering acclaimed Papa's action a scandal. Mama rose. Papa strode after her to beg, 'Can you not stay?'

In a low voice, she replied, 'We are dressed for a family occasion. I need to fetch my other kerchief to better cover my face so I can serve our guests.'

He ignored everyone watching to kiss her, on her mouth! Oblivious to the collective gasp that ran along the tables like a shock wave, he said, 'Enjoy the occasion as planned. I'll serve them.'

While he unwittingly had everyone's attention, he took his place at the head of the table and apologised for the delay. After he'd said Grace, Papa picked up our Christopsomo, smelt it appreciatively, and held the celebratory bread high to bless it, a signal for other family heads to do the same. When Papa took slices of the wonderful bread to his unusual guests, a crotchety great aunt stopped him.

'I understand the point you are making, Pappas, but two of them are Turks!'

Without pause, he replied, 'There's no need to worry. The assortment of food is so great they'll not need to touch pork.'

This brought smiles of amusement, until another great aunt called out, 'Wait, Pappas, it will not do.' He turned with dismay on his face, to hear, 'Their table isn't set for guests. Please, give us a few minutes.'

His taunt shoulders relaxed, and with joy Papa said, 'God bless you!'

Even while our plates overflowed, people anticipated

post-Christmas food such as delicious brawn made from pig's head, sausages made from intestines stuffed with rice, raisins, and liver, and finally lard to spread on our mid-morning bread during olive picking. Not one piece of those pigs was wasted, although I spent ages trying to find the oink in the meat juice that Grandma told me she'd put there.

As our meal concluded, someone's grandpa banged the table. Once hush fell, he thanked everyone for their contribution and complimented the women for the fine feast. Then he adopted a serious tone.

'We now come to the most important part of the day for some special people.' I glanced over to Manos, knowing that this was the one day of the year when he was happy to be called by his full name of Emmanuel. Sure enough, Manos wore an expectant grin as the man continued. 'Dusk on Christmas Day signals time to celebrate those with their name day today and tomorrow. Let us see all of you called Xristina, Christos, Chrisoula, Hrisa, Emmanuel, Kostantios, and Panagiota.' Clapping and cheering drowned the noise of eleven chairs scraping as people, ranging from grandparents to babies, went to the front. Men raised a glass to them, and we all chorused 'Many Years'. The oldest celebrating female happily accepted fresh roses from a granddaughter, and the two youngest, another Manos and a Chrissi, each received an inflated pig bladder to kick about. Surprisingly, I wasn't jealous as I looked forward to my name day in June.

When the sun passed behind the mountains, the air quickly chilled. People started to move. Men sat near the fires with the remainder of the *raki* and wine, although I was amazed that there was any left as they'd been at it all day. Children ran about with playmates, while the elders and unmarried girls made for their homes, and, of course, the women cleared away. As sudden darkness fell some men tuned up lyres and bouzoukis, others lit torches set in the wall or placed oil lamps on the tables. Their flickering light, and the promise of music, added more magic. It was now past curfew, so Papa escorted his guests to where they planned to sleep. Although he expected the guards to be lenient, he wanted to be on hand if trouble arose. That made Grandpa laugh – he thought Turks were afraid of their own shadows after dark. When Papa returned I was almost asleep, and in my drowsy state relished his beard against my face as he carried me to my bed on the sofa.

On New Year's Eve, I sat in the kitchen watching adults play cards for points, but that didn't reduce the excitement. My job was to top up *raki* glasses and *mezes*. When Papa judged it nearly midnight, he cleared a space on the table for our Saint Basil cake. In vain, I hoped he'd comment on the way I'd decorated it with almonds in the shape of 1813 by the Christian calendar. After theatrically counting how many people were in the room, Papa used Mama's large knife to cut the cake into enough slices, with three extra for Christ, the house, and, of course, Saint Basil. After a prayer, each person ate carefully, hoping to find the hidden coin. I always got the lucky slice!

Shortly afterwards, our guests took their leave, and Grandma commented on the cold, fierce wind.

'Blowing in from Russia,' stated Papa.

'It's not their weather we need,' grumbled Grandpa, 'but their forces would be useful to oust the b...ouch!' We all laughed, very aware of the expletive Grandma had expelled with a sharp elbow. Then it was off to bed. It wouldn't do for anyone to be awake when Saint Basil came. It was so difficult to sleep with butterflies of excitement in my stomach, anticipating delivery of a new pair of clogs filled with a small toy: perhaps a carved whistle or a rag doll. Years later, I realised the clogs were second-hand, a recent coat of beeswax making them appear and smell new.

*

Thea clearly enjoyed Rodanthe's tale. She laughed in all the right places, and asked many questions to understand more.

Rodanthe added, 'Now I realise I took family life for granted.'

As sadness masked the girl's face Thea reached out to hug her and said, 'I really enjoyed hearing that. It must have been wonderful to have a proper childhood. What happened next?'

4

USURPED

Of course, such festivities had a payback time. During the next four weeks, all donkeys, mules, carts, women, and children were employed olive picking. Even Papa, dressed in his everyday cassock, joined us. Only Grandma stayed behind to prepare vast amounts of food for later in the day. It was the first sunny day since Christmas, one of those days when everyone was anxious to get outside. Mama enchanted me with a story about a bird called a halcyon, with vivid turquoise, blue, and rose-pink feathers. Legend has it that this bird enjoys fourteen days of calm weather each January to lay her eggs safely, and it was certainly one of those days.

Adolescent youths showed strength and daring to climb trees and shake branches until olives fell. Women and girls, hot under their skirts and kerchiefs, completed the backbreaking task of picking up fallen olives to drop into huge aprons. How we envied those youths in the trees working with uncovered chests. Yes, the lads' women pretended not to notice! They were distant cousins, or friends of friends from other villages. I thought it strange, and wondered if they had no trees closer to home. A cousin excitedly told me these lads hoped to catch a glance of the girl their matchmaker had suggested for them. It was hard to see how it helped them, as the girls were chaperoned, demurely dressed, and veiled.

Once the women had tipped their apron contents on to mats in the shade, we children picked over the olives to discard twigs and leaves, before ranks of men used great shovels to fill hessian sacks. Vigilant tax assessors, who would earn a good percentage, made a careful note of which family provided each sack, and therefore how much tax they owed.

After this, the olives went on two authorised routes. For the first, men from the olive oil soap company, owned by Turks in Megalo Kastro, piled sacks on to large horse-drawn wagons. Once full, they set off on their slow route to the port at Agios Nikolaos for a boat to the city. The second permitted procedure used every available donkey, mule, and handcart to carry the best quality batches uphill to the aga's stone olive press for processing. All households, whether Christian, Turk, or Jew, valued the tasty oil, with the lowest quality going into oil lamps. Often a grandpa discreetly slipped away with a sack of olives on his shoulder, heading for home where each grandma used their 'special recipe' to ensure olives were available to eat all year. Everyone had a great time – a winter working holiday.

Towards the end of olive picking I developed a cold, so Mama thought it a good time to introduce me to embroidery, although bloody spots from my pricked fingers soon rendered the cloth unusable. What a treat, though. Mama cosseted me with hot cordials, and rubbed my chest with a paste of pungent eucalyptus leaves to help me breath. It was almost worth malingering, but when Great Grandma's walking stick again tapped in time with Dove's hooves, I grabbed my snack and rushed to the door, anxious to beat Manos in our resumed daily race.

On reflection, our time in the panniers was always going to be limited. At first, when our foreheads bumped the edge of the panniers, we stood on tiptoe to peep out. Then our noses bumped, and then our chins. Finally, when our heads were clear of the rim, we climbed in and out via a wall or chair. All the same, it was a shock when two ugly toddlers usurped us.

I swung around in surprise when Manos said, 'Do you want to cuddle one of my nephews, Rodanthe?'

In utter disbelief, I shouted, 'Have you gone mad?' In confusion, Manos looked from me to Great Grandma, who hugged him.

'The twins are so snug in their nests. Follow us, and play with them when they wake.'

There was no way I was going, so I sat on our doorstep. I doubted besotted Great Grandma would even miss us. Poor Manos was a picture of indecision. Eventually he held out his hand to suggest we run to catch up. To show my disdain, I picked up a stick to rake the line of ants that marched out of our door, each carrying a tiny breadcrumb, to disappear into a crack in the opposite wall. As planned, this annoyed Manos, so following Dove was no longer an option. He pulled the stick from me, snapped it in two, and flung both pieces along the street. I rushed to pick them up. Not fast enough! Manos raced ahead to snatch up both bits.

I had a strong punch! Manos fell, doubled up in pain, and stared at me with tears in his eyes. It didn't satisfy me. I kicked his shin, which must have hurt even though I had my feet wrapped in rabbit skins instead of wooden clogs. He rolled on his back to clutch his leg with a dramatic howl.

I goaded, 'Don't be a sissy. Fight back.' Before he had a chance, a door opened to reveal his aunt in an angry hands-on-hips pose, complaining that we'd woken her pa. We sullenly walked away as Manos rubbed his eyes then nose, mixing tears with snot that he wiped down his britches. Remorseful, I proffered my less than clean nose rag.

To my horror, he turned and snarled like a whipped

dog, 'I'm not using anything of yours, you dirty *malaca*.'

I guessed it was a bad word, and was shocked that Manos knew it and had directed it at me. Before I thought of a retort the next door opened to reveal Manos's sister, Maria. She thought Manos had fallen and fussed around to check for bruises. We soon learnt how exhausted she was with baby Nikos now that she was already expecting another, and how it was so kind of Great Grandma to take care of her twins. To move us on she pushed almond biscuits into our hands and kissed us goodbye.

Neither of us spoke, uncertain how to restore our easy camaraderie, so we sat in silence by the fountain. Although I felt sorry, I wasn't going to say so. Instead I suggested we go to the village. This made Manos twitter, as his mama forbade him to go out alone. Already on my way, I shouted, 'What's the worst she can do?' Desperate for inclusion, Manos ran after me as I strode purposefully towards the village. Now instead of indignant, I was exhilarated. We were free!

*

Like a child enjoying a folk story, Thea approved with a loud, 'Bravo, Rodanthe! Tell me more.'

5

GRANDPA DAYS

Opposite the spring was a *kafenion* with a whitewashed inside spruce enough to pass Grandma's inspection, not that a woman would ever enter such a male bastion! We usually passed by earlier of a morning, when tables and chairs placed outside were empty. Now they were full of men who sipped coffee, smoked, or played backgammon, all talking loudly, and most rhythmically clicking worry beads. With slight hesitation, I led the way.

'Manos? Rodanthe? Come, kiss Grandpa.'

It was difficult to trace the source of the voice from among the men with their leathery, weather-beaten faces. All wore moustaches, some long and straggly, some so bushy they hid the noses they aimed to enhance, and a few were dapper, neatly clipped, and waxed. Many grew beards, and all had their heads covered: two with handsome black fezzes at jaunty angles, three with hoods, and the remainder with loosely woven black cloths wound turban style, oddly decorated by escaping sprigs of hair. Each man wore a dark shirt with a voluminous waistcoat over wide, baggy britches thrust into much repaired goatskin boots.

Helpfully, Grandpa called, 'Here, at the back, in my favourite seat. Come this way.'

We ran into his outstretched arms to enjoy a fine welcome from his tickly whiskers as he loudly kissed us. Then he set us by his chair with a flourish.

'What splendid grandchildren I have. What a family. Half of Kritsa must be down to my grandpa!'

'Or mine,' said another. 'Come, Manos, surely I deserve a kiss too. Give Grandpa Babis a hug.' That's when I realised it was unfair – Manos had another grandpa. Our grandpa Nikos sat me on his knee and called out to the person boiling coffee in a tiny *breki*.

'Stop the coffee, Spanos. My grandson Manos has made an allegiance to your *kafenion*. Let's have *raki*, and warm soumadha for my grandchildren.' We grinned at each other, unable to believe our luck, and then sipped to relish every drop of our sweet almond cordial.

The old men, all politely called 'Grandpa', drank their *raki* with *mezes* of olives, lupin seeds, sliced artichoke with lemon, tiny bite size rusks, and cubes of cheese that Spanos produced as if from thin air. Their already loud voices gained volume as the fiery liquid warmed them. I'd never seen this odd Spanos before. His uncovered hair was long, as if in mourning, and his apron matched the one Grandma wore. Perhaps he ate too many cheese pies, because the taunt fabric of his apron suggested breasts beneath.

I watched the relaxed men. Grandpa Babis stroked his beard in an absent-minded way; Grandpa Nikos had crumbs in his; another braided his long beard, while another...

I swung around to look at Spanos. The sun had never tanned the pale face, and instead of a beard or moustache, Spanos had rosy apple cheeks to please any girl. I concluded that, unusually, a woman ran this business, and her patrons had nicknamed her Spanos, meaning beardless. I felt instant empathy with this person. Manos and I were often mistaken for a pair of brothers or sisters. When Spanos passed by, I thanked her for the soumadha, told her it was delicious, and left a pause where it would be usual to say her name.

She beamed, and in an odd pitch said, 'You're welcome,

Rodanthe. Your papa baptised me Michalis. I'm pleased to meet such a polite girl.'

Men roared with laughter, and one chimed, 'Michalis! Well, well, Spanos, and we thought you a heathen eunuch!' In a huff, Spanos flicked crumbs with his cloth to ensure they fell in the man's lap.

Not understanding, I turned my thoughts to the fact that Manos shared Grandpa Nikos and had Grandpa Babis. I felt cheated. 'What about uncles, aunts, and cousins?' I demanded. 'Does he have more of those too?'

Grandpa Nikos gave a strange answer. 'In Kritsa, yes, but you have many more.' With a grin, he added, 'We'll never be sure how many.'

An elderly man, apparently asleep in the corner, spoke without opening his eyes. 'That old devil, Nikos? God obviously has no use for him. His brood is related and interrelated. I'd not admit that part of my family!' All the men laughed and tapped the side of their noses. Grandpa laughed too, and intriguingly told us we both had relatives living in a secret place where those whom Turks called thieving *klephts* made their homes. This was where his own ancient grandpa Nikos still lived.

With a grin, Grandpa said, 'If you promise never to tell Great Grandma, I'll take you to visit him one day.'

Despite this amazing revelation, I excitedly realised I had a trump card. 'Surely my Papa must have family?'

'Ah yes. Settle down, and I'll tell you a gruesome tale.'

My papa's family hailed from a remote area on the south of Crete called Sfakia. It suited Turks to leave the wealthy Sfakians alone, as they were great sailors who travelled to distant lands to return with all manner of stock that delivered high taxes for Turks.

It seems Papa's great uncle gained an overseas education,

so people called him Daskalos, meaning teacher, and this evolved to become Daskalogiannis. By 1770, Daskalogiannis had four merchant ships, and was mayor of the region. As ever, there were dreams of shaking off the yoke of the Turks, and Daskalogiannis responded warmly to suggestions that he should finance a rebellion with support from the Russian fleet. The revolt began in March 1770, and, full of bravado, the rebel's gained initial success. However, Russian support never materialised, and brutal Turks defeated 1,300 of them.

In the aftermath, Turks arrested the wife and daughters of Daskalogiannis as hostages, along with one of his brothers. Megalo Kastro's pasha made this brother deliver a letter to assure Daskalogiannis of fair treatment and the release of hostages. Thus assured, Daskalogiannis surrendered with seventy of his men. It was a foul trick, and Turks skinned Daskalogiannis while he was still alive. All through his agony, the stoic and pious man suffered in dignified silence.

I heard Manos sniffle, and realised his grief put him at risk of mockery from the men, so with relief took the opportunity to make amends, and help him save face.

'Use my nose rag, Manos, your cold is still bad.'

I sat in adoration at Grandpa's feet, and he ruffled my hair as he spoke. 'You still have a great aunt and cousins working the land below Faneromenis Monastery. Your papa visits them when he has business with the abbot.' Grandpa also explained that Daskalogiannis had more brothers who, along with many others, fled Sfakia by boat to sail around the eastern end of the island to our north coast. Two boatloads of refugees set up home and called their new hamlet Sfaka, while other settlers took over deserted houses in Agios Nikolaos, left empty when the original Turks forcibly moved inhabitants from the coast. When some Sfakian lads married Kritsa girls, they took them to work for the abbot at Faneromenis.

After a swig of *raki*, Grandpa added, 'Sadly, your papa's ma died giving birth to him, and his pa a few years later. His aunt nursed him until he was old enough to attend the monastery's school. I think the abbot of that time hoped he'd join them as a monk. As you know, he chose the priesthood and village life instead.' Then Grandpa smiled proudly, and added, 'Once Mathaios heard my Irini sing he was entranced, so asked around to find out if she were already betrothed.' Obviously used to having a dog at his feet, Grandpa frequently passed down slivers of cheese while he spoke; just one reason why I fell in love with him that day. It was hard to hide my disappointment when fat drops of rain splattered down to act as a signal that it was lunchtime.

Mama assumed Great Grandma had returned us early due to the rain. As a treat, she let me sit by her loom to thread bobbins and use her silver knife to cut threads. When she got into the rhythm of the weaving, Mama sang to help the shuttles fly, so I asked, 'Is that what you sang when Papa noticed you?'

Mama's shuttle hand stopped abruptly. A pink blush made her pretty. 'Who's been telling tales?'

Offhandedly, I said, 'Oh, Manos and I met Grandpa Nikos.'

An odd smile played on her face as she said, 'I hinted that a certain novice had twinkly eyes, and your grandpa set about matchmaking.'

This puzzled me. 'How did Papa hear you from Faner omenis?'

'In those days, women from all around made a pilgrimage to the Panagia of Faneromenis on 15 August. I set out for our special expedition with aunts and grandmas the previous afternoon, and walked all night to take matins with the monks. We made our special prayers, then broke our fast with a huge feast in the shade of the monastery wall. The schoolboys and novices served our food and serenaded us in a holiday atmosphere, so it seemed only fair to sing to them.'

'So Papa was there?'

'Indeed. My mama noticed we couldn't stop talking to each other, and sent your grandpa to make the match.' Mama laid her knife on her hand from the tip of her middle finger to the base of her thumb. I was so used to seeing it I'd not realised the filigree handle was a work of art. 'It was my betrothal gift from your papa.' With a huge smile, she followed with, 'My most important treasures are my silver knife, my loom, my large kitchen knife...Oh, and my Rodanthe, of course!'

Manos and I soon fell into a new pattern. When Great Grandma and Dove clattered towards our homes, we rushed outside to create an illusion that we went too. Once they'd passed out of sight, we set off to do chores, a wonderful idea originated by Manos. On the first day, Manos timidly knocked on his aunt's door, and when she opened it he didn't give her a chance to berate us.

'Hello, Aunt. I'm sorry we disturbed you yesterday. Can we collect your water from the spring?' Her sour face was a picture of confusion, and two full water jars later we were richer by a biscuit each. Next stop was Manos's sister, Maria, where we gained a couple of apples as thanks for her full water jars.

The original inspiration for chores hit Manos when he was worried that his ma would be angry that we weren't with Great Grandma. He hoped that she'd be proud when neighbours passed comment, and think we spent the whole morning helping women instead of just two each day. With our work complete, we set off to explore. When I wanted to go to the *kafenion*, wise Manos suggested that if we only went there infrequently, the men would welcome us as a diversion rather than regard us as pests. He was right!

Men's chatter was different to that of women. A familiar phrase was 'Those bloody Turks'. Their refrain was as regular as the hallelujahs in a church service, and usually at the end of a sentence, just like 'Amen' at the end of a prayer. Manos invented a game to play where we sat with our eyes shut and listened hard to guess who spoke, which was not as easy as it sounds as they often all talked at once. Then, after a final 'Those bloody Turks', they all fell silent until one of them found a reason to call for *raki*. When conversation slackened, men fetched their pipe from a wall rack to fix to the flexible hose of a *narghile*.

*

Rodanthe helped Thea imagine the scene. 'Listen to the stream. It reminds me of men sucking on pipes to draw tobacco smoke across cool water, along the hose, and into their mouths, generating gentle bubbling sounds as they puff contentedly. We called them hubble-bubble pipes, and longed to have a go.' Fascinated, Thea urged Rodanthe to continue.

*

Some men studied their next backgammon move, and always someone picked their nose, carefully inspected the result, and then wiped it under their seat or on their dog. Then the conversation would go something like this:

'...Indigestion. That's the trouble, those bloody Turks.'

'My wife too. Her voice in the dark says, "You can stop that. Those days are past, and I have indigestion".'

'Give her *raki*. It cures all, including the mange on my dog.'

'I use it to disinfect used beehives before a new queen.'

'They had a queen in England once, sorted out the Spanish invaders. Perhaps we need one to oust those bloody Turks.'

'It was the Spanish who discovered potatoes in the Americas. Grow lovely they do, up in Kroustas.'

'Don't pretend you have learning.'

'My son told me. He attended school at Faneromenis.'

'Too much learning gives folk ideas above their station.'

'Think about the old baker. He gave his sons too much education. Cost him a fortune, so he's still working to pay off his debts. One son set off to sea twenty years ago, to join the Frenchies fighting for freedom. One is a pappas on the mainland. His youngest acted like a city gent, and went off to Megalo Kastro to work in the bloody soap factory. Makes me sick just to think of my fine olives going into soap to wash a Turk's arse!'

'My great uncle still owes tax arrears from when he was sick. I can't understand how he is responsible for paying head tax for his lad, who might be dead for all he knows. Once a man runs off to the Americas there's no more news.'

'Gives me indigestion just thinking about tax. Let's count: head tax, land tax, produce tax, meat tax, grain tax, sales tax, purchase tax. They'll introduce death tax next, those bloody Turks.'

'No wonder so many bow down. Those bloody Turks.'

'I'll tell you what will cause indigestion. Some of the sultan's elite force of janissaries will supplement our local aga's troops. Apparently the aga lost face when a report stated he was too lax as a regional ruler and his relationship with us is too soft!'

'I'm sure the pappas and imam are convivial enough to stop things getting out of hand.'

'It's my name day today, shall we have a *raki*?'

'So it is. Spanos, bring *raki*. Cheers, health to all, and pox on those bloody Turks.'

One day, as we tried to work out the rules of backgammon, we sniffed a dreadful smell. 'Hey, Manos, cut that out!' As Manos loudly protested he wasn't the culprit, a collective burst of laughter rang out. His grandpa patted his shoulder.

'Never mind. It was bound to have been old Manolis. He calls each of his dogs Manos. It stops him forgetting his own name, let alone that of the dog. Besides, only he can produce that toxic mix.' Their chuckles ended when a man walked past, and whispers put me in mind of the women's scandals.

Grandpa Nikos called, 'Hey, Alexomanolis, will you take a *raki*?'

'No thanks. I drink with Mardati Yannis. Your inaction condones the Turks. At our *kafenion* we plan to oust them.'

I expected the men to be insulted, but instead they all said with one voice, 'Bloody Turks!'

*

Although Thea was enthralled, she was concerned about Rodanthe's mind. Her smile seemed false, at odds with her glassy eyes and unpredictable moods. With a private prayer that the girl's physical condition would take a long time to heal, Thea kept her talking.

'What are Kritsa houses like? I've only seen a few local stone dwellings.'

Rodanthe pointed at the candle. 'Our houses cling to the hollow of the curved hillside in uneven tiers, like wax drips. Stone houses shore each other up in narrow streets, and thick walls keep homes cool in summer. In winter women hang colourful wool rugs over unglazed windows and ill-fitting doors.' Rodanthe was oblivious to her tears. 'Our un-plastered two-room home is in the poor area of herdsmen, and some cousins live in Pergiolikia a small enclave above us. Our house has one individual touch, in the form of a decorative cross. Grandpa carved it in the stone lintel above the door when Papa became the pappas.' After a sip of fragrant herb tea, Rodanthe continued. 'Homes in the street behind us were hurriedly built with a single room to house refugees. I'll tell you why.

'A previous aga took a tour of the area and recognised the strategic importance of a pass in the cliffs at Mardati, a hamlet that used to be below Kritsa. He declared the villagers must leave, so his militia set a house aflame to emphasise their commitment to the aga's command. The brutes probably expected fire to galvanise folk to leave; instead, they retaliated with anything from pitchforks and brooms to old firearms. Their brave resistance angered the troop, who killed indiscriminately and set fire to the church where women and children sheltered. Only twelve adults and fifteen children remained alive to move to Kritsa.

'Believe me, Thea, if I were a man I'd certainly drink at Mardati Yannis's *kafenion*. No wonder it is a place for the hotheads to congregate!'

'That sounds appalling. As the Panagia's ears I hear of dreadful events, that's why I enjoy your happier memories. The atmosphere in the *kafenion* must have been spoilt once Alexomanolis had passed.'

'Yes. Manos suggested then it was time for us to move.'

*

A four-legged bush lurched from side to side as it came towards us with a two-legged one close behind, so we guessed the twins were nearby. We perched by the spring, certain that Great Grandma would stop for a drink and hopeful that she might have a tasty morsel in her apron. Dove walked right past us, heading for his stable, anxious to have his load lifted. I was sad at this. Four years of daily companionship, and it was if he'd never known us. Great

Grandma just mumbled as she waddled by.

Shortly afterwards the twins arrived. One carried a few bedraggled mauve anemones and the other a couple of twigs. When they saw Manos they ran to him, eager for a hug. It was odd to see my playmate in the role of an uncle as he asked where they'd been. One boy explained that Great Grandma had toothache and needed to see the blacksmith tomorrow. I grimaced at that; she must have been desperate if she intended to have her tooth pulled. The other twin said the motion of riding in a pannier made him sick so now he rode on the saddle. That made me dislike the little brat even more – Angel Day was the only time we'd ridden on Dove's saddle.

Worried the twins might enjoy being with Uncle Manos, I reminded them to catch up with Great Grandma. As they ran off, Manos teased that I was jealous of them. With an indignant 'Not so' I pushed Manos backwards. He hit his head on a tree. In retaliation, he pushed me. I kicked his leg then darted away, expecting Manos to give chase. Instead, he moved away to sit down. I called him a sissy with no backbone for a fight. With his fingers in his ears he made an annoying 'La, la, la' sound. His passiveness increased my anger, so I scooped up a handful of small stones to fling in his face.

A large hand caught my wrist. As the stones dropped, I heard, 'God will forgive you, Rodanthe. He always does, but I am very disappointed in you.' Dismayed, I watched Papa walk away. Why did he never catch me being good? I knuckled prickly tears and gave Manos a grudging apology. He ignored me and headed home. I poked my tongue out, confident that our spat would soon be history.

The next day I gave Manos my breakfast crust to feed the ducks, and as we passed the *kafenion*, only Grandpa Babis was there. In answer to our wave, he shouted, 'Hey, Manos, we're going up the gorge. Will you both join us?'

We punched each other's arm in delight, and realised that we'd nearly missed the opportunity as Grandpa Nikos and others had left already.

Grandpa Babis led us down a street of rough steps leading to Church Rock, a communal gathering place. Papa had once told me he dreamed of building a proper church there, and with its heavenly eastern view over the plain, the sea, and the Thripti Mountains, I understood why. We often played there. Our favourite game was horses, when we galloped around to mimic troops in the fields below. When they practised with firearms, we shot back at them with stick rifles.

Mama was already on the rock, packing a basket with sheets that she'd bleached in the sun. We'd almost reached the steep descent when her voice reached us.

'I know where you're going!'

Grandpa Babis reacted like a guilty boy. 'I've a new crook bending, and I thought they'd be interested.'

'Yes, I'm sure! Have a lovely time, children, and give my love to the cousins.'

When Manos turned to me, eyes big and round, I understood his unspoken question. With no idea of the answer, I shrugged and said, 'It's an adventure!'

We zigzagged down the steep cobbled path, and then followed Grandpa Babis down an even steeper trail that continued to the foot of the gorge, where he led us across the riverbed to clamber up the other side. Grandpa Babis explained, 'The first part of the gorge is only for vigorous young men, so we'll start on this trading route and then rejoin it via another entrance.'

For a while, the path was so steep we couldn't spare breath to speak. By the time we paused, we were facing sea. Proud of his heritage, Grandpa Babis told us how past rulers of Crete, called Venetians, had named the bay

Mirabello, meaning beautiful, and improved trade between communities by laying cobbled routes over long-established footpaths. He added that while this brought prosperity, Venetians outlawed Orthodoxy and insisted that everyone became Papists. With a wry laugh, he added, 'It proves people should be careful what they wish for. When Turks ousted Venetians, they allowed people religious freedom to return to Orthodoxy.'

The track was wider at this point to allow us to walk either side of Grandpa Babis, who pointed out how the main cobbled path weaved down to pass a hill with two rounded humps, and then on down to the plain called Lakonia via ancient wide-cut steps. Next, he helped us to see huge white stones just visible under trees, and explained they were relics from the ancient people of Lato who once lived on the hill.

Like a teacher, Grandpa Babis explained that our island held a strategic position in the middle sea. As excellent sailors and administrators, Venetians brought wealth and order to the island. They designated the four hamlets around Kritsa a single village. By the time the Turks invaded, 450 years later, Kritsa's growing population had reduced the gaps between enclaves to create a shape that looks like a scorpion when viewed from a distance. The sultan in Constantinople had a lavish lifestyle, as did his pashas, agas, and beys. These all maintained huge numbers of troops, paid for by the sweat of local folk.

Grandpa Babis's voice became emotional. 'If they want land, they take it. If they want workers, they enslave them.' He paused for breath, then sadly added, 'They abuse women and quell their dreadful lust with our children.'

Indignant, Manos said, 'Cretans should kick the Turks out.'

His grandpa nodded. 'We might. More men align to Mardati Yannis. Enough of that now. Look up there, a proper snowy mountain.' To move us along, Grandpa Babis pointed to a distinctive rounded outcrop, and asked us to name it. Manos beat me with a loud 'Kastello'. I was just about to laugh at him and say that the bluff of red battlement shaped rocks above Kritsa was Kastello, when he received a congratulatory pat on the back from his grandpa.

'Well done! People who've never set foot out of Kritsa think our village has the only Kastello. Folk see that unmistakable round shape from many angles. We'd best cease our chatter now. Follow me.' He led us down a steep track between trees, carpeted by yellow oxalis. At an abrupt end, we dropped into the alien environment of the gorge.

Sparse shrubs studded opposing sheer rock faces, each topped by a dark line of trees. White fluffy clouds scudded across a vivid blue sky from west to east, and it took another hour for sunrays to penetrate the gorge. Clever Grandpa Babis challenged us to race him up to the narrowest part of the gorge. Thoroughly excited, we jumped from rock to rock to avoid the constant stream flowing towards us, or scrambled along the shale bank. Every so often we paused to catch our breath, and then, as soon as Grandpa Babis came into view, we waved and ran off again, until we reached the narrow pass.

Over millions of years flowing water has smoothed the rocks, and now the overhead sun reflected off sprayed droplets to create rainbows. Steep and slick, the boulders were difficult to climb, so Manos valiantly made several laugh-filled attempts to shove me up to the ledge. Eventually I clambered up, then reached back to pull him up. We felt triumphant with a hand on each side of the narrow rock gateway. Water cascaded over the rock ledge to gurgle and splash as Manos punched the air.

'Ha! Grandpa hasn't even rounded the last bend.'

His last word was still echoing about the gully when his smile faded and he clutched my hand. 'I think we're being watched.' Fear is contagious, so when a shower of stones fell noisily into the pool, we shrieked. Above us, at least twenty goats, frozen in shock, glared. We posed no risk to their fast, agile feet, so they bounced away, and we solemnly sealed our agreement not to tell Grandpa Babis we'd been spooked by goats with a shake of grubby hands.

Now the terrain either side of the stream became flatter and wider. Wheat grew beneath olive trees, interspersed with scarlet poppies and tall daisies that swayed in a gentle breeze. An unexpected sound of barking dogs funnelled through the gorge to alarm us. With unspoken agreement, we gathered pebbles ready to aim at any dog that reached us, for we'd both heard tales of feral dogs that terrorised sheep, goats, and remote folk. We sat under a shady tree to await Grandpa Babis, and showed him our stones, proud of our foresight. He assured us, 'No one will be bitten, just stay in single file behind me,' then walked off. He didn't need to tell us twice!

As we crested the next rim, a wondrous scene of hundreds of sheep and goats astounded us. What a din! Eight vicious dogs corralled the animals. These snarling curs stretched their individual rope tethers, each set in the ground by wooden stakes, to form bare patches, worn to dust by scrabbling paws. Manos was quick to comprehended the relevance of narrow strips of grass between each mongrel, and dashed after his grandpa. I'll admit to churning nerves in my stomach as I followed, not helped by savage hot breath on my ankle.

Attracted by the commotion, Grandpa Nikos appeared with Manos's brother, Aimilios, and Cousin Lukas. This triggered a clear memory of Angel Day, and I grinned in delight as Lukas swung me to ride on his back and chase after Manos who 'rode' Aimilios. Despite the first pair's head start we soon caught up, and by the time Lukas lowered me to the ground, breathless with laughter, I'd elevated him to hero status. No wonder I was disappointed when Aimilios said, 'You nearly missed us. We're off to Kritsa.' Although Manos asked his brother to stay, a bemusing outburst of laughter from nearby men quashed his question when Aimilios added, 'I've got to get Lukas to the spice man before his dick drops off!'

As the two men left us, both grandpas guided us to a trestle table set in the shade, surrounded by men sitting on an assortment of chairs, or benches made from planks across tree stumps. Two women sat at the far end of the table preparing a mound of greens, and, contrary to custom, they freely conversed with the men. Then I noticed two women working at another table to roll pasta and place it on a large cloth to dry.

Grandpa Babis saw my gaze, and licked his lips before saying, 'Pasta, I love it. Something else we can thank those Venetians for. I don't know what I like more, pasta or rice for *pilaf.*'

Too overawed to answer, I turned to Manos and mouthed, 'Who are they?' He shrugged and whispered in his grandpa's ear. In response, Grandpa Babis grinned, tapped his nose, and stood up to kiss the eldest woman on her cheek.

'Thank you, Sophia. That coffee was good. Is the old man up to visitors?'

'Of course, he'll enjoy your village news. Lunch will be ready when you get back. I think you'll have a better appetite up here, the air is fresher without contamination from Turks.'

Another man I recognised from the taverna responded, 'I'd drink to that, if I had *raki.*'

A shepherd chortled and answered, 'I'm just going for some.' His response brought loud cheers.

Grandpa Nikos rose. 'Not for me. I'll go with Babis, it's time I saw my old man again.' Manos and I simultaneously asked, 'What old man?'

'Do you remember I once told you my grandpa Nikos is still alive? He was born in Kritsa, and his life sounds like a tall story. Come, I'll tell it as we walk.

'Then, as now, shepherds herded their beasts and sons up to Katharo's pastures to escape the heat of summer. When Nikos was a youth, and due to marry the next winter, his pa took him to trade prime stock with shepherds on the south slopes of the Dikties, high above the shimmering Libyan Sea. It seems this lad had been too friendly with his betrothed, for her angry pa arrived on Katharo to demand the irresponsible lad bring the wedding forward, only to find he'd disappeared. Unbeknown to the angry man, the erstwhile lad and his pa were enjoying the hospitality of a village called Kalamafka. As the youth hadn't seen this village before, he went to visit the crystal spring that kept the valley lush. Here he met a pretty maid, her kerchief askew and tears on her cheeks, anxious to find a missing sheep. Five months later, her angry pa was in Kritsa to demand the lad marry his daughter.

'Back on Kathero, shepherds worked together to establish a herd of juveniles, and spirited them away to the secret place where we've just enjoyed our coffee. Men fled to that place in the early days of the Turks and took stolen sheep to set up a smallholding. The klephts of Grandpa's day expected the shepherds, so it didn't take long before they were all under shady trees, *raki* in hand. Women and girls appeared to set up tables and produce a selection of *mezes* for their guests to nibble while a young pig cooked over a fire pit. Now, these girls were bold and wore their kerchiefs to show their tanned faces. Inevitably, the youth of our story noticed the lass with the most sparkly eyes, and fell victim to the klepht Captain's teases. Of course, he apologised for his lingering gaze, and then almost burnt away when the girl kissed him. Legend has it she boldly told him that klephts didn't hold with repressed village customs, and led the lad away while the meat cooked.'

I hung on every word, certain Grandpa wouldn't have told the tale had our parents been nearby. Despite his hot blush, Manos sought clarification.

'So, let me get this right. The lad had babies with the Kritsa girl, the lass from Kalamafka, and now the klepht's daughter. Phew, what happened? Did he bow down to take several wives?'

'Well, the rogue married the Kritsa girl and bigamously married the one from Kalamafka to run two households, confident neither would meet. Each of these unions produced six children, and one of these was your great grandma. That's not all: as a result of annual visits to the klephts he had more secret children, and the Sophia you just met is a daughter.'

Confused, I asked, 'If it was secret, how do you know?'

'Great Grandma's matchmaker unwittingly caused a scandal by suggesting a half-brother as her husband, so the rascal had to own up. After this, Great Grandma forbade mention of klephts, and never spoke to her pa.'

Chuckles from Grandpa Babis drew attention back to him. 'I should admit that my family tree, like many others, includes klepht progeny, so Rodanthe's pa has to work hard to ensure close family members don't marry.'

Still absorbed in this dramatic account, we stepped out from a canopy of trees into a yard to view a stonewall covered in a unique crop of twenty walking sticks and shepherd crooks, all suspended top to tail. Lengths of leather bound each bend, and a steel nail acted as a ratchet, each turn increasing the tension to form an elegant curve.

My grandpa shouted through the open doorway of a single-room stone house, 'Hello, Nikos old devil. Are you decent?' Not awaiting a reply, he strode into where a wizened, frail man sat in an armchair. A woollen cap covered blind eyes, and he twisted a magnificent snow-white chest-length beard in gnarled fingers.

He rasped, 'I like visitors. Who are you?'

'I'm a grandson, another Nikos. I've brought two of my grandchildren, Manos and Rodanthe.'

I stroked the old man's hand, and then squirmed in embarrassment to hear, 'And I'm Babis. Is my stick finished? You promised me another, but you're running out of time.' I gasped, expecting the grandpa to be offended. Instead he laughed.

'Take one, and choose another for the boy. The maid too if she wants one.'

Of course I did!

Back under the trees, Sophia's table groaned with the weight of food, and such a splendid meal needed plenty of *raki*. The cheerful noise level rose, with many tales of cheating the taxman, until somnolent diners, slept leaving us free to explore.

I copied Manos as he beat his stick on a row of wooden troughs, and our odd, resonating tune brought ten rust coloured piglets from the prickly undergrowth. With excited oinks and squeals, they snuffled their snouts into troughs, then snorted in disbelief that the troughs were empty. Next, we wielded sticks to scythe into bushes covered in purple cones of flowers, causing them to fly into the air along with brightly coloured butterflies. To our delight, some of the largest yellow butterflies landed on our outstretched hands, and we marvelled at the delicate black lines tracing mosaic shapes over their fragile wings. Their tiny feet gripped the minute ridges on my fingers, their antennae quivered in a breeze too slight for me to notice, and their long tongues shot out to curl back in a split second. Thrilled, we walked slowly to show off our new pets.

An eerie hush greeted our return. Each man crossed his chest piously, and gave a fervent 'Panagia Mou'. We stopped in confusion, and looked at one another for a clue to our mischief. Grandpa Nikos said, 'Blow them away, and send a kiss after them. Your pretty catch brings a message of love from someone who has died.' Reluctantly we did as he bid, and when one butterfly moved to my shoulder Grandpa brushed it away as if it were a troublesome wasp around autumn grapes. This episode spoilt the atmosphere of leisure and drove the men about their business, or, like us, to return to Kritsa.

The long day of excitement caught up with us, and our slow pace caused us to fall behind the main group. We each clasped a grandpa by the hand and trudged along, lost in our own thoughts until I voiced mine.

'I've had a lovely day, Grandpa, but now I'm worried Papa will be angry. I ate meat during Lent.'

In Grandpa's eyes I could do no wrong. He hugged me close to reassure me. 'Remember that place is secret, so it's like it never happened.' Then, to distract me he pointed out bats that fluttered above. However, our fabulous adventure had proved too much, so Grandpa carried me up the final steep, dark climb...

*

In distress, Rodanthe whispered to Thea, 'When I told you about village life, I didn't tell you the way we broadcast news of death is to prop a coffin outside the house.'

Aghast, Thea covered her mouth with her hand. 'Panagia Mou! Whose?'

'We'd only walked past two houses in our street when the lack of noise struck me. Without candles in windows our alley was so dark that Grandpa almost knocked into the coffin by Great Grandma's open door.'

Thea clutched the girl's hand. 'What had happened?'

6

INNOCENCE LOST

Grandpa Babis took a spill from the pot on the hearth, lit it on fire embers, and then used the bright flame to light a candle on the mantelpiece, illuminating Great Grandma laid out on her bed in the corner of the kitchen. With no kerchief to restrain it, wispy grey hair framed her swollen face and stuck in her forehead's deep, bloody gash, already attracting buzzing flies. Most shocking of all, a dead child lay in each arm.

I'd been in homes of the dead before to run errands for Papa, and always the house and street had been full of people paying their respects or settling down for the overnight vigil. It was inconceivable that the sad trio were alone.

Grandpa Babis broke our stunned silence. 'Nikos, sit with your ma. I'll see Rodanthe home and take Manos to our Maria. My poor girl must be distraught. I'll return when I know what's going on.'

There was no one in the street. It seemed as if an unseen hand had scooped everyone up. Dogs and cats went about their business unperturbed, and chickens scratched in stinking refuse. Beneath houses, domestic ewes and goats bleated in discomfort, long past milking time. At Maria's house I expected an anxious crowd. There was no one.

Grandpa Babis went through the open door, into the kitchen and then the bedroom to confirm the house was empty. Through a voice thick with tears, Manos said, 'Listen, it sounds like baby Nikos is with my aunt next door.

Those sound like teething screams.' We followed Manos into his aunt's house with difficulty; a man lay sprawled behind the door.

Immobilised by shock, I gagged on appalling smells. Grandpa Babis stepped over the man's body to lift Nikos from the cloth cradle that hung by ropes from a ceiling beam, intended to lull him to sleep. Instead, his thrashing had twisted the sling to leave his head unsupported, and now each scream of distress increased the likelihood of the cradle throttling him. Grandpa Babis handed the terrified baby to me as he spoke to Manos.

'Help me, this grandpa breathes.'

I took a candle and went next door to clean the baby. Maria's outdoor shoes were on her doorstep, and a pile of beans lay on her kitchen table next to a pan of mixed vegetables. A milk pot hung in the fireplace with an acrid stink where it had boiled over; all clear evidence that Maria had left in a hurry. I clumsily changed the baby's swaddling and found his wooden feeding tube. It took me a few practices at stoppering the top of the tube with one finger to limit the amount of water mixed with honey reaching Nikos, so by the time I carried him next door the old man was in his chair, snug in a blanket.

Grandpa Babis took Nikos and beckoned me to follow him. After he'd laid the mite on the bed, he lifted me to sit on the edge, my feet not reaching to the floor. He sat to hug me close and share what he'd learnt. A boy had run to Maria with news that one of her twins was badly hurt, so she'd hurriedly left Nikos with her aunt. According to the old man that had been mid-morning, and when Maria failed to return her aunt went to search. Some hours after this he'd tried to reach the baby, and that was when he fell. With an extra hug, Grandpa Babis told me Manos had checked my empty house as well as his own. Now I was to stay with the baby and not leave unless someone I trusted fetched me. I was so stunned I didn't even question why Manos got to go with his grandpa. Thoroughly exhausted I curled around the baby, ignored the lumpy bed's rancid smell, and slept until Manos startled me.

'Rodanthe, wake up. Janissaries have imprisoned folk behind the harem.' Without a pause to make sure I understood, Manos rushed on. 'The janissaries had a parade. Their cannon carriage collapsed and crushed people. Then there was a fight. When the janissaries made arrests, people protested and rushed to the marketplace.' Now wide-awake, I begged Manos to tell me more. He was relieved to share all that he had learnt, despite several pauses to wipe his eyes.

Manos grabbed my hand to emphasise how scary it was when he and Grandpa Babis returned to Great Grandma's house to find Grandpa Nikos had vanished. Cautiously they'd crept through shadows towards the *kafenion*, and Grandpa Babis had whispered he thought someone was inside so he went to check. First, he'd instructed Manos to whisper the Lord's Prayer ten times, and made him promise that if he was still alone at the end he should run back to me. On his eighth recitation his grandpa returned and guided him to the *kafenion* to meet some of the men who'd been with us earlier, plus his brother Aimilios, Cousin Lukas, Mardati Yannis, Alexomanolis, and two other hotheads armed with ancient matchlock guns.

Those who'd returned to Kritsa ahead of us had declared they needed a *raki* to wash dust from their throats so cheerfully piled into the *kafenion* to find what they had initially thought was a group of armed men threatening Spanos. Their relief that it was men that they knew was short-lived. Mardati Yannis explained that when he and his men stopped to drink at the nearby spring they found Aimilios, clumsily binding Lukas's hand. After hearing news of the terrible bloodshed Mardati Yannis was anxious to get the wounded man out of sight, so helped Aimilios drag his friend into the *kafenion*.

✻

Rodanthe rubbed her forehead then clutched Thea's arm. 'I was so bewildered Thea. I remember I put a hand up to stop Manos and demanded to know what had happened. Manos had just stared at me as if he couldn't comprehend that I didn't know. Then he collapsed to the floor in a sobbing heap. I sat with Manos, and held him until he eventually started to explain the full horror. Then I cried with him.'

✻

Earlier in the day, Lukas had met Great Grandma in the market place with the twins. She was in distress from toothache and cross with one of the twins because he'd dirtied some cloth bags. It seems the boy ran off into the path of janissaries. He died, crushed in a melee of cannon and horses. Next, Turks had attacked Christians to trigger a riot and mass arrests. Those at the *kafenion* had only learnt about the death of Great Grandma and the second twin when Grandpa Nikos had joined them, but of course he couldn't give any details. By the time Manos arrived, Mardati Yannis was urging everyone to help him free those imprisoned. Lukas clapped Aimilios on the back with his good hand and stated that he'd be facing trial if his cousin had not dragged him away, so now it was only right to go to the aid of others.

That's when Manos stopped abruptly and noisily chewed his lip to mask his renewed sobs. I pulled back the bed cover, gently pushed baby Nikos to the far side, and then hauled Manos up to join me.

'Come here, you're shivering. Don't worry about crying, just tell me.'

Cocooned, Manos continued. 'Rodanthe, your parents, my mama, and grieving sister are taken.' Unable to speak, I concentrated on the guttering candle. Kind Manos reached for my hand, then told me of the heated discussions among the men.

Mardati Yannis and the six men aligned to him wanted to storm the harem. The other six, including Grandpa Nikos and Grandpa Babis, wanted to wait until morning, and then send representatives to talk to the aga. Mardati Yannis had encouraged them, 'Come, let's use the night to our advantage.' With a wry laugh, Manos reported how jaws had dropped when Spanos had declared he agreed with those urging caution. Spanos reasoned that the aga would lose out if the Christian folk were not available to pay taxes.

Mardati Yannis answered, 'After the way a Turk sliced you I'd have thought revenge would taste sweet. You think you've caused deadlock, Spanos, whereas our two guns give us the upper hand.'

Then Manos shocked them. 'No, I make eight. Your weapons will worsen the situation.'

Mardati Yannis sneered, 'So, young man, what's your plan?' Despite the awful situation, I laughed at Manos's answer.

'Wait until morning. The women of the harem will be desperate to use their privies, and will demand Christians be cleared from their yard.' After heated discussions that is what they agreed, so Manos had run back to me. Utterly exhausted, Manos slept.

*

Instinctively, Thea took Rodanthe into her arms and held the sobbing girl until she calmed. 'Ah, my poor Goldfinch, so much pain. Let it out now. Tell me, what happened next?'

*

The next morning I took baby Nikos to his home just as my aunt helped Maria stumble to her bed. My aunt took Nikos from me and settled him at his mama's breast. 'Thank God for you, Rodanthe. Run home now, your mama needs you.'

Mama was cold. She'd knelt with the captives all night while Papa had worked a miracle to calm the group. Being the Wednesday of Easter Week, Papa had improvised the correct service and followed it with a loud prayerful vigil. When the harem shutters had slammed shut, the prisoners recognised Papa was leading a pious act of defiance, so, keen to keep the women in aga's household from their sleep, all Christians increased the volume of their responses.

I led Mama to her bed and snuggled alongside, disappointed that her chilling information brought no comfort. Most folk gained release just before dawn. Those detained faced the judgement of the kardi after Muslim morning prayers. Even before Mama could nap, the high-pitched tones of the muezzin called his faithful to their prayer mats, and acted as our signal to join the silent column heading for the market place.

Apart from *kafenions*, all other trade ceased. Turks gathered under hastily erected awnings; most had brought a stool, chair, or mat for their comfort. Tables stood ready to receive coffee cups, and many had a *narghile* between them. In a holiday atmosphere, boys weaved about to sell nuts, pastries, and paper fans. In contrast, Christians sat on hard ground amidst dust and refuse, already too hot from the early morning sun. I sat between Mama and Grandpa Nikos near the dais containing the aga, imam, kardi, and janissary captain. After the defendants and Papa had been ushered to the front, the kardi stood, banged his staff, and assumed instant attention to read from a long parchment. Although Papa had used his schooling in the Turk's language to teach me simple phrases, I couldn't make sense of the kardi. Blank faced Turk traders also showed their lack of comprehension, because most village Turks were Kritsa born so used our dialect. Not that it made a difference to us; we called them Turk whether they were fresh from Constantinople or had recently bowed down. At a brief nod from the kardi, his clerk of the court commenced proceedings.

Papa took a step towards the dais to a gasp of fear from the assembled Christians. 'Esteemed Kardi, may I speak before your clerk starts?' Two janissaries barred his way, while the kardi stroked the thin black moustache that decorated each side of his mouth in a unique fashion.

'Speak.'

'Your Eminence, I'd like to translate so that local folk may understand what passes.' Papa held his gaze steady until the kardi turned to speak to the aga and imam in low tones.

The kardi returned to glare at Papa with a sharp, 'Yes.'

'*Teşekkür ederim.* Thank you.'

'People of Kritsa, horrific events need to be examined so that I can pass judgement on behalf of our esteemed aga, as Allah wills. My reputation as a hard but fair man should reassure witnesses, satisfy those who have been wronged, and terrify those who brought discord and death.' A low mulberry branch cost the kardi his fez as he retook his seat, earning jeers from Christians. His clerk promptly retrieved the fez, gave it a brush, and handed it to the kardi, who pushed it in place so fiercely he winced. Silence fell as the clerk read the accusations, leaving pauses for Papa to translate.

'The Christian woman, Maria, stole three cloves from the spice trader. The mute servant of the spice trader used his sword inappropriately to kill a child. Five men from Pergiolikia set filthy dogs on janissaries, and thanks be to God, janissaries killed two of these ruffians. Four unidentified Christian youths attacked a group of our sons before they ran off, leaving two dead and two injured.

'Additionally, and in accordance with the law, the pappas seeks our kardi's permission to remove the deceased non-believers from the tax list, and authorisation to bury their eight carcasses before they cause offensive stink.'

Unexpectedly the kardi rose. 'I also meant to announce the captain's request to revive the custom of enforced recruitment of Christian boys to his janissary, along with women and girls for domestic duties.' In the collective Christian sharp intake of breath, Mama gripped my hand until it hurt. The clerk ignored the crowd's reaction and called the spice trader, Malachi.

The long curled toes of the spice trader's green slippers bounced as he strode, their jollity so misplaced. Malachi used flowery language to say he valued his reputation, and asserted he'd dealt fairly with Kritsa customers for over thirty years, no matter their religion or value of purchase. Then he pointed to a manacled man.

'My mute bodyguard is a freed slave. He uses his sword as protection when we journey. Never before has he unsheathed the blade in a village.' At this point Malachi wiped his eyes, and said it was tragic how his mute's attempt to help had had such dreadful consequences. I swear he dabbed his eyes with a red silk handkerchief for theatrical effect. After a final loud sniff, he continued.

'Maria always drove a hard bargain, and offered chicken, cheese or other goods when she had no money. Yesterday she wanted three cloves, without coin or barter, to ease toothache. Women often ask for a gift to ease pain, perhaps ginger for stomach cramps, but I'm a trader so always refuse. That's when her unbecoming shouts disturbed the peace, and the child clambered from the donkey saddle to pick a fight with my young grandson. The pair tumbled into the street, just as the parade headed towards them. My man recognised the danger and went to save the boys. Thankfully, he managed to seize my grandson. Remember the mute cannot call out, so when the wretched donkey blocked his way he prodded it through a pannier with his sword. Of course, we were appalled to learn a child slept in the basket. Such a tragic accident. However, the woman was unaware of the bolting donkey. She just took advantage of the commotion.' With a sigh, the spice man paused, as if it gathering his thoughts. 'If Maria had intended to purchase or barter, the sleeping child would be alive. Instead, she stole cloves, ran, fell, and hit her head on a rock. Allah's will was done.'

Uproar followed. Turks jeered, and Christians called for compassion. In his angry haste to stand, the kardi's gilded chair toppled with a clatter, and he seemed not to notice his fez fall again.

'Cease your clamour. Call the woman's defence.'

All fell silent as Cousin Lukas made his way to the front. Each person he passed gave him a touch to signal solidarity. This time, Papa acted as a translator in reverse to explain that Lukas had been to Malachi to purchase healing ointment. Although Lukas ignored ribald comments from the crowd, he looked flushed and agitated. With one hand in his pocket, Lukas used the other to touch his cheek while he described Great Grandma's severe toothache. She had hoped to barter for cloves to gain relief until the blacksmith could draw her tooth. Uncharacteristically short tempered, she'd snatched tiny white cloth bags away from the small boy on the donkey, stating they were for the spice man.

Although Lukas watched his feet throughout his testimony, he looked up when the kardi snapped, 'What use are bags to Malachi?'

Staring defiantly, Lukas explained, 'If accepted as barter the merchant could sell them as gift bags, perhaps for a nutmeg. This proves Great Grandma had no intention to steal, and...'

The kardi interrupted. 'Malachi, did this Maria offer bags as barter?' Malachi's single 'No' needed no translation. In the ensuing pause, the kardi's penetrating gaze bore into Lukas, who studied his feet again, shuffling from one to the other. He didn't even raise his eyes when the kardi asked, 'How did you bruise your handsome face?' Rubbing his nose, Lukas hesitantly explained he'd taken too much *raki* the night before so had walked into a door.

'No, that's not good enough! Show respect. Stand straight, take your hand from your pocket, and face me.' Reluctantly, Lukas revealed his bloody, rag-bandaged hand, and when forced explained he'd been clumsy chopping wood. When the kardi's eyebrows shot up and froze, my chest pounded until I snapped my mouth on a hissing sigh of relief at Lukas's dismissal. My grown-up hero shot a defiant scowl across the assembly, then dashed to sit by hooded Aimilios.

Next, the clerk called the janissary lieutenant, who needed no encouragement to speak.

'When the will of Allah sent an earthquake to Megalo Kastro three years ago, rubble destroyed our cannon. Imagine that, a city janissary corps without cannon! Initially we rescued survivors, shored up buildings, and prevented looting. Since then we've been rebuilding. Now it's time to resume our key task of keeping the sultan's peace to improve his prosperity, may Allah protect and preserve him. We are pleased to be in Kritsa as part of our training regime, and aim to bolster the local militia in light of lax administration in these parts.' The lieutenant was either unaware of or indifferent to the aga's glare. 'The wide fields beneath Kritsa give us room to exercise, and I'm pleased to report that our archery results, plus expertise with all types of blades, are first class. Our precision with grenades is improving at pace, and now that we have a replacement cannon from Arabia, we practice to reach high levels of accuracy.'

I recalled how Manos watched from Church Rock and then bored me with details of how many men it took to lift the cannon on to a special carriage with huge steel-rimmed wheels.

The lieutenant continued, 'Our pace makers led the way, followed by the troop, and finally six horses pulled the cannon. A large rock in your poorly maintained street caught a carriage wheel, and the axle snapped like a twig. Believe me, the blacksmith's head now feeds the crows. I don't accept shoddy work! Carriage horses reared in fright, the shaft broke, and two beasts fell. The knock jolted a cannon ball out of its recess to crush a child at the roadside. He didn't stand a chance. It was the will of Allah, praise be to His name. Brave lead horses tried to continue uphill, but the weight of the carriage and fallen animals made it impossible. They kicked out in panic, and crushed the haberdasher and two of his customers. Worst of all, we had to destroy two fine beasts – a tragic loss.'

Murmurs in the Christian crowd became disruptive, and, at a barked instruction from their captain, the janissaries came loudly to attention. It seemed they might enter the throng, so Papa begged for calm.

The lieutenant continued, 'Following this tragedy, a mob set dogs on fine young men. Of course my troops acted. We killed some rabble and their filthy dogs. I have to say, I can't understand why you Muslims allow dogs.'

Finally, the kardi raised his hand. 'I don't need your opinion, only facts. Stand down.' When the lieutenant marched to his troop in the shade, we yearned for such relief. The early April heat drew rank body odour from the crush of people to exacerbate our thirst and hunger.

The next man called was to defend the hunters from Pergiolikia, a hamlet at the top of Kritsa, and as he stuttered, in obvious distress, my papa advised him to take deep breaths and speak slowly. Hesitantly the trembling man explained that for the past two weeks he'd worked for his cousin, the blacksmith, where his task was to chop wood to feed the hungry furnace. Subconsciously he studied his calloused hands, and then mumbled that he didn't actually witness the accident. He'd run uphill to investigate a commotion to find a group of lads fighting, and when he saw his Pergiolikia friends nearby he'd called them without realising they had hounds. Bravely this defender offered his opinion that the fracas would have ended quickly if janissaries hadn't joined in to kill two Christians and most dogs. Then, as an afterthought, he added, 'It's lucky the breeding pair survived, their bloodline is renowned throughout Crete.'

After a few words with the captain, the kardi turned to the defender, who was still visibly shaking. To be honest, even I sensed he hadn't told the whole story. With his fierce stare fixed on the uncomfortable wretch, the kardi demanded, 'Point out the youths in the brawl.'

Without hesitation, the man turned to point out lads sitting in the shade. 'Those three, plus two who are being nursed by their families, and two who sadly died.'

'Now point out the Christian brawlers.'

'Sorry, Kardi, there was such confusion. I cannot.'

I noticed Lukas and Aimilios whisper while the kardi repeated his question. At the same reply, the kardi raged, 'You're lying. What's the use of a defence who won't tell the truth? Lieutenant, arrest him.' Impotent protests ran through the Christians.

Next a youth limped up to answer his summons. Flushed with excitement, he gushed his statement. 'Seven of us, including Ibrahim, a recent convert, went on a trip to Elounda on the coast. We took donkeys to carry our haul from the saltpans. We brought some whetstones too, for the knifeman and carpenters. Imagine Ibrahim's excitement – he'd never left Kritsa. He enjoyed bathing in the sea, and learnt of a family who would accept a convert to marry a daughter. Ibrahim was keen to tell his parents of his travels and good fortune at finding a wife. Not that he'd met her, of course! Back here, Christians taunted Ibrahim as we passed, and threw unclean meat. Like us, and in self-defence, Ibrahim raised his fists against Christian daggers, until men with dogs overwhelmed us.'

As the Turk drew breath, the kardi asked him to identify the attackers.

'I can't, they wore hoods.' A wave of the kardi's hand sent him back to the shade.

Next, the kardi and Papa had a direct and heated exchange. Papa turned to face us. 'The kardi asks me to name the Christian brawlers. I wasn't a witness so cannot. I'm therefore required to ask those involved to step forward.' An awkward silence, accentuated by cawing crows, drew another exchange between the two men. Then Papa sighed and shook his head sadly. 'I implore the culprits to own up. Assuredly, God will forgive you. If you don't show courage and admit your actions, the kardi will hang a random selection of eight youths.'

Uneasy quiet led to murmurs and anxious glances as heads twisted to view who else was in the crowd. Not renowned for patience, the kardi rose to his feet and pointed at Lukas. 'I'll take him as the first one, and...'

One of the oldest men at the gathering hauled himself to his feet. In the bewildered hush, his thin voice spouted nonsense. All around, adults questioned each other with raised eyebrows, and gave silent shrugs in answer. Mystified, Papa paused to check that the man really did want the kardi to hear his words, and gained an emphatic 'Yes'. As Papa reluctantly translated, Christians cried out in horror at the man's stupidity.

'It was me, Stavros. I'm sick of feeble Christians losing their faith. In my anger I struck Ibrahim.' Derisive laughter rang out from the Turks. The kardi shouted at Papa, as enraged as if he'd put the word's in the man's mouth. Through Papa, he told Stavros to stop holding the court in contempt. Stavros continued to stand, restating, 'I'm guilty.'

Now apoplectic, the red-faced kardi struck his fist on the side of his chair. 'I'm no fool. Who attacked our sons?' Before Papa could translate, a pair of elderly brothers caused a commotion as they helped each other stand.

'And us, we helped Stavros. It's time for Christians to fight oppression.' With arms around each other for support, they walked unsteadily to stand by their comrade, who watched in open-mouthed amazement.

Wearily, the kardi slumped into his seat. 'Who is the fourth man?'

An unseen man called out, 'I am.'

'Who is that? Show yourself.'

'Sorry, Kardi, I took a tumble fighting. Perhaps the lieutenant can help me.' Now even the Christians laughed. Although Aristidis was once a renowned dancer, I'd never seen him walk unaided. Due to his bent body his eyes continually searched the ground, so it was impossible for him to face the kardi. Despite the desperate situation, it was comical to see the lieutenant's confusion. He clearly hoped for an instruction, not wanting to appear stupid by assisting a deluded liar. In the following pause, the three old men shuffled over to Aristidis, and, short of breath, Stavros turned to the kardi.

'We've seen too many Christians persecuted. God miraculously answered our prayers to give us the strength of young men. God willing, we'll do it again.' Before Papa translated, all Christians stood to cheer, and I joined in, not understanding the old men's sacrifice.

Anxious janissaries surged forward to hit out indiscriminately with the hilt of their blades. This frightened Papa who begged for calm. The chaos was over almost immediately, and stunned silence fell when eight janissaries dragged our old heroes to the shade. Such was my innocence, I thought that the militia were kind to get the men out of the sun. By the time Captain Hursit stood to attention at the dais, the welcome shade was just reaching me. This handsome captain wore clothes similar to the lieutenant, except his silk waistcoat was a fabulous, bright sunny colour, like a goldfinch's flash.

*

Thea gasped at the implication of this revelation and asked a question. Locked in a world of her own, Rodanthe ignored her, continuing her account in a flat monotone.

*

Captain Hursit explained his troop and servant numbers had depleted in Megalo Kastro due to deaths from injury or disease, so he wanted Christian boys to train as janissaries. He also wanted men to labour, women to serve, plus girls for men who wished for a wife. When Papa translated this, he added a caution to stay calm and not to give janissaries cause to beat anyone. His advice was timely as tempers were rising, agitation increasing as folk digested the captain's demands for fresh meat, eggs, cheese, vegetables, olive oil, grain, rusks…Some brave souls interrupted to call out their complaints that the captain's preposterous proposals would impoverish the village. To calm the situation the kardi halted the captain. Once there was respectful silence, the kardi stated that he was well aware that the village's welcome guests had need of supplies, and that he would consult with the aga over an appropriate quantity. The captain realised he'd been dismissed, so made three separate courteous bows to the aga, the kardi, and the imam, before marching towards his troop that came rigidly to attention with a loud stomp of booted heels.

The aga had evidently decided it was time to leave the kardi to consider the evidence, and left the dais with his entourage. This left the kardi resting, with his chin in one hand, for so long I wondered if he slept. Eventually he sat up, and the buzz of muted conversation ceased. In anticipation of an angry reaction to his judgement, he took pains to remind the assembly that his decision was final. He warned that any unseemly reactions to his verdict would bring arrests.

Despite this warning, Christians rose up to plead for mercy when the kardi announced, 'Maria had no means to pay for the cloves that she was so desperate for. By taking them, she was a thief. Amputation of her hand posthumously will brand her as such, for eternity.'

This was the first time Papa's voice betrayed his emotion. 'Quiet please. Remember, many people await the kardi's judgement. Sit quietly now, don't prejudice events.' Mama fumbled in her apron pocket for her nose rag. The kardi continued and Papa translated, as if deaf to the distress all around.

'With regard to the mute, he acted to save a life. He was not to blame for the tragic consequences so is free to go with Malachi. Not so, defender of the men from Pergiolikia.

The men you spoke for clearly set hunting dogs on the janissaries. You chose not to tell the truth, so you will share their fate. The janissaries will use all of you as targets when they next practice with grenades. Janissary corps travel with surgeons, so my decision will allow them to review the effects of these weapons to learn how best to treat men who suffer future injury.'

Papa translated the kardi's words blandly, as if explaining the weather. 'Muslims are permitted dogs for hunting, so I'll award the breeding pair to Captain Hursit. Apart from these two, I decree a total cull of dogs. Every bark after five days will cost each man, woman, and child a sack of grain.'

As Papa translated, he kept his emotions in check, and many of us took this as a sign of his agreement to the outcomes. We were wrong.

Papa's translation continued. 'Swine are abhorrent to us. From this day forward, the penalty for keeping pigs, or possessing their filthy flesh, is banishment from Kritsa. Such action will cause loss of tax revenue, so I'll seize all goods and chattels belonging to an evicted person, and enslave their families.'

With a pause to sip water, the kardi ratcheted up the tension. 'As for the hooded villains, I've given them much thought.' Then he turned to face the frail huddled group. 'You freely admitted your part in the fracas, although I doubt your assertion, so you must bear the consequences. Watch as I cut my white silk handkerchief into four pieces. Each of you will stitch a patch of it on your shirt, above your heart, and tomorrow janissary archers will use you for target practice.'

Totally ignoring howls of protest, the kardi addressed the janissary. 'Listen to me, archers. In groups of four, aim at each man simultaneously. If you hit a patch of silk, you'll earn enough to pay for your uniforms. I guess most of you owe a tailor or moneylender, if not both. The villagers will repay this amount, via their pappas.' A collective gasp of dismay appeared unheard by the kardi. 'The bodies of men fed to the grenades belong to the surgeons. Those with arrow wounds can go to their families for burial.'

Before this chilling information had been absorbed, the kardi demanded all Christian boys and girls between the ages of seven and fourteen line up on either side of the dais in age order. Mama clutched my skirt as I naively rushed to take my place in line, anxious to gain a rewarding glance from Papa. Arranged as required, smaller girlfriends and cousins stood to my left, and the older, taller ones to my right. Mirrored by the line of boys, we were like two flights of steps. There were twenty boys, with Manos fourth in line, and eighteen girls, where I was seventh in line. I had no idea we were in danger until I saw Grandpa comforting Mama. Clearly irritated, the kardi prompted Papa twice before he continued translating.

'The practice of taking young Christian lads as janissaries is from the past. Is this how you were recruited?'

The captain stood to answer. 'Yes, Kardi. If I'd not been liberated from my parents at the age of seven, I'd not have found the teachings of Prophet Muhammad, peace be upon Him. In accordance with custom, they selected one in five of the boys from my village. We soon learnt we belonged to the sultan and worked hard to do him proud. It took most of us to the age of twenty-four to gain full acceptance as a janissary, when we qualified to accumulate our own wealth and take a wife. Now I sleep secure. If I die fighting for the sultan I'll go directly to paradise.' The captain threw out his chest, emphasising his pride. 'I'm the only recruit from my part of Albania to earn such rank, thanks be to Allah.'

'These days a man applies to join the janissary, often via the sponsorship of kin within your ranks.' The kardi thought aloud as he weighed up how to make his selection. Should it be the six youngest boys because they'd be more malleable, or the six oldest to provide useful resource immediately? I looked across at the row of boys, and realised they didn't know whether to be excited or scared. Then the possible consequences hit me. If they took Manos, I wanted to go too. Life without him was unthinkable.

Finally, the kardi turned to Papa. 'Call the wives and families of the condemned and dead Pergiolikia men.' It took some time before they stood close together by Papa, like frightened sheep herded into an unfamiliar pen. 'All of you must leave with the janissary. Take all you can carry. I'll speak privately to those standing before me. Everyone else, leave.'

This was confusing. We children stood before him, so did he mean we should stay? Mama resolved the issue. She grabbed me and Manos by the hand, then ran out of the market place. We were almost home when terrible screams rang out. We both huddled close to Mama. When another scream rent the alley, Mama spoke for the first time since we'd left the court.

'Sounds like you'll soon be an uncle again, Manos, earlier than expected. Come to my kitchen.' Once indoors, Mama recognised our greatest need was for sleep, so we slept on her bed while she prepared food.

In a community where people live so close to each other, we are adept at switching off when loud voices, full of anger, break the peace. Usually it is all over in a flash, and if you later ask what was wrong a blank expression meets your question, the exchange forgotten. On this difficult day, I awoke to find my parents arguing in hissing whispers, while tension hung like a curtain between the kitchen and bedroom. From my pillow, I saw Papa slumped in his armchair by the fire, facing Mama who stood with her back to me, pointing rigidly at the door. Obviously weary, Papa rose and straightened his cassock. Just before leaving, Papa stopped to say something, just three quiet words, and then he smiled the way he never smiles at anyone else. I sensed the moment was critical; then, with a sob, Mama ran to embrace Papa. Her unbraided black hair reached past her waist, and Papa tenderly stroked her tresses, his eyes shut. I glanced at Manos, suddenly aware that I'd love him to hold me like that when we were older. Papa had disappeared when I turned back to the kitchen, and Mama stood in our doorway to watch him go. She shrugged, tied her apron, and picked up her broom to give our floor the most vigorous sweep ever seen. I recognised my intrusion would be unwelcome, so feigned sleep.

Soon afterwards, I sensed Mama in the bedroom. I expected her to stroke my face to wake me. Instead, she reached under the bed to pull out her cedar wood trunk. Intent on her task, she didn't notice me take the few paces to the kitchen. She sat on her heels to empty the box and placed a silver candlestick to one side. Next she held her finest black kerchief, gently stroking it as if it were a small bird, then, with a sigh, she carefully unfolded it, and used her knife to cut off the coin edging that she placed by the candlestick. With a flash of comprehension, I realised Papa needed valuables to pay the kardi. What I didn't understand were her words as she closed the box.

'Oh, Rodanthe, more of your dowry disappearing. I'm so sorry.' By the time she replaced the box I was back on the bed, apparently asleep.

I heard another woman enter the kitchen. They held a soft, rapid conversation. The door closed. Mama's distraught sobs took me to her on her sofa. She grabbed me close, and buried her face in my loose hair. I thought she'd never let me go. Her tears wet my neck, so I wriggled free to take her a drink. Distraught, she stared into the cup, not bothering to wipe the tears dripping from the end of her nose into the water. I passed her my nose rag, but with both hands still on the cup she didn't take it. I wiped her eyes and fetched a wet cloth to wash her face. All the time she just sat passively, allowing my clumsy attempts to make it better, whatever 'it' was. When she found her voice it was barely audible, as if to lessen the impact. I soon realised she needed to tell me before Manos woke, because the dreadful death tally that day had increased by two when Maria had died giving birth to a premature stillborn baby. I later heard that her husband had kissed baby Nikos, their only surviving child, and then walked out of their house. I thought at the time no one knew where he had gone.

When I saw Manos beam in delight as his papa woke him I felt ill, crushed by the leaden weight of knowing his smile wouldn't last. Our house fell silent, and Mama remained on the sofa, as if asleep with her eyes open. I just held her hand. Eventually she stood to say she wanted to support her sister, and mourn with her family as an aunt and granddaughter rather than as the pappas's wife.

When the sun disappeared over the mountains behind the village it left an immediate chill, matching the mood of those bringing valuables to fill trestle tables set up on Church Rock. Papa's deacon was one of the few men able to read and write, so he took receipt of money, valuables, and foodstuffs, making careful note of who'd donated what. Someone had tacked blankets together to form a canopy that draped from the palm trees to provide shelter for the coffins. Some, like Great Grandma's, were of polished wood, purchased years before then kept flat at the back of the carpenter's workshop ready for quick assembly when required. Others were rough wood, hastily constructed to cope with the unexpected demand. With no known kin, the haberdasher lay wrapped in one of the Egyptian cotton sheets he'd hoped to sell in Kritsa. A handcart held a bespoke coffin, and as we filed past to pay our respects everyone choked with emotion at the grim contents. Now at peace with her tragic family, Maria had a twin in each arm and a tiny girl across her breast.

Dusk deepened as the murmuring congregation awaited direction from Papa, his dark silhouette dramatic against the backdrop of pink tinged mountains that reflected the setting sun. Everyone expected funeral proceedings to start, so shock and anger met Papa's announcement of a delay. The imam insisted on interring dead Turks before the day was out. In light of this, the kardi aimed to prevent disruption by Christians, so refused to authorise our burials. To deflect rising anger, Papa proposed that he start the Easter Thursday service. Most people stayed where they were, so Papa took the crucifix out of the church sanctuary, and then brought it to Church Rock to complete the service. Afterwards he encouraged women to continue the tradition of covering the epitaph (representing the funeral bier of Jesus) with flowers. With a stroke of genius, he urged us to collect flowers to adorn coffins in preparation for the funerals the next day, Good Friday.

By the early hours, there was no bloom left in Christian Kritsa. Each cherished pot of chrysanthemums, roses, and geraniums rendered bare stems. Trailing jasmine, sparkling white lilies, freesias, and orange blossom all provided heady fragrances. Bright dots of colour came from tiny wild orchids, violets, iris, and buttercups from the fields, their gathering lit by moonlight. White boughs of early blossom from hawthorn bushes put gatherers at risk, until a knife removed their long hard spikes. Vibrant but delicate poppies, white, mauve, and scarlet anemones, red and white hibiscus, and slim, elegant gladioli were all collected in armfuls by eager children. With floral shrouds for the epitaph and coffins complete, we slept fitfully on the rock with the heady bouquet of flowers as a soothing blanket.

Villagers rise early and are blasé to the sight of a dramatic dawn heralding the sunrise over the Thripti Mountains. However, this morning God staged a spectacular sunrise to gain our full attention. First, as Orion strode away, a faint outline of the mountains became visible, their tops covered in frothy cloud that hid their rounded summits from view. Behind the mountains, sky lightened to grey, and then gained an apricot hue that rapidly deepened to vivid burnt-orange. The clouds, lit by heavenly fire, took on molten red outlines, leaving the mountains black in contrast with a pool of blinding liquid gold at their feet. When the sun appeared through a gap in the fiery clouds, it directed an astonishing shaft of pink sunlight to illuminate the flower-strewn coffins, its rosy glow making a dramatic prayer of hope. Then, as the widening beam brought light to the fields below Kritsa, eerie drums started a roll call. Unbidden, we gathered at the edge of the rock, and when Mama tried to coax me away, Grandpa stopped her.

'Let her witness their sacrifice.'

Three men shuffled into view, each prodded along by an impatient janissary towards four posts stuck in the ground. Janissaries then carried a bent form to join his comrades. Increasing sunlight illuminated the white patches on the captive's shirts, and brought into view the sixteen waiting archers. The drummers' beat rolled louder and louder, coming to a crescendo that ended abruptly to amplify the morning music of crowing cockerels, barking dogs, and bleating sheep, along with the deep bass notes of braying donkeys. Archers took up their stance, their bodies facing away from us as if ashamed. I saw the archers stretch their bows taut, and imagined each of them with one eye closed, squinting along the length of an arrow to judge their aim.

Standing on a jutting point of rock, Papa hoped the men saw him signing the cross, whereas I hoped they had their eyes tightly shut. A shouted instruction to 'Take aim' carried on a light breeze. Instinctively we knelt, sending prayers to assist the final moments of those brave men. In flight the arrows had no sound, but as each struck its mark a keening wail went up from the watching women to drown Papa's final sacrament.

Drums rolled, and janissaries formed two groups for a macabre contest where representatives of each took turns to hurl grenades at the unfortunate souls staked at regular intervals across the training ground. Each janissary rode his horse at full pelt, his grenade flaring. As he neared the victim, who was facing last painful breaths, he flung his grenade to arc through the air. Then the janissary exercised great skill to swerve his horse from the blast and avoid the spray of debris and body parts that spun skywards. Cheers accompanied each new blast from the watching troop, with an echo of anguished cries from the rock. When the field below fell quiet, eight grim faced Christian men wheeled handcarts to collect the remains of those struck by arrows. Later, when the funeral procession started, the coffins of our four martyrs had pride of place, dramatically covered solely in red flowers.

I found the prospect of ritual final kisses in the graveyard too much to bear, so kissed Cousin Maria, her babies, and Great Grandma in a personal tribute. I gently placed a bracelet of flowers and basil around Great Grandma's severed wrist, a gesture of love that filled me with overwhelming rage. I kicked at a rag doll, discarded by a younger girl, sending it flying to land under a bush. Without thinking I retrieved the doll, then tore it into pieces as I ran to the overhanging edge of rock, where I screamed down at the killing fields.

'You filthy Turks. You dirty malacas. You murderers, I hope you all die. This is what you deserve!' I was oblivious to my hot tears as I watched the rag pieces flutter away. My rage then evaporated, replaced with misery at Papa's dreaded words.

'God will forgive you, Rodanthe. He always does, but I am very disappointed in you. Remember, Jesus said we should turn the other cheek, and the Lord's Prayer says we should forgive those who trespass against us.' I froze in shock until Mama led me away from danger and Papa's chilling displeasure.

Angry debate rose from people on the far side of the rock, and seeing Manos there I went to join him. I hoped to convey sympathy and take comfort by holding his hand, a gesture spoilt by rude comments from an older boy that caused Manos to blush and hurriedly drop my hand. I recognised that asking Manos the cause of the heated discussion would cause him more embarrassment, so I listened and hoped to pick up the thread. It was hard as many spoke at once.

'Everyone enjoys eating roast spring lamb on Easter Sunday as a symbolic treat, a tradition. Apart from this, it makes economic sense to wait until autumn when beasts yield more.'

'A summer on the mountains, eating grass and fragrant herbs, gives a rich taste to the fat marbled through their meat.'

'Ah, that's the problem. Turks have no taste!' The familiar refrain followed: 'Those bloody Turks!'

'It will be hard to save beasts to trade if they take two thirds of our lambs and kids.'

'How will I bake *kalitsounia* pies on Easter Sunday? They want our flour, oil, and cheese.'

'Pappas Mathaios has no fire in his belly. When we asked him to lead us in civil disobedience, he said the retribution would be harder than our current circumstances. So perhaps he agrees with the kardi's decisions if he won't challenge them!'

I scanned the crowd, hoping Papa wasn't nearby, and then it got worse as a coarse voice said, 'The pappas told me the kardi had been wise in his judgements, showing a balance of strength and compassion to ensure the aga didn't lose face.'

*

In her anguish, Rodanthe clutched Thea's arm, and said, 'I never really understood what Papa meant. I guess I never will.'

After a few moments, Thea said, 'I think the kardi ensured a swift death for the brave old men. By gifting the Pergiolikia families to the janissaries he ensured they wouldn't starve, and removed potential trouble from the village. What did other people think at the time?'

*

The wife of Mardati Yannis raged, 'Just imagine, the families from Pergiolikia bade farewell to their men hoping for a good dinner of hare stew. Now their enslaved wives and children will get no compassion. I bet those young girls already wish for death!' Furious support encouraged the woman to continue. 'I dread to think what it will be like for our children. We used to grumble and moan about life under our aga, but we didn't walk in daily fear for our lives. This captain warned the aga to keep us in tighter rein, and raise more taxes. The pappas says leave things to settle, and he'll talk to the kardi to try to renegotiate the levy, but my Yannis says the time is right to fight back.'

A male voice called out, 'My son was promised to one of those Pergiolikia girls, and I had my work cut out preventing him from launching a raid to snatch her back. His death would have been certain, for no good result.'

Another male responded, 'Ugh! Surely he'd not consider her once she'd been used by a Turk!' Female voices rose to protest that the shame belonged to the Turks not the girl, and begged for ideas on how to save her and the others. Men responded with the single opinion: the women were lost.

Our sombre procession followed the flower decked epitaph and coffins to wind down to the graveyard beyond the village. Not a Turk was in sight, but we felt their eyes peering through shuttered windows. On reaching the graveyard, I saw the caretaker had already opened the family vaults of the bereaved.

Once everyone had squeezed into the graveyard, Papa gave the Good Friday service, then, after only a brief pause for water to soothe his croaky voice, he conducted the funerals. Despite the colossal amount of flowers now in the cemetery, their scent was insufficient to mask the decay from so many open tombs, and I felt sorry for Papa as he blessed reeking graves, apparently immune to noxious smells and spores. His sermon was heavily themed towards forgiveness, and I disloyally realised that many of the congregation would have thought more of their pappas had his bias been fighting the good fight. Thanks to divine intervention, the sermon wasn't the most memorable part of the day. Winds gust through Kritsa at any time, and often a single blast wreaks the most damage. On this day, a tumultuous gust was heaven sent.

Papa had reached the part of the service for final farewells when a roaring squall raced from the sea. This blast raged through trees, and swirled Papa's hat away. It went up and around, caught on a thermal like a buzzard, and the same updraft took the blooms from the coffins. All eyes turned skyward, watching the flowers going ever higher. As the maelstrom lost power, the hat and torn petals fell slowly, like large, wet snowflakes. Its job done, the gale became a breeze, leaving the graves and congregation beautifully covered. Papa may have intended to say more; instead, he fell to his knees for a private prayer, and mourners took their leave with the constantly repeated refrain 'May their memory be eternal'.

On my exit, I walked past Sly Fanis on his lonely seat on the wall, and he spitefully tripped me. Shocked more than hurt I got to my feet, wondering why a distant adult cousin I knew only slightly was so horrid. He looked away to pretend it hadn't been him, and the direction of his gaze was towards Lukas and Aimilios in earnest conversation with other men. When I saw his scowl I realised they'd intentionally excluded him, so Fanis had lashed out at me.

It wasn't until dusk on Easter Sunday that I realised the nature of the grisly plot the other men had kept from Fanis.

Meanwhile, the dawn of Holy Saturday passed unremarked. I'd slept with Mama, and had expected Papa to move me to the sofa when he retired, so I was pleased to wake still with her. Snores from the kitchen told tale that Papa had sat to remove his boots, and then fallen asleep for the first time in over sixty hours. Luckily, the Holy Saturday service is late evening, so Mama and I crept out to maximise his rest.

We went to visit my aunt, who was at her wits' end trying to find a wet nurse for Nikos as well as cope with her grief. After an hour, I welcomed the errand to tell folk that Church Rock was the venue for the Resurrection Service. Many women commented that, in light of our troubles, they'd had no opportunity to make *mageiritsa*.

*

Puzzled, Thea asked what *mageiritsa* was. With a grimace, Rodanthe answered, 'It's a traditional soup made with vinegar and offal to break our fast in the early hours of Easter Sunday. I don't like it.' Then the girl giggled, and said, 'Some women swore me to secrecy, and showed me batches of red dyed eggs they'd kept from the janissaries, acts of defiance to ensure children had a treasured egg to knock against that of another on Easter morning. The previous year, Manos had owned the unbroken egg in our contest, so I hoped someone had saved one for him. I wanted revenge.'

The mention of Manos kindled more memories.

*

I'd not seen Manos all day. With a jealous pang I realised he now spent more time with boys, and, as I'd learnt yesterday, my presence easily embarrassed him. Almost immediately, grim faced men led a motley collection of dogs past me. Most dogs barked excitedly as they bit at unfamiliar bonds, and wagged their tails at the unexpected adventure, unaware it was their last. With sudden insight, I knew Manos would be at the *kafenion*. Spanos had recently adopted a pup and Manos was besotted with it. Spanos always made Manos so welcome, I think he loved him as the son he could never have.

A broom rested across the *kafenion* doorway. I stepped over it, called out my hello, and headed for the brushed dirt courtyard. A patch of dug earth told me I was too late. A cross, made from two twigs and a piece of twine, gave clear sign of Manos's involvement. The list of deceased animals that had benefited from a special Manos tribute included an old dog that used to guard chickens from weasels, two puppies that unwittingly swallowed poison, a litter of unwanted kittens, mice rescued from cats, and three baby birds found below a nest destroyed by hooded crows. There had also been burials for his green lizard, plus a pot full of chirruping cicadas he'd hoped to keep till spring. For me, the premature death of this soft pup was the final straw, and I cried openly until I reached home.

I was so relieved to find Papa still in his chair, and hoped he'd let me sit on his knee, but there was no response to my 'Papa!' He was as I'd left him, only now his chair faced the cold remnants of the fire. Beads of sweat covered his brow, and wheezy breaths sounded dreadful. Perhaps he sensed my presence in the kitchen and mistook me for Mama, as in his sleep he croaked out a feeble 'Irini?'

I ran to my aunt's home to fetch Mama, then trailed her as she sprinted back. I timidly watched from the doorway as she helped Papa into bed, then gently washed his face. When she noticed me, Mama said, 'Don't be frightened, Rodanthe. Fetch fresh water to make dittany tea, it's a cure-all.'

Right from the start of the Easter service, it was evident that Papa struggled. He needed frequent pauses to ease coughing fits, and his usually clear voice was barely audible. Coughs echoed through the congregation as people cleared their throats, as if subconsciously trying to help him. With perfect celestial timing, a gibbous moon rose over the Thripti Mountains just before midnight. It started with a silver speck, and within the short time it took Papa to light the Holy Flame and declare *Christos anesti* – Christ is risen – the moon was up. Next, Papa lit the candles held by those nearest him, and then, with a flare of gold, each of them lit another's candle.

The Holy Flame flowed swiftly through the congregation, with the moon adding a silvery sheen to eerie flame-illuminated faces. As the last candles danced to life, exciting crackling sounds of a bonfire on the leeward side of Church Rock took over. Orange flames illuminated the traditional effigy of Judas that swung from its gibbet, with its heels already singed. The crowd shielded their candle flames and formed a semicircle around the blaze to enjoy the heat. Fire swallowed

Judas's legs in seconds, but his body, stuffed with different material, took longer to burn. Bright flames gave luminance to an instantly recognisable face, and as comprehension hit the crowd that our Judas wore a distinctive moustache and fez, a mocking cheer rang out, followed by a collective cry of 'Christos anesti'. A spark caught the stolen fez's silk tassel, and a blue flame sizzled up its length to elicit another loud cheer, and an irreverent cry of 'Christos anesti, and pox on bloody Turks.' Even subdued by the heavy pall of mourning, we enjoyed that moment of mirth.

By morning, fever had rendered Papa insensible. In different circumstances I'd have been sent to Grandma, but she had enough worries supporting my aunt so I stayed by Papa to hold his hand. When an awful rasp, deep in Papa's, throat signalled his last breath, his lips were already turning blue. I stared in horror at his bulging eyes, and it took a few seconds for the dreadful implication to register.

I screamed, 'Papa! Papa's dead.' Mama was only a few steps away preparing more dittany tea, and she reached his bed in a heartbeat. She jerked Papa's arm to pull him across the bed. His head hung down, almost touching the chipped *kazani* we used as a chamber pot. Then she banged his back, hard. At her second strike, a huge gobbet of rust coloured sputum shot from his mouth to plop on the floor. He sat up, gasping for air, then collapsed back on his pillows in a fit of painful coughing.

Bad news travels fast so we soon had visitors, each carrying their personal panacea. Grandpa Nikos brought *raki* infused with honey, as did Grandpa Babis and two uncles. Papa would certainly have been insensible to his plight if he'd consumed all those tonics! Despite her other worries, Grandma sent Manos in with carrots and a twist of paper containing cayenne pepper, plus instructions for Mama to make a broth to feed Papa every hour. A great aunt brought bitter tea made from olive leaves sweetened with honey and cinnamon to ease coughs, and our deacon said prayers in confidence that God would save his faithful servant.

In a community such as ours, affording the physician isn't usually an option, so Mama was astonished when Spanos paid Samuel to call. When Mama expressed her gratitude, Spanos made light of his generosity.

'It's the least I can do. Your wonderful man found me beaten and left for dead. He even made Sly Fanis return the purse of coins bequeathed to me by a rich patron. Once I regained my health, he helped me complete the formalities to buy the *kafenion*, and I know that he encouraged customers not to take their pipes elsewhere. Best of all, he brought me to Jesus.'

Samuel diagnosed Papa with a potentially lethal condition called pneumonia, and although he doubted the power of *raki* and honey, he thought the remedies suggested by the women would be helpful. To these, he added a recommendation that Mama use a large sheet to create a tent over a pan of boiling water containing crushed eucalyptus leaves, and sit Papa under the tent twice a day to breathe the beneficial steam to loosen mucus in his lungs. It scared me when Samuel told Mama to avoid Papa's breath, put his soiled nose rags onto the fire, and then wash her hands to prevent the spread of infection. As Samuel took his leave, he noticed me huddled miserably on the sofa, and coaxed, 'Help your mama. Collect eucalyptus leaves.'

Pleased to have a specific task, I set off towards the trees by Kavousi Spring, and found Manos hunched in a miserable heap on the steps of his sister's empty house. Careful not to mention his tears I asked him to help me, and as we walked along he explained how he felt invisible. Everyone asked his ma how she was coping, but no one recognised his distress at losing his sister and nephews. He told me he'd looked for his pa and brother, but they'd disappeared along with Grandpa Babis. With a humourless laugh, he added, 'I expect they've gone to Uncle Raki, and...'

An explosion boomed high above Kritsa. Sick with fear, we cowered against the harem wall. With the trauma eclipsing the day, we'd both forgotten that Christians illegally exploded black powder on Easter evening to remind God that we celebrated his reawakening. Smoke, tinged brown with particles of earth and rock, billowed on a light breeze. Once we realised what it was, we settled to enjoy the contemptuous display.

We scanned the cliffs, hoping to glimpse men priming the next detonation. Instead, our reward was eyes full of grit from the first explosion. We had just surmised that perhaps the men thought one token gesture was enough when eight explosions, sited close together, flared simultaneously. We held our breath in anticipation of the blasts that came a few seconds later to leave our ears ringing. As before, the plumes of smoke billowed out, but this time each blast had a flaming centre, rapidly widening as it fell. We didn't have time to wonder. A gory mess rained down. Suddenly we had evidence of what Lukas, Aimilios, and friends had been plotting. Clumps of burning fur and chunks of bloody dogs splattered over the hillside causing us to run, shrieking in terror.

*

White-faced, Rodanthe paused. 'I can't tell you any more tonight, Thea, this is more exhausting than I imagined. I'll take some fresh air to clear my head, and then sleep.'

7

AFTERMATH

Pain in her hand woke Rodanthe. Her taut red and shiny skin had stretched so much that pus seeped through the scab-covered stitches. She tentatively sniffed at her wound, fearful that suppuration might lead to gangrene. When Thea found Rodanthe cooling her hand in the pool, she was mortified.

'I should have removed the stitches. I'll brew a pain relief. I've an onion too, so can make a poultice to mash with thyme.'

'That makes sense, I know of the antiseptic properties of thyme. I'd prefer dittany though. Do you have some?'

'No, what's that?'

Rodanthe expressed surprise that Thea hadn't heard of the celebrated herb, and then shared the myth.

'Aeneus, son of the goddess Aphrodite, was involved in the battle of Troy, part of ancient Greece. Afterwards, he went across the sea to another country called Italy, where he helped found the great city of Rome. Those were not peaceful times, and Aeneus was seriously hurt in an archery duel. Luckily, Aphrodite kept watch on her son from afar, so saw Aeneus fall with dreadful wounds. Aphrodite raced to the mountains of Crete to cut dittany for a tea. This drink expelled the arrow and eased his pain to allow Aeneus to return to his battles. Now folklore says goats forage for dittany to heal their wounds.'

'If they are mountain goats it will explain why I wasn't aware of dittany. The village of Vrisses on the ridge above Choumeriakos is the highest I've been.'

'Yes, I'm sure it only comes from the mountains.'

'Panagia Mou! A mountain woman used to make regular pilgrimages to the Panagia, and her offering was usually pink flowers with hairy stems and downy leaves.'

'That sounds like dittany. Is she likely to visit again soon?'

'No. Her husband, Captain Kazanis, runs a fierce band of brigands known as *palikers* in open rebellion of the Turks. I think she took her baby and fled to escape retribution.' Even as she spoke, realisation struck Thea. 'I might have dittany!' It took a while as Thea rummaged through her storage area, anxiously watched by Rodanthe. Eventually, she passed over a bundle of dried and faded blooms that crumbled in Rodanthe's hand to release their distinctive aroma.

'This is it! Oh, Thea, there's so much. Can I make a tea of it too?'

'Take as much as you need, then show me how to prepare it. I just thought that woman brought pretty flowers to the Panagia. Good job I'm a hoarder!'

Thea noticed Rodanthe wince as she removed the stitches, so chatted to distract her patient. 'At first I thought the Panagia delivered you here to tend the chapel with me. I sensed you had no kin, and thought it an attractive solution.' Thea sounded wistful. It was evident that she longed to have someone to care for. With the sudden realisation that her future didn't lie in the quiet forest glade, Rodanthe changed the subject.

'Of course, Thea and Dora! You worked together to tend the icon. I expect Dora knew the legend of Saint Theadora, and named you for her.'

'Really? Tell me.'

'Ancient Russian priests banished icons as idolatry, and one of the fiercest critics of these beautiful pictures was Emperor Theophilus. When the Emperor died, his widow Theadora became regent. Like us, Theadora knew people didn't worship icons, but treated them as pictures of friends who helped explain God's word. This holy woman put an end to 120 years of heresy to restore hidden icons for all to enjoy. On the next first Sunday of Lent, the patriarch of Constantinople led great celebrations to give thanks for the restoration of the icons.'

'I'm sure you're right. Dora had a great sense of humour, and I can see how that idea would have appealed to her.'

This conversation allowed Rodanthe to put recent thoughts into words. 'It's a worry to know what to do when I leave you. What do you think?'

'You'll need to find a community, start a family. For now, though, drink your dittany tea, and tell me how people got on with their lives after that gruesome Easter.'

*

Colossal griffon vultures arrived the next day.

These scavengers glided out from their feeding grounds above Katharo Plateau. They circled lazily on high thermals, tracing mesmerising spirals against the cloudless cobalt-blue sky. Their effortless motion went on for hours with hardly a wing beat among them. Finally, a brave bird plunged to feast, rapidly followed by others. Of course, Manos climbed the cliffs to observe them.

When Manos met me later, he hunched over with his arms outstretched to imitate the vultures' massive wingspan. Bubbling with excitement, he described how each long, gangly neck ended in a frilly ruff of white feathers beneath the head. As usual, whatever the situation, Manos made me laugh. He mimicked the disgusting grunts and hisses made by feeding birds, and then mimed their ungainly hops, with wings outstretched, to move from one grisly morsel to the next. What a contrast to their graceful flying! Finally, he impersonated the flocks of argumentative hooded crows that arrived to pick fights with the larger birds. Our laughter was a short interlude from raw grief.

Disgusting flies came ten days later.

Debris quickly became a stinking breeding ground for flies. Their fast reproductive cycles soon created huge swarms to hum over the village, and even cover food in our hand. My aunt kept baby Nikos under a sheet tent, otherwise his cradle gained an awful buzzing shawl. A deadly consequence of the flies was the bloody flux. At first, death struck like wildfire without discrimination between Christian, Jew, or Turk.

Samuel still visited Papa at that time, and he reported how Turks minimised contact between people to reduce the spread of the disease. The imam cancelled prayer meetings and urged his followers to redouble their already high standards of personal cleanliness. When the aga left for Megalo Kastro with his women, it reduced commerce and therefore interaction among the Turks. Christians knew the imam called on the Prophet to support Muslim mourners, so the fact that Papa was too ill to conduct funerals left folk feeling 'robbed' of their due to add anger to their grief. This anger led to rumour and counter rumour against the men who'd blasted dogs across the village. To make matters worse, the kardi offered a bounty for the perpetrators' names.

One evening, when Samuel was in the bedroom to check on Papa, our door burst open. An exhausted Aimilios dragged a limp body inside, and heaved Lukas on to the sofa.

Immediately grave, Samuel attended to Lukas whose arm had swollen to double its usual size, its taut skin an ominous, dull brown. As Samuel gently removed a rough bandage, I gagged at the sight and smell of suppuration. Fully engaged in his task, the physician issued brisk instructions.

'Rodanthe, fetch fresh water. Irini, find clean cloths and help me wash Lukas to bring his fever down. Aimilios, find me twenty maggots. We might save his hand.'

The physician agreed to waive payment until Lukas could assume responsibility for his debt, and Mama agreed to nurse him. This meant Lukas needed my bed on the sofa, so Mama sent me to Grandma for a few days. To soften the impact, she couched it as an adventure to include a night under the stars. Full of excitement, tinged with fear of the unknown, I adjusted my rucksack over my shoulder, and submitted to Mama's thorough check. Yes, I'd packed a warm blanket. No, I'd not forgotten my hairbrush. Yes, I'd wash my face. No, of course I wouldn't forget her. Yes, of course I loved her. Finally satisfied, Mama kissed me goodbye with tears in her eyes.

Manos was fascinated to hear how Samuel used maggots to eat rotten flesh. Not so Grandma; she was appalled. Tut-tutting, she hurried away to share the news.

*

With a squeamish sound, Thea said, 'Maggots! Really?'

'I know, it sounds unbelievable. Samuel was sure it was the only way to save the hand. Do you remember I previously described helping Grandpa with the slaughter?'

'Yes, indeed. Your Grandma scolded you for using a knife.'

'Well, when Grandma returned to check on Manos and me, she found us sitting in the shade of a tree wondering what to do next. She beckoned us to her in a conspiratorial

111

manner, quite unlike her usual behaviour. She gave us both a sewn kidskin, the type used by shepherds for carrying water, with the instruction to scavenge around and fill both bags with maggots. We gawped as if Grandma were mad when she winked and waved us off. With lots of giggles, Manos shared his thoughts that Grandma intended to give the janissaries more than they expected. So, with an evil grin I bet Manos that I'd fill my bag the fastest.'

*

After shepherds had identified animals to meet the janissaries greed, the apprentice lads herded all remaining sheep into pens. Then men of all ages bent under shady trees from dawn to dusk for three days to separate bleating animals from their coats. We children peered over armfuls of heavy, stinking fleeces as we staggered to throw them on handcarts. Once, when we passed Grandpa Babis, Manos called, 'Hey, Grandpa, where did all these sheep come from? They didn't winter in the village.' Relieved to take a moment's break, Grandpa Babis came close and urged Manos to look where he pointed.

'I bet you can't see a rocky cleft in the hills. Look beyond the gorge, to the right. There's a hidden stream-fed valley, a natural corral for wintering flocks. It's out of sight, but under Turk noses.' Grandpa was delighted that we couldn't see it. 'Right, move on, you two, these sheep won't shear themselves.'

Two days later, we'd gained promotion! We were proud to be herders on the trek up ancient paths to Katharo. When our path passed through a forest of stumpy trees, we were amazed to see goats climb up them to nibble leaves. After that, we seemed to be constantly saying 'Wow!' The panorama now included five great headlands that thrust into the incredibly blue sea, with such vivid white rims I expected to hear waves crash onto rocks. Instead, I heard frantic barks and howls.

At the next bend the cobbled path opened out on to a wide, long-established resting area for transient flocks. There were stone pens, wooden troughs full of rainwater, and a cacophony from twenty dogs, each straining at the end of a rope leash. Gruff shepherds, well used to masking emotions, broke into wide grins as they anxiously sought their own dog, and then bent to fuss it, enjoying their excited welcome. No wonder I was confused; I'd seen the horrific demise of village dogs. Manos rushed to tell me the best dogs had been spirited away from Kritsa under cover of the Easter Sunday explosions. I guessed his 'That's one in the eye for the bloody Turk!' was copied from his grandpa.

With the dogs back in control of the flocks, we continued at a faster pace, until the path narrowed between white rock towers. The incredible noise from so many animals in a constricted space created a blanket of separation. Their constant movement bowled me along, and I stumbled over uneven surfaces, very aware that a fall would leave me crushed under streaming hooves. When the animals funnelled on to a wide, grassy area, the constant movement eased. Although minutes earlier I'd been hot and sweaty, I was now chilled and hungry. After a short rest, Grandpa moved on, and I responded to his whistle as obediently as his dog, but less eagerly as I doubted my ability to walk much further.

Only the shame of confessing fatigue kept me going, and I soon lost sight of Grandpa. When darkness fell I trudged on, confident as long as animals passed me that I was on the right path. I stopped in sudden fear. Sheep surged past in bright moonlight to disappear over a dark drop. Nervous of a descent into the unknown, I put my faith in a passing ewe, grabbed her leather collar, and ran.

My fall was inevitable.

Grandpa's dog reached me first, its loud barks bringing him to the right thorn bush. Chuckling at my predicament, Grandpa pulled me out and swung me onto his back like a sack of olives. When Grandpa reached the camp he sat me near firelight to tend my cut legs. I guessed herders shouldn't cry, so bit my lip, hard.

Savoury meat roasting on posts around the fires soothed my discomfort. That succulent mutton was the best I've ever tasted. Greasy juices flowed down my chin, but I've no recollection of sleeping. The next morning, Manos woke me to marvel at snow-topped peaks forming a statuesque backdrop to the plain. Close by, donkeys cropped lush knee-length grass; to the right, spectacular blossom covered fruit trees; and, all around us, adventure!

If a child has a paradise, then that fabulous carefree summer was it, although, unbeknown to us, Grandpa had us under surveillance. He gave Manos a square goat bell to wear on a leather thong around his neck, and me an oval one from a sheep. At that time, we didn't realise a shepherd recognises the bell of each animal; the tinkling soothes when all is well, and alarms when a note is missing. After days filled with new experiences we enjoyed musical evenings, and when the men danced, the increasing height of their leaps correlated to lowering levels in *raki* flasks.

I yearned to join Manos as he learnt to dance, and encouraged him with loud shouts of 'Bravo!' For some strange reason, dancing was the only thing denied me, and when Grandpa returned from a few days trading without us, I complained that it was not fair. He took my face in his rough hands, and for a scary moment I thought he was about to cry.

Instead, he said, 'Many things in life are unfair.' Then

he clutched me close. 'Now, little lady, find your weary old Grandpa some supper.'

Cooler days of autumn signalled time to round up animals for the descent to Kritsa. I was suddenly keen to reach home, and by mimicking the long, loping stride of the men, I maintained the lead. Joyfully I rushed into the house, and then stopped in shock. I hardly recognised the frail man Papa had become. I wished he'd say he was pleased to see me, but instead he said, 'Ah, Rodanthe, God has kept you well. Mama is relieved to have you home. I'm such a burden.' It was a shock to hear his hacking cough leave him so breathless. Mama absent-mindedly passed him a clean rag, and stoked his hair.

'Mathaios, what a thing to say. You're no burden. Let me help you to the table.' To welcome me, Mama had laid out her best cloth and three matching plates. If she hadn't drawn attention to our sparse fare, I wouldn't have noticed. I was just happy to be home.

Tales of my wondrous summer gushed like water from a spring. I'd fed crumbs to tadpoles in the receding river, traded with Kalamafka shepherds, snared rabbits, won at catapult shooting, and learnt to make cheese. Best of all, I'd ridden donkeys back and forth until Grandpa declared me good enough to be a drover. To aid my description of daily aerial displays by falcons, kestrels, buzzards, and vultures, I waved my hands around, earning a reproving comment from Papa.

'You make me dizzy, Rodanthe. Come and sit by me.'

Delighted to have his undivided attention, I gave Papa the most astounding news of all: Uncle Giannis had discovered a giant molar tooth in shale at the edge of a river, and no one had a clue what manner of beast had lost it. I'm sure Papa was interested, but after a long cough he slumped back in his chair with his eyes closed, totally exhausted. I didn't know whether to leave Papa or continue talking to him.

Mama saw my confusion. 'Mathaios, try this cheese that Rodanthe made. It's the most delicious that I've ever tasted.' I thought I'd burst with pride when Papa weakly agreed.

Given licence to enjoy such a glorious summer, my dreams went no further than hoping for a return visit next year. Then I became aware of the tension. With a barely discernible nod, Papa moved towards the bedroom to rest. I recognised it as a pre-arranged signal to leave me with Mama, so I nervously asked her how her summer had passed. I sensed her distress. The longer she took to reply, the more I chewed my lip. For the first time I noticed her gaunt, hollow-eyed face. She hugged me close, and then told me that Grandma had succumbed to the flux. Grandpa had kept the news from us, and when we'd thought he was away trading, he'd attended the funeral. There was no chance for me to ask any questions, as Mama continued her litany of the dead. At first, she named each one gently, allowing the loss to register. Then, in an increasingly dull tone, she listed those who had passed, mentally walking down each street to make sure she remembered them all.

I asked after Lukas and Aimilios. Mama explained that, as far as she knew, they were alive. Lukas hadn't lost his arm to gangrene, although for some time she'd feared the worst. He'd been on the road to recovery when Aimilios had stealthily knocked at the door to say the kardi had issued an arrest warrant in their names. Someone had declared the pair responsible for blasting dogs across Kritsa, and therefore accountable for the bloody flux. When the militia couldn't find the culprits they'd swept through households, confiscating foods put aside for winter and killing domestic goats and chickens, as if for fun. Although no one had absolute proof, word had it that Sly Fanis had turned traitor to name Lukas and Aimilios. Within days of the harsh reprisal, Fanis bowed down and became Omar. As a Turk, with a bulging purse, he was free to leave Kritsa, and he'd declared that he was off to make his fortune.

During the next four hungry years, I lived a sheltered life among women to learn the basics of traditional weaving, sewing, embroidery, and cooking. This included learning how to stretch scant rations to include the various men that Papa invited to join him most nights. Papa fed men who ordinarily passed most of their portion to hungry children, and took the opportunity to dissuade them from bowing down. It was a losing battle. The imam made it clear that the well-fed, chubby children of the Turks were happy to welcome new playmates.

My joy at that time came from Papa. He'd taught me to read, write, work numbers, and use the basics of the Turk language when I was small. Now he stretched me in both Greek and Turk languages. Complicated grammar and spelling became like a game, but, as ever, I felt inadequate in front of Papa as he always found room for improvement.

My twelfth summer was particularly difficult. Fettered by our customs I was always in the company of women. When Mama commented that Manolis was soon to leave Kritsa to attend school, it took me time to realise she meant Manos as he'd adopted an adult form of his name. That summer, the thick house walls lost the battle to keep the inside cool, and even our sparse furniture was warm to the touch. Most mornings passed in the shady street with other women, companionably chatting over sewing or crochet. I blushed with pleasure when our neighbour, Roula, commented on the embroidery I'd applied to a waistcoat, a gift for Papa. Then I burned in embarrassment when she teased, 'Is that for your intended, Rodanthe?'

When Tinker had brought confirmation of a school place for Manos, he'd also had an envelope for Papa. Incredibly, this letter was from the first pappas of Ierapetra, a port on the south coast. Papa had read the note aloud.

'Dear Mathaios, First Pappas of Kritsa,
Please forgive this direct approach, and be assured that it is on the recommendation of our mutual friend, the abbot of Faneromenis, who believes you will seek an educated husband for your daughter. After studying at Faneromenis, my son, Alexos, was schooled in France to qualify as a doctor. He has reached a stage in life where I'd like to recommend my son for your consideration. I understand your daughter is of a tender age, so a long betrothal will be mutually beneficial as Alexos will shortly accept commission as a ship's surgeon. It will...'

Mama had noticed my stricken face, and had broken in, 'Of course, Papa won't say yes. You're far too young.' I'd held my breath as the page slowly lowered to reveal Papa's frown.

'Well, it won't hurt to investigate. Once Alexos finishes at sea he might move to Kritsa. I'll visit Ierapetra, when I'm fit.' Without a word, Mama had taken a water jar, stormed from the house, and slammed the door so hard that the cups on the dresser rattled their disapproval. Papa had then carefully refolded the letter and placed it in his pocket.

As my cheeks cooled from Roula's good-natured teasing, I realised Mama must have shared the news of my suitor. In an attempt to hide my mixed emotions I bent over my task, and felt relieved when Mama sent me to fetch a rabbit to stew. I guessed that she wanted me out of earshot.

With Turks persecuting Christians without fear of reprisal, food was scarce, so rabbit became a staple but boring meal. I hated the shrieks of a rabbit about to have its neck wrung, so set about it quickly. Unfortunately, the doe I grabbed was a fighter. She raked her foot along my arm. As my blood flowed, I dropped her and then gave chase. Trapped by houses on either side of the street the frantic doe ran towards the spring, then sped towards Church Rock and freedom. I rushed after the rabbit, then halted in shock to see Papa sprawled under the palm tree.

'Papa! What's the matter? Did you fall?'

'Rodanthe, don't roam alone. Go home.'

Blood streamed down his face from a misshapen nose. This, together with a blackened eye and the awkward way he held one arm protectively across his ribs, told of a cruel beating. I tried to support him to stand. He pushed me away.

'Run, Rodanthe. For God's sake, go.'

I turned to see what was frightening him. Omar and three cronies strolled around the corner, laden with stolen jars of *raki* and sacks of food. I froze in fear as Omar shouted, 'Hey, you still here, Grandpa? You got what you deserved. That will teach you to use my new name.' As the brute passed, he aimed a spiteful kick at Papa. 'Get out of my sight, or we'll give you another dose.' I screamed and dropped to Papa's side.

Despite his pain, Papa shouted, 'Seek forgiveness, Fanis. I'll heal, but God saw your foul deeds. You'll burn in hell for eternity.' This retort caused Omar to turn, and, despite his spiteful bravado, his cowardly face blanched. That might have been the end of it had an ugly, bent dwarf not made a lewd suggestion to me with an obscene gesture. A huge turbaned Moor pushed him out of the way.

'In your dreams, Bilalis, a cat like that needs a real man.'

Omar seemed driven to look tough in front of his rough comrades, so sprinted to grab me. At the same time, Papa realised he was about to faint. I heard him shout, 'Please, God, save her!'

I ran. Omar caught me. He used one arm to clutch me close, while his free hand pulled my face for a rough kiss. 'Come on, lads, we deserve a bit of exercise. My cousin here is energetic!' He threw me to the ground, and shouted, 'Come on, one of you, open the honey pot! Hurry up, she's lively.'

Despite my adrenalin-fuelled thrashing, Omar overwhelmed me and held me at an awkward angle to ensure I saw the men drop their sacks as they walked towards me, loosening their britches. The Moor shouted a command to the fourth man.

'Hey, hold that infidel. He can watch his daughter enjoy an exotic stud.' When the huge man lowered his bulk towards me, he balanced on his toes and one hand, using his other hand to fumble in his britches. His face was so close to mine I saw hair from his nose tremble as he drew breath. My spit got his eye.

'Lovely, a spirited lass! Hold her tight now, Omar.'

'Let her go.'

Taken by surprise, the man hesitated long enough in his awkward stance for Manos to kick a leg from under him. At the same time Omar's grip eased slightly, giving me just enough room to bite his hand, hard. With a shriek, Omar pulled his hand away. I followed through to dig my elbow in his ribs. Suddenly free, I curled in a protective ball in anticipation of a beating. Instead, Omar joined the thug who struggled to restrain Papa, and swiftly kicked Papa unconscious. The Moor wrestled Manos to the ground, then sat astride his chest to throttle him. The other oaf rained in kicks, urged on by maniacal shouts from the tiny man. Overwhelmed by hatred and a powerful need to protect Manos, I joined the fray.

Mardati Yannis found us. When he lifted me, he retched at the bloody mess covering my face. Then he saw the gaping hole in the back of the Moor's head, smashed like a ripe watermelon, and the gore covered rock at my feet.

'My God, Rodanthe, what have you done?' Mardati Yannis ran to hurl the incriminating stone over the edge of the outcrop. The last thing I heard was his horrified yell.

I awoke in Mama's bed, disorientated and alone. Not aware of my sedation, I stumbled into the kitchen, then stared at my other set of clothes airing on the chair by the fire. Vaguely I realised I stood in my petticoat. I found out later that Mama had fed my bloody clothes to the flames, washed my face, and put me in her bed. Then she ran to my aunt's house where, despite his grave injuries, Papa tried to bring solace.

I expect Mama thought I'd sleep much longer. With no one to stop me, I walked unsteadily towards the spring. Women fell silent as I passed. Their whispers started before I was out of earshot. Children laughed and played in the alley. Scrawny chickens pecked away without concern, a solitary goat bleated in its stall, and, through an open door, came the unmistakable sound of a loom. This normality was surreal.

Like a sleepwalker, I reached the crumbled edge of Church Rock. Its broken shrubs gave up a heady fragrance to denote the place where frantic men had so recently scrambled. Gentle noises reached me: bleating sheep in fields below; mewing buzzards in a clear blue sky; cicadas, chirruping in this warm June evening. Then, louder than all of this, the remembered echo of a sickening scream.

Dreadful Omar and his brute had taken Manos by his arms and legs, swinging him back and forth over the edge to gain momentum, encouraged by Bilalis's ghoulish shrieks. I'd run futilely towards them as they propelled Manos into the air. My anguished scream had echoed his mercifully short, terrorised one. Now, from my vantage point on the high edge of the precipice, I tried to gauge how far Manos had plummeted. Although Samuel assured me that Manos's broken neck had meant instant death, I feared he said that for my sake. I leant forward to see the broken tree that had caught Manos, and, when the loose earth shifted under my weight, I rejoiced to share his fate. My saviour was Spanos. Distraught at the death of his young friend Spanos had also needed to face the drop. He grabbed me to hold me close, and when Spanos's tears splashed onto my face to mix with mine, we had no need for words. That was just as well; my ability to speak had frozen.

Despite great discomfort, my brave, disfigured papa conducted Manos's funeral service the next morning. I had no tears left, just choking anger that made it impossible to speak. When Papa praised Manos's courage, I was deaf to his words, lost in memories. Of course, I couldn't imagine witnessing anything so awful again. Once home, Mama helped me on to the sofa, and there I remained, locked in silence. I ate and drank mechanically, and slept with the aid of Samuel's potions.

After two weeks, Papa couldn't bear it. He took control.

*

Oblivious to her tears, Rodanthe had let the memory jinnee out of its bottle. Had she looked up, she'd have seen that Thea wept with her.

Rodanthe continued.

8

BANISHED

Dove stood in our kitchen, ears flat in fear. Earlier I'd watched Mama pack examples of my work, including a blanket woven with elaborate patterns and an embroidered tablecloth, into a pannier. On top of these, Mama had placed a set of clothes that Cousin Maria sadly no longer needed, a wrapped cheese, and several dry rusks. Throughout these preparations for my banishment I'd sat on her sofa, watching in disbelief. It became real when Mama sat close to me and passed me her ornate knife.

'Take it, my Rodanthe. Use it daily, and remember how much I love you.' Then her voice failed and she fled to her bedroom, sobbing. With no hope left, I swallowed the evil tasting concoction that Samuel had delivered earlier.

I needed to climb on to the table, so moved a chair closer to clamber up, and almost fell as the potion took effect. I kissed the handle of Mama's farewell gift and ran my thumb lightly on the blade, but lacked courage to use it on my wrists. Instead, I placed the blade in its leather sheath and tucked it in my apron pocket. Finally, I stepped from the table to crouch inside the largest pannier Grandpa could find. When the placid old donkey shifted to counter my weight, my knees rubbed on the rough basket, so it was going to be a painful journey.

Mama was still sobbing on her bed. 'Who'll keep me company in my slavery of grief? I'm desolate. No, Mathaios, I'll not kiss you.'

Papa tucked a blanket around my shoulders and lightly stroked my hair. 'Rodanthe, my sweet, you've kissed your mama. Now, dear child, we must flee.' Then Papa shut the pannier lid, opened the door, and led the donkey soundlessly down the street; the sacking around Dove's hooves effectively muffled his steps.

Fresh air threatened to revive me and negate Samuel's opiate syrup, until the rhythmic bumps of the pannier against the donkey's flank sent me to oblivion even before we'd left the outer limits of the sleeping village. Turks didn't venture out at night, so we passed unchallenged. I'm sure Papa was in great pain as he trudged uphill through the mild, windy darkness to reach Kroustas, the village at the top of the steep hill, just out of sight of Kritsa. Unbeknown to those villagers, my dishevelled Papa limped in a wide berth of the main street. When the path eventually led Papa downhill, the altered motion pressed my face against the pannier to wake me.

My discomfort was immediate, and any attempt to move futile. With an instant pang of loss, I remembered why I'd crushed myself in this basket womb. In a reassuring tone, Papa told me I'd done well and that he knew a safe place to stop. Soon spots of the morning sun filtered through the basketwork to dance on my face, fresh fragrances told me Dove walked over herbs, and birdsong indicated we passed trees, so I was surprised when the brightness was suddenly snuffed out. We were inside a musty cave, where Papa opened the pannier and held my hand to help me step unsteadily on to a rocky ledge. The effect I knew as pins and needles now felt like red-hot pokers, sending me stomping about to bring life back to my limbs.

Papa slumped on the ledge, rendered unrecognisable by exhaustion and swelling. The anger I'd felt for him, fuelled by Mama's distress, melted as I realised that despite his dreadful injuries he was taking a brave step to save me, and my reputation. I'd sworn the Turks hadn't soiled me, but gossips weave their own tales, and Mama worried that I'd lose any future suitor. Nevertheless, she was devastated at Papa's decision to lodge me with his elderly cousin below the Monastery of Faneromenis. I knew once Papa had settled me that he intended to conclude the bargaining for my betrothal, hence the gifts of my work for my potential ma-in-law. Mama had clung to Papa's knees, the floor awash with her hot tears, to plead that, at twelve years old, I was too young to send to unknown kin. She'd lost.

I took food to Papa. 'Will you say Grace?'

'Ah, you've found your voice. Thank God. This cave is cool and dark despite the heat of the day, so we can sleep here.'

That evening we were thankful for bright moonlight to illuminate our way down a dry riverbed of large, pale stones. The downhill part of our trek ended just past dawn near a wide, flat space Papa called Kalo Chorio – Good Town, obviously named by people with an ironic sense of humour. Three deserted wooden shacks leant clumsily against each other on the far side of a stagnant pool, overseen by a snow-white egret elegantly standing on one black leg to preen his feathers. Then a high-pitched whine heralded a cloud of mosquitoes. It was worse than any nightmare as a dense fog of tiny stabbing insects attacked our ankles, face, and hands. Even Dove brayed and bucked in pain. On reaching a glade rising away from the foul water we tried to rid ourselves of the pests in our clothing, but our frantic scratching brought hot spots of blood rather than relief. Papa's cut face proved irresistible to the mosquitoes, and his already distorted features swelled at an alarming rate. It seemed a final straw for Papa as he raged, 'I've never encountered such vile pests. They're the work of the devil.

I've not used this path before, and I thank God I'll not use it again.'

'Papa, you visit the monastery at least twice a year, so why use a new route?'

'If we used the trading path someone might see us. I expect the kardi will call you to give evidence at the inquest into the death of the Moor.'

'Well I hope there will be an inquest for Manos too!'

'Sadly not, Rodanthe. We live in a world where a savage is mourned publicly, whereas a murdered Christian youth is of no consequence.' In an attempt to lighten the situation, Papa gave a grimace that he probably intended as a smile. 'Mardati Yannis told me about this route. He said those huts at Kalo Chorio would make a good overnight spot, and then he laughed. Now I know why!' Despite needing rest, the irritation from so many bites made sleep impossible, and after scratching for an hour, Papa made ready to move.

'Come, Rodanthe, I've a fantastic idea. Follow me.'

Shortly afterwards, Papa guided us into a dry water-course. Conversation through bite-swollen lips was difficult so we trudged downhill in silence, the increasing heat making our discomfort worse. Gradually I became aware of an unfamiliar noise. It was a soft, low sound, like a rhythmic heartbeat, more discernible with each step. Then I noticed an odd tang in the air. Our path was narrow, flanked by tall poisonous oleander with fabulous heads of bright pink flowers. With a brief sniff, I realised these were not the source of the smell. When I faced an immense barricade of giant green rushes, I pushed my way through, and then dropped to my knees in prayer.

The spectacular vision of a stony tree-fringed bay and the refreshing salty breeze that cooled my face were heavenly. Coloured bands started with a dark line that fused heaven and sea, then merged into a stripe to mimic the clear lapis lazuli blue of the sky, before melting into bright turquoise tiers of waves that chased each other to the shore. I marvelled as foam-topped arcs rose then crashed onto the beach, with the retreating water dragging tiny stones tumbling backwards. By the time Papa reached me, I had my clogs in one hand and skirts high in the other as I paddled in cool water to soothe the red bites on my feet.

With an uncharacteristic wink, Papa stripped off his surplice and blouses, then kicked his boots away as he strode to the sea. I'd no idea Papa could swim, so was anxious and enthralled as he propelled through the water, each stroke showing a glistening arm. When he headed back, I relaxed on a rock, and once the stinging sensation of water on my bites had passed, each drenching brought sheer delight. When Papa emerged, he struggled to speak.

'I enjoyed that, although I should have remembered my battered body is not used to such exertion.'

'It was exciting to watch. How did you learn?'

'When I was a schoolboy we snatched opportunities to rush down the mountain, swim, skim stones, build rafts, catch fish, cook on the beach, and sleep under the stars before the long slog up to attend the first service of the day.'

'Who taught you to swim?'

'Ah, what memories you stir. Our beach had a deep rock pool, used annually as anchorage for boats collecting carobs. I learnt to swim the same way as other young boys: older lads dropped us in. They assured us it was holy water so we wouldn't drown. Actually, all mammals can swim, so I just did what comes naturally and splashed to the side. Then, to show I wasn't scared, I jumped back in. Style came much later.'

I was truly happy on that shore with Papa. We aimed stones at foaming wave tops. We laughed and shrieked as large waves caught us, then spluttered to rid our mouths of salt water. Eventually, lulled by the swell, we each stared out across the bay, deep in our own thoughts. My gaze, like a moth drawn irresistibly to a flame, moved towards the mountains where Kritsa nestled. A choking lump in my throat threatened my newfound ability to speak, so I jumped at Papa's suggestion that it was time to move on. We quickly forgot the cool sea as we trudged up a rocky track. Only the promise of a meal with Papa's aunt kept me going.

Where the steep path broke over a peak, giving way to a flat grassy area, I noticed an odd smell of a sweet roast. Horrified realisation dawned when we found eight burnt-out dwellings. Distraught, Papa rushed over each threshold as if willing someone to be alive. Instead, we found charred debris, fallen roof beams, a broken chair, battered sooty pans, and the singed remains of a bed. In one house, a plate rack hung at an angle from a single nail, its fragile blue plates now a pile of shards on the ground. I was staring at the mess in bewilderment when Papa came up behind me.

'Savage janissaries have been here. I pray to God some folk made it to the monastery.'

He didn't say another word until we reached the monastery's stout wooden door. Reinforced by a sheath of metal studs, it stood firm in a Roman arch, an effective barricade against all comers. Here Papa used his staff to bang out a coded pattern of knocks. A small window high up in the gate tower opened to reveal a tonsured head.

'Who is it? Oh, Mathaios! Thank the Lord.'

Wizened Brother Michalis was so frail I was amazed that he could swing the door open. He rushed to hug Papa as if he were a boy. Once introduced, he clasped me. 'So this is Rodanthe. All these years I've listened to your papa's tales of you, from perfect babe to mischievous toddler, and now young woman. Thank the Lord I lived to kiss you.'

The heavy door closed behind us with such a thud that the timbers of the gatehouse shook. This caused a shutter over an unglazed window in the west wall to swing open, allowing a golden shaft of setting sun to illuminate dust motes as if they were fireflies, and now the monk saw us properly.

'Who hit you? Oh, this child's face is a mass of sores. Come, let me tend you both. What brings you here now? Did news of the slaughter reach you? God in his heaven must have his plan, but a mortal like me cannot understand.'

In a cold voice, Papa said, 'We saw the remains of the hamlet. Please save the details for when my daughter sleeps, as she has had enough grief.' I almost ventured a question, then realised Papa's plans for me were in tatters so clamped my mouth shut.

After stabling Dove, I went to the kitchen where Brother Michalis provided soup, and then he sat with me as we both strained to overhear the abbot and Papa talking in armchairs set in front of the range. I heard that some of the younger men from the now ruined settlement had been landing rebel supplies at a nearby port when, by unfortunate coincidence, janissaries were at that dock to receive Arab horses. After cruel torture at least one of the men disclosed where their families lived, and retribution was swift. Although it was all shocking, I'd not expected an abbot to swear.

'Bastard janissaries left while the buildings burned, without testing our stout walls and reinforced gatehouse. Piled in one blazing home we found eight men, five boys, and twelve charred females. Two surviving old women were in another. Damn Turks!'

Papa glanced towards me. 'What of the younger women?'

'I expect the janissaries' pockets bulged after selling them.'

I thought Papa needed comforting, so I went to sit at

his feet as he asked after the two survivors. He clasped my shoulder as the abbot explained how his cousin had died without regaining consciousness. The other, called Anna, needed constant care. The abbot said, 'I know it's not seemly for Brother Michalis to tend her, but I've no option.'

Tentatively, I suggested, 'My Papa needs to go to Ierapetra, so I could care for Anna.'

'Anna's in the cramped space above the schoolroom. Your daughter could share with her. It's a decent distance from where the brothers and boys sleep.'

'I'd be very grateful if Rodanthe could stay with you for ten to fifteen days. When I conclude her betrothal, I'll make it part of the bargain that she lives with her future ma-in-law until she reaches sixteen. I'll set off tomorrow.'

Without further discussion, Brother Michalis led me towards Anna's gatehouse bed. Candles flickering in niches around the monastery's church on its high rock augmented the starry night to light our way. I'd stopped, entranced by the dancing flames, when Brother Michalis gently turned me to face into the darkness.

He quietly said, 'Kritsa is directly over there.' All I saw was the outline of mountains under the moon, but he'd triggered an idea.

'Brother Michalis, I'd like to light a candle in case Mama's looking.' After that, love shone across the distance each evening. I never missed once, not even when gales snuffed the flickering light before I was two paces away.

Anna lived in a separate world, trapped inside her mind. I squeezed into her narrow bed, and was frightened in case I disturb her as I scratched at my sores. She made no sound until morning, when she sat up and said, 'Hurry up, girl, there are goats to milk,' and repeated this every day.

Although I'd risen at dawn, there was no sign of the fifteen monks and eleven pupils when I went to the kitchen to find breakfast. I thought of Grandma as I wiped my finger along the large, roughly-hewn table. She'd always said that cleanliness was next to godliness. If Grandma was right, these monks were unaware of it. By midday, when the first two brothers walked into the kitchen, the place gleamed, and smelt of beeswax, lemon juice, and elbow grease, mixed with the piquant aroma of vegetable stew. The brothers introduced themselves, and explained how the abbot had spoken of me after the midnight service. He'd told them how I needed refuge until Papa could arrange my betrothal. With wonder in his voice, one brother said, 'The sweet maid has transformed our kitchen, and that delicious aroma says lunch is ready. Can she spend her mornings in here instead of the sickroom?'

Apparently, the abbot enjoyed his meal, so agreed I could use the kitchen.

When afternoon sun shone through the west-facing window of our tiny bedroom, I took books from the schoolroom to read aloud while Anna sat with her crochet. Each day, Anna made a fine and intricate lacy runner, like the one we used at home to decorate a shelf edge. Each night, I unpicked it to roll the cotton back into a ball for her to use the next day, and saw the once white thread quickly become dingy grey. In the evenings, when I lay in my dark bed to overhear the lessons below, I kept count of how many times I answered a question before the boys. I gave myself double points if I answered when none of them could.

One evening, frustrated by the lack of response over an easy question, I shouted the answer. The boys' tutor, Brother Dimitris, called out, 'Well done, Rodanthe, but if you are going to disturb our peace you should join the class. Then you can raise your hand in an orderly fashion if you wish to answer.' I was overjoyed to join the boys, despite the scowls from some of them.

On the twelfth morning, Anna failed to wake. It wasn't the fact that she'd died that upset me as I knew it was inevitable, but I was horrified to find I'd slept soundly next to a corpse. Papa returned two days after Anna's death. I expected him to come and find me; instead, he went directly to the abbot. I was peeling a mound of potatoes as Papa crossed the courtyard, and it was a shock to see his bent, old frame. It was clear that, although his bruises had healed, Papa wasn't well. Suddenly I felt nervous, and I expected his summons. Later, when he did speak to me, I had to feign ignorance of what he told me, because, thanks to Brother Michalis, I already knew more than Papa chose to share.

Always a gossip, dear Brother Michalis had listened outside the abbot's study, before unashamedly sharing the news with me. On his arrival in Ierapetra, Papa had enjoyed a warm welcome from Alexos and his pa. As custom dictated, Alexos's pa led discussions to explain how, once married, I'd keep house and, if blessed, nurse children, while my husband built a career in the French navy. It seemed that Papa had to persuade them to agree to me reaching the age of sixteen before marriage, and, with a twinkle in his eye, Brother Michalis said, 'With a dowry like yours I expect they'd wait until you're twenty!' I might have asked what he meant about my dowry, but the monk chatted on, anxious to get to what he considered the exciting bit.

Apparently, Alexos had left the two men toasting each other with brandy while he went along the street for a few minutes, and returned with a buxom woman bearing trays of food. With a chuckle, Brother Michalis said, 'Your pa choked on his drink. He told the abbot that blaming the brandy fumes hitting the back of his throat was easier than expressing dismay that the woman was not Alexos's ma, but his aunt. It seems his ma died years ago, and your papa has unwittingly struck a bargain that you'll act as housekeeper to your pa-in-law.'

'Don't worry, Brother Michalis, lots of women keep house for their pa-in-law.'

'Just think of the implications. Your pa was at his wits' end. He told the abbot that, because there is no prospective ma-in-law, you can't stay in Ierapetra before your marriage, and he dreaded taking you back to Kritsa.'

'Oh, yes, I see what you mean. Brother Michalis, you have an odd grin on your face. What is going to happen to me?'

'Our abbot has always had a soft spot for your pa, and he's certainly been impressed with you, so he suggested you stay here, at the monastery.'

'And Papa agreed?'

'He was very uncertain until the abbot explained how you've taken over the kitchen, and that Brother Dimitris enjoys teaching you. That shocked your papa, and he was concerned at the boys' reaction. Ah, Rodanthe, that's when I gave myself away! They heard me laughing at the way you have jerked certain boys out of their complacency.'

I realised that, apart from the fact that I'd rather be in Kritsa, I was enjoying myself, and I loved the incredible opportunity to attend classes. I noticed how Brother Michalis watched me intently, hoping that I'd be pleased. I said, 'How ironic. It's not appropriate for me to stay in a town house and act as housemaid to a single old man destined to become my pa-in-law, but it's acceptable for me to live and work at a remote place with nearly thirty men and boys.'

With a wink, Brother Michalis said something very odd. 'I think your pa's gold Napoleons clinched it with the abbot.' Having no idea what he meant, that comment passed over my head. I was deep in thought, considering the daunting prospect of raising children with their papa absent and no army of supportive grandparents and aunts.

Later, Papa was clearly agitated as he explained I was to marry and go to Ierapetra as planned, but not for three years. He didn't give reasons, other than that it was to give me time to finish growing up. He added, 'Meanwhile, the good abbot has been kind enough to offer you his continuing protection, and, as long as there are no complaints from the boys, you can attend school.' Without giving me a chance to comment, Papa rushed on, probably fearing I'd ask awkward questions. He reassured me that he'd visit the abbot regularly, at least twice a year, so it would be easy to keep in touch, and reminded me that Tinker would pass on letters. Then, sounding miserable and exhausted, he said, 'After all, time will fly, and then Mama will travel to Ierapetra to attend your wedding.'

As if to underline he'd brook no discussion, Papa pointed to a large package, as big as a full olive sack, wrapped in fine leather and enticingly bound with pink silk ribbons. 'Alexos sent you this gift. The weight greatly troubled Dove. Alexos bids you send him letters, he appreciates the fact you can read and write. Now, I must go.'

I tried to think of something appropriate to say, and my pause caused Papa mistakenly to think I was about to argue. He snapped, 'As God's my witness, Rodanthe, I've tried. Hopefully in time you'll realise I did my best.' With that, he turned away. I think something irritated his eyes, for he rubbed at them furiously as he went.

An hour later, I watched from the window above the gatehouse as the hunched figure of Papa walked away, leaning heavily on his staff. My thoughts urged him to turn to wave, but no, Papa didn't think of that.

Curiosity won the day, and my package was open before Papa was out of sight.

My Dear Rodanthe,

Your papa and mine think we shall be well suited. My papa was disappointed that I did not seek a church career, so the thought of me marrying the daughter of such a renowned pappas serves him well. True, I am a good fifteen years older than you are, but vanity tells me I appear younger.

Since playing in the docks as a small boy, I've been besotted with the idea of travelling. The great Napoleon visited our town the summer I was eight, and I hid to watch his boats take on supplies for his crew and army bound for Egypt. I even saw the great man. A huge entourage surrounded him as he walked past in full regalia to spend the night in a nearby house. Once he'd left the port, security was reduced, and I managed to get close to the ships. I came across a long line of wounded and sick men queuing to enter the surgeon's marquee. Each exited with clean white bandaging, brandishing a crutch or a medicine bottle. From that day, I wanted to be a ship's surgeon.

Napoleon generated fear and respect in equal measure, and in his wake medical schools flourished as his ships and armies always needed surgeons. I will enjoy sharing tales of my many adventures with you, and, God willing, our children.

I do hope you will like our house. You will find it so different to the close confines of a village. My papa's church is the opposite end of town to the fort, but he still complains that he hears the muezzin calling from the mosque. I think the market will delight you. Exotic goods come in from Africa, so there is always something interesting to see. Antics of monkeys will make you laugh, and brightly coloured parrots will amaze you with their ability to speak. A vibrant blue one says hello in six languages, and a scarlet one squawks, 'Look out, I'm watching you'. They draw a crowd so that the trader can sell his wares.

Your mama kindly thought to share samples of your handiwork. Although her message to me was that your skills would continue to improve, I think they are delightful. My mama did not weave, so I'll buy you a loom as a wedding present. However, I get ahead of myself. This package is a betrothal gift.

Your papa explained some of the great troubles you have all suffered in Kritsa, and how the traditional betrothal ceremony in your home was not possible. Believe me, the ceremony was very proper. I'm very aware as a betrothed man that I have so much more responsibility. I'll not let you down.

I understand Christian folk in Kritsa now wear permanent black of mourning. That is commendable, but not for my bride! I trust that among this selection of silk bolts you will find something suitable for a trousseau. Perhaps, if there is something left, you might make me a waistcoat.

Exchanging letters is a great joy, so I hope you will indulge me. Meanwhile, I send sincere thanks that you accepted my offer of marriage. I hope to learn more about you in the years before our wedding.

Your betrothed, Alexos.

I knew I shouldn't lie, so thought hard about my reply, not wanting to say anything that might cause a rift between us in years to come. It was difficult, though. Alexos was unaware that I now had sanctuary at the monastery. I took days over my letter, rewriting it several times. This became my habit, so not only did I keep each letter from Alexos, but my response too. It's no wonder I remember most of them. My letter was ready when Tinker next called for a night of prayer.

My Lord,

Thank you for the honour of accepting my hand. My papa says you are a handsome and kind man. The silks are beautiful. I'll enjoy working on them, and of course I'll make you a waistcoat.

As you are aware, I accompanied Papa to the monastery to visit the abbot. Now I'm betrothed it's been decided that I'll remain here as a housekeeper, and attend school so that I'll be a better companion for you. Like most Kritsa folk, I'd not left the village before so have a very narrow view of the world. I was not aware of Napoleon or a land called France. There is a library at the monastery and I've permission to read. Brother Dimitris likes my keenness to learn, so he has pointed out some books that I might find useful.

Most exciting of all, Brother Dimitris showed me a globe, and helped me plot the country called France. Now I see how tiny Crete is. It made sense why conquerors plague us when Brother Dimitris explained we are a strategic jewel in the middle sea.

I have a cute kitten that follows me everywhere. I call him Alexos, so hope you are not offended. He chases sparrows, so I wonder what he will make of the wonderful parrots you describe – I look forward to seeing them.

Best wishes, Rodanthe.

*

Wrapped in memories, Rodanthe fell silent, heedless of fat tears running down her face. Instinctively, Thea reached to comfort her.

'Leave me be! You make me too comfortable. I must leave. I need to kill the bastard who ended my life.'

Thea had previously experienced how quickly the girl's

mood could swing between grief, explosive rage, hysteria, or silence, and was uncertain of the best way to help. Inspired, she said, 'Here, take the water skin, Rodanthe, you must be thirsty from talking. What a life you've had! I'd like to hear more another time. Now, come to my store. I'll show you items that you might want when you leave.'

In poor light at the back of the cave, Rodanthe passively watched Thea clamber up the craggy wall to reach into an awkward crevice. 'Catch this bundle, Rodanthe. It's your britches and bloody blouses. You can give them a wash later. Now, take these from me. Carefully, don't stab yourself.' This time it was two silver handled blades, one coated in dried blood. Rodanthe realised the time had come to confess.

'You must guess that harbouring me brings you great risk.'

'Hush. Now stand aside, I need room to manoeuvre this wooden chest to reach a hole in the rock beneath it. It's where I hid items from your horse. No, don't try to lift it, you'll hurt your ribs. I'll manage.' As Thea lay on her stomach to reach her treasure, Rodanthe watched in wonder. Piece by piece the hoard appeared, including an amazing long-barrelled flintlock gun, a powder pouch with paper shot cases, a huge scimitar, and a fine leather saddlebag. Realising the light was too poor for Rodanthe to see properly, Thea helped her carry the hoard to the front of the cave.

Here they took turns to aim the fantastic gun at imaginary targets. First Thea, her thoughts full of grouse, hare, and pigeon, then Rodanthe grimly imagined a single man in her gun sight. Reluctantly the girl agreed that Thea should hide the gun and scimitar; they were far too conspicuous. Next, Rodanthe turned to the saddlebag to pick through its contents, reporting, 'Everything is useful.

There's a tinderbox, a pouch of grain, a liquor flask, several nuts, and...Oh, Thea, this is bizarre! Look at this kerchief. It's mine. I lost it months ago, fleeing Turks.'

As if Rodanthe were in a trance, the wooing words of her vile bridegroom, Hursit Pasha, instantly came back to her.

'Your honeyed voice haunts me. I've loved you since your singing first entranced me. Sing for me now.'

With a frown, Rodanthe remembered her puzzled question. 'When did you hear me sing?' Her new husband had explained it was when he'd visited Kritsa's aga to request permission to marry one of his many daughters. Always haughty, the aga had laughed off the suggestion, stating his daughters would marry born Turks and not an ambitious Albanian janissary. Full of anger, Hursit had ridden off the wrong way to pass Rodanthe's house, where, busy at her loom, she was defiantly singing to speed her shuttle on its way.

Intrigued by the shadow of a man on horseback across the window, Rodanthe had stepped into the street to see a lone rider disappear around the corner. She was still pondering why a Turk was in the Christian area when three more had ridden up at a great pace. Her neighbour's grandson was sitting squashing a crust into his mouth, oblivious to his danger. Rodanthe had snatched the child and run, desperate to escape flailing hooves. She'd squeezed into a narrow gap between houses with her wriggling armful howling in protest. As she ducked in, an overhanging bough had torn off her kerchief. She'd not even realised it was gone. Instead, with her chest heaving, she'd cupped a hand over the child's mouth to quieten him. Bulky clothing had prevented a man from reaching into the gap, then Omar's dreadful voice had snarled, 'Damn, I've missed this opportunity. I'll keep your kerchief as a memento!'

Frozen in fear, Rodanthe had remained hidden until the toddler's cries brought Roula, his grandma.

'How many times must we tell you not to sing? You put us all at risk.'

Months later, in the bridal chamber, Hursit had told his bride he'd kept the kerchief that Omar had presented to him as a talisman. Now Rodanthe shook her head, as if to erase the memory, and muttered, 'He's dead, and my life's in tatters, all for song.'

With a gentle touch to the girl's shoulder, Thea asked, 'What is it, child? Is there a ghost in that saddlebag?'

Her kind voice brought the girl back to the moment. With a shudder, Rodanthe said, 'This cloth brought back a memory I'd prefer to forget.' Then, to prevent further questions, she rushed out to wash the stolen clothes in the pool, where it struck her that she should be able to get a good price for them once she left Thea.

Impressed with the cleanliness of the clothes, Rodanthe spread them over bushes to dry, then sat in the weak sun trying to quieten her busy mind. When Thea joined her with a welcome herb tea, she said, 'That washing put me in mind of school, and the embarrassing second letter I sent Alexos.'

Always keen to hear more of her friend's past, Thea said, 'I'll sit on this rock to listen. Go on.'

My Lord,

I've told the boys in the monastery school that next time you are in Crete you'll box their ears for being unkind to me. Pavlos laughed and said no man in their right mind would want me for a wife. He said that he would write to warn you. I don't think he will, but just in case I will tell you my side of the story. He is so unkind because I answer more questions than he does, and I have only just started lessons.

I sleep in a tiny space above the schoolroom, so I have

peace once the boys have gone. This means I am always in class first because I just climb down the ladder. Brother Dimitris left the key to his big cupboard on the desk, so I thought I'd peek inside. There were books with squiggly illegible writing, and books I could read including a bible, a book on mathematics, and a fabulous book of animal drawings. There was a fierce lion, a green parrot, a hump backed pack animal called a camel loaded with an Arab merchant's stock, and a panther (a huge cat) sat with her baby that had a face like Alexos. (Not you, my fast growing kitten.)

Suddenly, it went dark as the door shut behind me. Pavlos shouted, 'You are a sneak. You cheat to get the answers by reading the books in secret. Well, I've thrown the key away and you will soon be dead. Then we won't have a smelly girl in class.' I do not smell – I had a wash last week. All the other boys laughed, and no one let me out when I screamed. Just when I thought I would die, Brother Dimitris saved me. It's not fair because I didn't do anything wrong, but I had to write out 100 times 'I must not touch things without permission'. Brother Dimitris said he would hit Pavlos with a stick if he were unkind to me again.

It is also not fair that boys don't have to wash their own clothes when they change their blouses and drawers every month. When I washed an under blouse for Pavlos, I put caterpillars inside – the ones that give you very itchy red spots. I hope you have enough money so that I can pay a girl to wash your clothes after we are married. But, if I have to do your things, I promise not to put caterpillars in them.

I hope you still want to marry me.

From, Rodanthe.

As Rodanthe anticipated, this made Thea laugh, and prompted the question, 'Did Alexos write often?

In a fond tone, Rodanthe answered, 'He wrote monthly. Some letters never arrived, and sometimes I got several at once. I learnt much of the outside world from his letters.'

'Can you remember another letter that you sent him?'

'I remember many of them.'

Dear Alexos,

It is not fair: the boys go exploring caves and leave me behind. This makes me sad, so I don't think I should stay at home when we are married and you go to sea. I have been getting good marks in geography. When you wrote that you had been to Piraeus, Patras, Ancona, Venice, and Gibraltar, I found them on the globe. I'd like to visit these places, so I think I will be a doctor and travel with you. Horrid Pavlos eavesdropped on me telling Brother Dimitris, and then he teased me, saying a girl could never be a doctor. He said the only time you'd want me near you would be if I was on my back with my skirt over my face. The other boys laughed.

I'd been sweeping the yard, so I chased Pavlos with my broom and hit him with it, hard. Papa was watching. He made me apologise to Pavlos AND the abbot – that was so unfair. Then Papa said you might not want to marry me if I don't behave properly. I can behave if people are pleasant to me.

Do you like vegetable stew? I make it a lot with whatever is ready. The monks and boys don't complain, but Papa said he'd never had cauliflower in vegetable stew before. With a sad face, he said, 'Ah, Rodanthe, there are so many ways that you miss your mama. She would have liked to teach you her recipes.' I said it wasn't fair that he should criticise my cooking, and took Alexos outside.

Brother Dimitris followed me. He said that Papa was sad that his visit had upset me. It was true, I was upset, and not just about the cooking. I tried to use a crochet hook and thread. Grandma had started to teach me, but had died before I learnt properly, so I made up my own pattern. I enjoyed working on a doily while sitting on a rock under a shady mulberry tree. I washed it carefully, and asked Papa to take it to Mama. He said, 'I've never seen such a doily, it resembles a spider's web.' I snatched it and threw it on the fire. I think a spider's web is very pretty.

From, Rodanthe.

Dear Alexos,

A trip to the Christian merchant quarter in Rhodes for a honeymoon sounds fantastic. None of my friends have ever done anything that exciting.

I asked to borrow Brother Dimitris's fat dictionary. He laughed when I told him you thought having a spirited and irascible bride would be good for you. I can't help getting angry if people are unfair to me. Papa says I should turn the other cheek, but I'm sure he doesn't know anyone as vexing as Pavlos.

I caught Pavlos when he tried to cheat at cards. I remembered what cards were out of play, and used the lesson on probability to work out what he might have in his hand. Brother Dimitris was cross with him and said he should own up. When the other boys said they didn't want to play with Pavlos anymore it made him very angry. He sat and sulked when the boys invited me to play with them against Pious Tinker. We used to play for points, but Tinker bet a bag of pistachios that he would beat me. We enjoyed the pistachio biscuits I made. Except for Pavlos – he refused to eat one. Papa said it was an unusual ingredient for a biscuit. I gave him some for Mama to try. If you let me play cards with you, I'll try not to always win.

I'm good at winning things – even if it does upset Pavlos. The boys had a competition with their catapults and I asked to join in. Pavlos said if I beat all of the boys, he'd give me his Sunday meat. My first shot went wide, and the boys hooted with laughter. That wasn't fair because a long time has passed since I won the catapult competition among the shepherd boys. I was sure the second shot hit the target. Pavlos said it didn't. My last shot brought the cone down, so there was no doubt. Our meat that Sunday was pork. Pavlos is a liar and a bad loser. He ran away with his plate to eat his meat.

I'll cook my special pork for you – the boys love it with a stuffing of stale bread, oil, onions, apple chunks, and rosemary. The abbot calls it Rodanthe's Roast. Can you collect recipes from other lands?

From, Rodanthe.

Dear Alexos,

Thank you for the garlic seeds. They grew well in my kitchen garden. Although I told the boys it was fashionable in France, they didn't like it at first. I carried on using it the way you described, and now they all say vegetable stew is bland without it. I fried some in oil to spread it on bread, and now we have this every Sunday for a treat. When Papa came, he said there was an appalling smell in the refectory. He wouldn't even try a tiny bite of garlic bread.

The news from Kritsa sounds grave. I'd like to go back to help Mama. I was accidently nearby when the abbot, Tinker, and Papa discussed the growing resistance. I told them that you'd met the Englishman, Lord Byron, in Italy, and that he was helping the secret organisation, Filiki Etaireia. Papa said, 'Rodanthe, don't eavesdrop, and don't repeat that. You put men's lives at risk.' I'm proud of you and wanted them to know that you mix with important people.

I've made good progress on your waistcoat for the wedding. When I showed it to Papa, he said, 'I wonder what your mama will make of that. The pattern is not of the tradition she'd have taught you.' I don't care, as long as you like it.

I don't mind that you've postponed our wedding while you're away on your important travels, and I do understand why you can't tell me so much about your voyages now. Stay safe.

Your, Rodanthe.

Emotionally drained, Rodanthe said, 'I'm cold, Thea, can we sit by the fire?' Without waiting for an answer she went into the cave to pile logs on the fire. The atmosphere was tense, and Thea sensed the girl was on the brink of telling what had brought her so far from home.

9

RENAISSANCE

The roaring fire captivated Rodanthe. Its flames conjured up pictures that served as fitting illustrations to the 'book' of her old life as it swiftly turned to ashes. A log flared then broke into pieces, to send up bright sparks with a waft of pine. Thea watched Rodanthe intently until the girl raised her eyes from the blaze to say, 'I've made up my mind, Thea. Tomorrow I'll set off to find a new life. Now I'll tell you what happened.'

*

Once it became obvious Alexos had postponed marriage indefinitely, I begged to return to Kritsa. I yearned to see Mama. I saw Papa go to the chapel with the abbot, and when they came out the monk said, 'Everyone will miss you, Rodanthe. It's been a pleasure having you here.'

I looked at Papa for confirmation. He gruffly said, 'Well, don't dawdle, collect your things. We'll leave in an hour. You'll have to walk fast as I've a man to meet.'

Frail Brother Michalis hugged me, and Bother Dimitris sombrely shook my hand. 'Goodbye, Rodanthe, it's been a pleasure to teach someone so gifted. I've a premonition that you'll need to make your own way in life, so your intelligence and resourcefulness will stand you in good stead. May God go with you.' Perhaps I should have been frightened at his prophesy; instead, I was thrilled to have

Papa hear those words of commendation. Of course, he didn't comment. In fact, he didn't say a word for the first hour of our trek, and then he stooped to take a stone from his clog.

'It's not the same, Rodanthe. Whatever memories you have of Krista are outdated. I don't want you to be disappointed.'

'You, Mama, and Grandpa are there. That's enough for me.'

'No child, you cannot imagine how dreadful it is. Folk are subdued and hungry. You mustn't venture out alone. Do nothing to attract attention. Turks need only the slightest excuse to maim, rape, or kill. Only last week a wretched man was ashamed to tell me that his family had resorted to eating "roof rats". He meant cats. Turks had beaten the wretched man for picking up rotting plums. They left him with a broken leg. Now he's so distraught at not being able to feed his family, it's destroying his sense of being. I doubt he believed me when I said that many other families eat similar stews.'

'How do you bear it, Papa?'

'I don't. I beg food from those who still tend flocks or turn over a piece of land for vegetables. I can usually persuade people to give me something, and then I share it out as fairly as possible. Some people hide from me as if I were a taxman. I know the pattern: it will take a week or two, but that man will bow down. Of course, his wife is only interested in the survival of her children, so she'll pressure him.'

'Can I help you with visiting, Papa?'

'No, I've even stopped your mama. It's not too late, Rodanthe, you can return to the monastery.' I kissed him and strode uphill. We didn't speak again, saving our breath to struggle up the steep ravine. Our prize at the top was a rest under the welcome shade of pine trees. Before he'd regained his breath, Papa gasped, 'A man will meet me here. It's the Yannis whose twins were killed the same day as Great Grandma.' Almost immediately, a figure emerged from trees.

Despite the man's foul odour, Papa hugged him, and then explained I'd left school to spend time with Mama before my marriage. I wasn't surprised when Papa steered Yannis a few paces away, and even then I sensed frequent glances in my direction as they sought assurance I couldn't hear. This Yannis seemed to be a hermit as his clothes were in tatters, his hair and beard matted with dirt, and, even at a distance, the fresh scent of pine couldn't mask his stink. Papa handed over a small cloth bag. I'm sure I heard clinking coins. When they parted, Yannis had only taken a few paces before he stopped.

'Hey, Rodanthe, I forgot to give you this. It's a letter from Alexos. I didn't expect to be able to hand it over personally. Invite me to the wedding.' With a wink and a grin, he was gone, leaving the surprisingly clean letter in my hand.

Without comment, Papa set off, and as we followed the track around the mountain I sensed his worry. Eventually, he shared brief details.

'There's a rebel group I've been part of for years. Mardati Yannis, your betrothed, and even the abbot are all part of our great network. The Yannis we just met lives in caves near here, and is a key link to provide an essential staging post for passing information across the mountains. As for me, I deliver messages and money to and from the monastery, as does the more frequently visiting Tinker.'

I grinned at my Papa, and said, 'At school we call him Pious Tinker, because he visits so often.'

'Yes, he's a good man. We buy weapons that come into small ports more accustomed to trading carob. Across

Europe, and especially in a country called England, there are men keen to free the Hellenic nations from the Ottoman yoke. Do you remember those men from below Faneromenis Monastery who were slaughtered by janissaries?' Without waiting for my reply, he went on. 'They were also part of subversive activities. Seeing how janissaries burnt out that hamlet in retribution was the final straw for me. Short of taking up arms, I do what I can, although I can't hate a man enough to break one of the ten commandments. I'm not proud of keeping this secret from your mama, but it's essential. Don't write of it in your reply to Alexos. That way you help to keep him and the other brave souls safe. Now hurry, we must be in Kritsa before curfew.'

Over the years I'd formed an easy style in letters to Alexos, but now, for the first time since my initial letter, I felt constrained, needing caution in case of prying eyes.

My dear Alexos,

Having left school, my reception in Kritsa was warm indeed. Mama didn't let me out of her sight for a week! While I love being home, the way Mama constantly suggests I do things in a more traditional manner is frustrating. What is the point of education if not to develop new ideas? The final straw was when Mama suggested I roll my pastry thinner. I snapped, 'If you're so worried about my skills, you should have visited me. I'd have appreciated a lesson then.' I immediately felt guilty, so now I keep asking her to show me things. Mama must have told other women her worries, because every woman in the neighbourhood has shared recipes to ensure you'll not starve.

Rest assured, I'm comfortable with your decision to accept a long commission on a boat bound for England. Papa told me about your special colleagues there. While

Mama's friends think you've jilted me, I'm satisfied time will prove them wrong. I have written quickly in the hope that you receive my letter before you sail. Enjoy your adventures, and keep safe.

Your betrothed, Rodanthe.

PS I gave my other Alexos to the newest boy at the school because he needed a friend!

*

Outside the cave, the sky darkened, while inside Thea sat rapt at the unfolding tale. Prompted by Thea's questions, Rodanthe said, 'Of course, you're unaware of events that altered history. I'll give you some background.'

*

Virtually a year ago, on 25 March 1821, following a series of abominations against church leaders and congregations, the bishop of Patras raised the Greek flag to declare revolution. Rebels adopted the rally cry 'Freedom, or death'. We were ignorant of these facts until May, when persistent knocks at our door woke us in the dead of night. Nothing good comes to the door during curfew, so Papa was at my side in seconds. He whispered, 'Sit with Mama. Bolt the bedroom door.'

If I hadn't been scared, I'd have enjoyed being snug with Mama as we murmured our speculation to each other. Mama concluded it wasn't an emergency, or Papa would have rushed out. Sounds from the kitchen told us he served his visitor *raki* and cold *mezes*. Soon a scraping noise indicated Papa had moved the kitchen table, so I guessed he took something out of his floor safe. I'm sure coins clinked. When I was sure Papa was alone, I went to the kitchen where he sat with a *raki* glass in one hand and his head in the other. He called Mama to join us, and then explained that our nocturnal visitor had been Mardati Yannis, who was too excited to wait until morning to share amazing news from the mainland. He'd come to seek Papa's blessing before taking his men to join the rebels. From his demeanour, it was obvious that Papa was wrestling with his conscience. Mama voiced my concern.

'Will you join them?'

'No. I won't bear arms.'

It was fantastic to help with the olive picking. I relished the jollity and companionship. By mid-January we'd finished, and I strolled uphill chattering with friends. My idyll ended when a lad raced up to say that Mama had somehow slipped and broken a leg. He assured me men had carried Mama home, so I sped off for Samuel, who thankfully came immediately.

Once Samuel arrived, Papa thanked folk who'd crowded into our house for their concern, then asked them to leave. With Mama on the kitchen table, Papa and I had to hold her still while Samuel manipulated her leg. I mistakenly thought I'd never again hear her suffer such distress and agony! With her leg set in wooden splints, Samuel instructed Mama to rest for at least six weeks. Even with doses of Samuel's opiates she suffered, so I was pleased when, three days later, eight women squashed into our kitchen to raise Mama's spirits.

Unbeknown to us, Tinker was secretly delivering bad news to Papa.

When Papa came home to find the women with us, I expected him to smile and leave us. Instead, Papa cleared his throat. 'I've grave news. Mardati Yannis and twenty patriots died on a raid in Ierapetra. Fortunately, Alexomanolis led most to safety.'

In the past year, many men had disappeared from Kritsa, so most women counted a son, nephew, or cousin with the rebels. Of course they clamoured for information. Papa ignored them, walked over, and held me.

'Rodanthe dear, Alexos is among the dead. You're bereaved, even before you're wed.'

Papa walked out of Kritsa through the eastern checkpoint, together with most Christian men and a good number of women, all determined to attend funerals of friends and relatives. From where I stood watching them leave, I sensed the guards' indecision. Although they shouldn't let folk leave, none wanted to be culpable of igniting a powder keg of trouble.

Back at our house, Mama and I worked companionably at the loom, where I sang quiet, melancholy tunes. A commotion in the street signalled the approach of drunken men on horseback. In all truth, I expected them to pass by. Loud bangs on the door said otherwise. An unknown voice, thick with alcohol, called out, 'Rodanthe, come to us. Your cousin has a rare honour for you.'

Then, the long remembered and hated voice of Bilalis sent shudders of fear down my spine. 'What if your grandpa is home? You might have misjudged things.'

Next Omar – of course he was at the centre of trouble – said, 'You misunderstand. Grandpa is a village term for an older man.'

Then the slurred voice again. 'Oh well, the fact Bilalis told the pasha he was your grandpa went well for you. Deliver the singing bird he pines for and you'll be well rewarded.'

'Go away, Omar. This is Irini. I'm alone at my loom. I have no coin or grain. My leg is broken, so I can't attend to you.' White-faced with fear, Mama pointed to the bedroom as she mouthed instructions for me to hide.

Next came Omar's pleading voice. 'Come, Rodanthe,

don't play hard to get. The pasha loves you. He wants you as his bride. I'll not go back empty handed. I'll have my men break open the door.'

Somehow, Mama had managed to pull the bolt across. The door splintered under force, and I heard the men were inside. I don't know who hit Mama to the floor, but her anguished cry had me at her side in seconds. My fingers traced a horrid pattern in pooling blood as I screamed at them to leave. An oaf pulled me up roughly, then bent me backwards over the sofa. Vile abuse spilt from his mouth, along with long threads of dibbling saliva. Incredibly, Mama found strength to cry, 'Leave my girl. Take me if you must, but please, leave her.'

The lout holding me dropped on to the sofa, pulled me on top of him, and said, 'Ah, this'll be good. Watch.' Despite the thickness of my skirts, I felt his repulsive hardness. I futilely struggled and kicked. He used one hand to keep my head turned to Mama, and his other to hold me tight. Mama's cries muffled as another beast kissed her mouth. Her eyes locked on mine, as if by doing so she might blot out the rape. Although I was sickened, I owed it to her to maintain that eye contact. After the first brute had finished with Mama, Omar hesitated before taking hold of her.

'I've waited over-long for you. All these years I've yearned for a look of love from you. Don't look at me with hatred, Irini…'

Like a deranged lunatic, Omar then screamed, 'You should have married me!' as he speared Mama's eye with his dagger. Her immediate ear-splitting shriek ceased abruptly. Omar stared at her, as if surprised that her agony was brief. My keening unnerved him. 'Don't grieve, girl! She got what she asked for!'

Sick guffaws followed, and the brute holding me called out, 'Fantastic job.'

Dazed, I realised the next voice was Bilalis's. 'Argh, just my luck, I'm poking a dead one. Why are they always dead for me? Never mind, at least she's warm.' Seconds later, when the disgusting dwarf grunted and slumped forward, Omar pulled him off Mama.

'Come on, there'll be hell to pay if we tarry.'

I screamed every foul oath I knew, and hit out as Omar took me into his grasp. I managed to rake his face with my nails, drawing a howl of rage. A satisfying stripe of blood stood out on his face, but it wasn't enough to stop him. The brutes bundled me into an empty grain sack, and even through my terror it registered this was no random attack. Once I was trussed inside the filthy sack, they dragged me outside, and with difficulty slung me across a horse. Nausea overwhelmed me, and my head bumped against the horse's flank with such a weight of blood it felt fit to burst. Each throb in my head repeated, 'Mama is dead.'

The brutes had chosen a difficult way to transport me, and soon Omar stopped and pulled me from the horse. He bound my hands behind my back and lifted me to sit in front of him as he rode. His head was so close to mine that his foul breath sickened me as he whispered what he'd enjoy doing if the pasha were disappointed with me. I refused to respond, and just held on to the thought that I might escape to tend Mama. I dimly recognised the route as the trading path I'd once walked with Grandpa, until the horse picked its way down the ancient stepped pathway from Lato to the lower plain of Lakonia. Once on flat ground, Omar cruelly whipped his horse to gallop.

When the men stopped for refreshment, I refused to drink. Omar wrenched my head back to pour water into my mouth, heedless of my choking. Then he emptied the remainder of the flask over me. 'That will wash the filth from you. Your spew stinks.' Drenched, my light blouse clung and became transparent, to bring obscene comments about the ripe fruit beneath it. My face burnt with shame as my grief turned to lasting hatred.

'I'll kill you, Omar, as God's my witness.'

He grinned, kissed me hard, spat in my face, and lifted me on to his horse. Before long, one of the horses behind us stumbled, his foot in a burrow, and in response to the thrown rider's bellow Omar stopped. He pulled me down and dragged me to the shade of a walnut tree, cursing all the while, before he helped the others. I knew Mama's knife was in my apron pocket; I'd been using it at the loom. I tried to reach it, chaffing my wrists raw in the process. The men spent so long attending to the lame horse that I took my chance to struggle to my feet and run. With my arms bound, keeping my balance was impossible, and I fell heavily. To my shame, I'd trapped one leg at an awkward angle with my skirt up over my face, exposing my bloomers. Omar's cry deafened me as he pounced, crushed me with his weight, and thrust his revolting crotch.

'Shall I test you out, my lovely?'

Foul Bilalis advised, 'Leave her be. Hursit will kill you.'

'Don't tell him, Bilalis, and you can use her too. If she dies, we can say she fled. My face is evidence she fought hard.'

'You'd not be so brave at Hursit's mercy. He can make death come to a man so slowly that you'd bite your own balls off to hurry it. No, leave her be, and dream of *raki* and women at your new brothel.'

With a yank that nearly tore my arm from my shoulder, Omar pulled me to my feet. 'Come on. If our esteemed pasha knew I had such thoughts of you he'd add me to his rank of eunuchs, at the very least.' Mortified, I accepted Omar's arm to take weight off my twisted ankle. Stunned by the shocking events, I sat passively in front of him as he rode. My thoughts stayed with Mama – was there a way I might have saved her?

Eventually Omar stopped, and spitefully pulled my hair to raise my head, then, in a deferential tone, said, 'Now, My Lady, appreciate your new home, and remember who brought you here. Such a fine Venetian arch, covered in welcoming red geraniums. What a fantastic mansion. Just imagine the luxuries that await you, the pasha's bride. You'll thank me yet.' Even before he'd finished speaking, a veiled woman came for me.

Despite my pride, I was grateful for the woman's proffered arm when she realised I couldn't bear weight on my foot. She welcomed me into a sumptuous boudoir full of heady scents. Overcome with dizziness, I fell and threw up over a delicate silk rug. Immediately concerned, the woman called two others, both heavily veiled, to genuflect before me prior to cosseting me like a beloved child. The woman sat next to me on the crimson sofa and made it clear her name was Suri. I stared at the floor and gave no indication I understood.

'Over there is your bath, warm water whenever you desire. There is a water closet too. No shared privy for you, My Lady.' I knew ritual bathing was integral to Muslim beliefs, whereas I only took a strip wash a few times a year when there was no snow on the mountains. Full of indignation, I decided that if this Hursit wanted me he'd have to appreciate the earthy scent of a village maid. The unwelcome thought of the forthcoming horrors of my bridal night wracked me with violent shivers.

One of the women opened a door with a flourish. 'This is a special room, My Lady, for you to weave or embroider in. Pasha Hursit has ordered you a loom and silks. It leads to your bedroom, My Lady.' This brought trills of laughter and colloquial teasing from all three of them. This time I truly didn't understand the words, although their clear meaning brought a hot blush to my cheeks. I bent my head to prevent them seeing how their teasing hit home. Suri drew me to my feet, and mimed that she wanted me to relax in the bath to soothe my ankle. I sat and ignored her.

After a murmured discussion, the women agreed to leave me, thinking sleep would improve my disposition. Using mime, Suri indicated I should rest and they'd return later, her attempt at kindness ruined as she turned a key in the lock. Stubbornly I ignored the tempting bath of warm scented water, and shut my eyes to the table of delicious food, including chilled lemon sherbet that I'd have loved to taste in different circumstances.

Due to a combination of need and curiosity, I used the water closet, a luxury beyond imagination. A cushioned seat rimmed a stone bowl, and a constant stream of water washed the waste away via a gully running to the outside. As I sat I heard horses, and men's voices, so realised the waste ran through stables directly behind this special room. The men's speech was clear, although I'd have preferred not to hear. Lewd comments and awful suggestions of what might pass on my wedding night made my blood boil. When the stable fell silent, I felt the wall where the waste channel exited, hoping for a loose brick to ease out. Thoroughly frustrated, I realised only a rat would get through that hole. With my mind in turmoil I sat again, and was still there when several men entered the stables, where they exchanged banter until the scraping noise of the door opening rendered them silent.

'...Ah, Allah be praised, we feared it was dreadful Omar come to check on us.'

'Or worse still, Omar and his twisted dwarf, Bilalis.'

'How do you two like this garrison?'

'Well, to tell the truth we are bored of not serving Allah,

praise be His name, as actively as before. In the south west, the infidels had had too much rope in past years, and our commander decided it was time to hang them with it.'

'How?'

'Last spring, the day the infidels call Good Friday, their captains met to discuss their situation at a monastery called Prevelli, in the south west. I was there. They knew me as a Christian, so they talked freely in front of me. I reported to my commander that they'd meet a week later, and of course I went among them again.'

*

When Thea gasped at the implications, Rodanthe said, 'Just imagine the damage this turncoat caused. He has blood on his hands. I need to get word out so that Christians can take revenge.'

Keen to learn more, Thea asked, 'What else did you overhear?'

*

This spy went on to explain how he knew about those responsible for fundraising and procuring firearms. Apparently, one man donated 400 kegs of black powder and opened a warehouse for food, clothing, and farming implements, and when the stores were full he sent a boat to Malta to sell stock and buy weapons. The spy's companions kept asking questions, not realising their words flowed through the wall, so the spy boasted about the hot reception Turks had given the Christians when they beached their boats at the foot of the river running down the steep gorge from Prevelli Monastery to the sea. With a sickening laugh, the unseen voice said, 'Palm trees grow on the riverbanks, right down to the beach. When we torched those trees, the flames lit the sky as if it were day!'

An envious voice said, 'Yours was a glorious strike for Allah, praise be His name, and we're in awe of your deeds. Did you kill the rebels?'

'Some got away by boat. We tortured those caught alive.'

Another man spoke, and his words echoed what Alexos had told me. 'They're stupid folk, thinking we're unaware of what goes on. We know of a supposedly secret organisation, sponsored by a lame Englishman called Lord Byron.'

Then the spy spoke again. 'The best news is that the sultan, may Allah preserve him in Constantinople a thousand years, has offered Crete to his Egyptian allies.' This last comment set off a round of excited discussion and speculation that turned my bowels to water.

'What about black powder? Will Arabs bring the stuff?'

'Yes, and cannon, plus men, horses, and kohl eyed women.'

Once again the door scraped, causing the voices to cease. This time the hated voice of Omar sounded loud and pompous. 'What are you slackers doing here in the stables?'

'Discussing the lack of black powder.'

'No worry. My friend Bilalis here brings intelligence of a good stock. Rebels transport kegs to the coast to meet the Mediterranean Queen. You janissaries should close the mill.'

With a wry sneer to myself, I derided Omar's ignorance: there was no such queen. A hot discussion reclaimed my attention, as an opinionated voice held sway. 'Listen, I've a plan. When I was a boy, I spent many hours mending fishing nets, and when I ate my bread I fed some to small fish caught in rock pools. A smart seagull watching nearby did not greedily snatch up the bread, as you would expect. Instead, he cunningly waited until several fish were nibbling the bread, and then he struck, catching a fish and the bread. We should act like this shrewd bird.'

'This sounds good. Come, let's get to the wedding feast and discuss it thoroughly before we share half a plan.'

Quiet rang loud in my ears, and my desperation to escape increased as I realised I must share what I'd overheard. I tried to ignore my inflamed ankle and limped into each room, trying in vain to find a glazed window that would open. When I reached the bedroom, I stopped in amazement. The bed was like a small room, hung with heavy tapestry curtains woven from red and golden threads. An exquisite pink silk gown, trimmed with white silk roses, lay across the bed. White silk leggings, slippers, and a small lace bag covered in fresh pink and white rosebuds nestled among the folds of silk. Intrigued, I reached for the beautiful bag to find it filled with exquisite rose petals. As I inhaled the heady aroma, I found it incomprehensible that the pasha had gone to so much trouble.

Early evening brought Suri and her women back, and they found me as they had left me. They tried hard to win me round by refreshing the bath with warm water. When I ignored Suri, she tried to manipulate me towards the bath. I slapped her face so hard that she fell. Her flailing hand caught my wooden crucifix, and as its cord broke my treasured cross flew across the room. Of course, Suri could move faster than I could, so when she stood with my cross held high while pointing to the bath her threat was explicit.

I limped over, and with my nose virtually against hers I screamed, 'You whore, give me that. Papa carved it to pass the hours of Mama's labour. I've worn it since a babe. Give it to me.'

She screamed in her vile tongue, 'Infidel, this is what I think of your evil symbol.' As she snapped my crucifix in two and flung the pieces into the bath, she yelled, 'Dirty bitch. Get in the water.' I rushed at her. The other two women had watched as if immobilised; now, with shrieks of fear, they ran to Suri's aid. They sensed one blow would never satisfy me. When my fist stopped in mid-air, all three of them were visibly shocked. I stood as if frozen. They each took a tentative step forward.

I yelled, 'Mama is dead!' and fell to the floor, howling like a hurt toddler. I'd suddenly realised that nothing mattered anymore. My precious crucifix was no more, and, like it, I no longer existed. I was dead to what was left of my family. The snapped crucifix might as well have been my neck.

As Mama is dead, I too am dead.

I lay passive on the bright silk carpet and let them strip and wash me, just as I've washed dead bodies. Once they were convinced that I'd no intention to fight, the women painted heathen swirls on my hands and feet. I meekly let them dress me in gossamer light layers of silk. It was my funeral shroud. My enlarged foot made it impossible to use the pretty slippers, so Suri cut two slits in one, and then eased it on to my foot. To their surprise, I voluntarily limped to the sofa to pick up the bag full of rose petals. I even heard Suri's sigh of relief.

Next, two liveried eunuchs carried me to the mosque. Standing by the imam, my bridegroom turned, and with genuine pleasure said in our dialect, 'My bride, you are so welcome. I'll make you happy.'

Using the language of the Turk, I replied, 'You might, if you drop dead this second!'

Hursit's face broke into a grin. 'Rodanthe, I love you. I didn't ask for it, nevertheless I must bear it. So must you. Imam, continue.' Then, without a word or gesture of assent from me, I was married.

Hursit carried me from the ceremony as if I was a fragile ornament, and in my exhaustion I remained placid. When he walked through the magnificent celebratory banquet set up in the courtyard, appreciative cheers and whistles met his declaration that the next two days were a holiday for all, as long as he was not disturbed for any reason during that time. Raucous innuendo about red roses on the bed sheets and continuous cheering dimmed to a murmur as Hursit shut the heavy door to my apartment with his foot. He looked genuinely happy as he tenderly laid me on the enormous bed, covered in fine silken sheets the same pink colour as my dress. My husband stroked hair from my face, then bent to bestow a light kiss.

'I'll not force you. I don't want rape. I want a wedding night to remember.'

His gentleness disarmed me and laid bare my anguish. My sobbing distressed him, and he begged me to believe he'd not been aware of how Mama had died during my abduction. 'Rodanthe, those brutes let me down. I'll strip Omar of the rank and privileges I've just bestowed. No, I can tell by your face that is not enough. You'll watch him hang later, after our special time.'

I was incredulous. How could he think that would buy me? Under my bland, wet gaze, this powerful man actually appeared nervous. He sat on an ornate carved chair by the bed and poured *raki*, as if for courage. He swiftly downed his drink, placed his wicked curved ceremonial blade on a table, and poured another.

Eventually my cries eased. He stroked my shoulder, and said, 'So, my dear one, how can we put this dreadfulness behind us?' He met my silence by filling my ears with beautiful words that would thrill any other bride. He'd long dreamt of this night, and wanted things to go well between us, so wanted to know how to ease my melancholy.

Without expecting him to agree, I suggested that he give me time to accept the situation and grieve overnight for my mama. His answer amazed me.

'Since I was first smitten by your heavenly voice, you

have filled my heart and my soul. What's one more night when we have a lifetime? My ears swear you have stolen the language of nightingales. At least sing.'

I did so, my song a sad lament for Mama. He watched me with such longing in his eyes that I rose from the bed, poured him another *raki*, and then repeated the same song over again, keeping his glass full until he lolled in his chair. When I bestowed a tender smile and suggested he take off his clothes to lie on our marriage bed, he needed no further encouragement. His eyes were wide in surprise as I limped to his side, still singing and inhaling the wonderful scent from my pretty bag. In blissful anticipation, he closed his eyes and smiled as I leant across him. His head lifted slightly to receive my kiss.

Crimson blood spurted across the silk sheets and down my bridal gown. With an amazing sense of release, I congratulated myself for daring to hide Mama's knife among the rose petals. His head slumped forward, and the wound in his vital artery ceased to bleed. It was a swift and tidy kill. I'm sure it would have earned a 'Bravo Rodanthe' from Grandpa.

I must have fainted, for I awoke on the stone floor. Perhaps the music and bawdy celebrations revived me. In a daze, I looked around and wondered why the sideboard held an obscene amount of food. Then I remembered that Hursit had asked not to be disturbed for two days. Slowly an idea formed. I'd wear Hursit's clothing to escape, in the hope that I'd be far away before the corpse's discovery. His clothing gave me boldness, until I pulled a boot over my swollen foot and realised I'd not get far. Rage welled. Everything about Hursit was evil. He and his kind had brought grief to those I loved over many years. His death did not set me free; he'd stolen my life. Distraught, I sank onto a chair and leant forward to rest my head in my arms, movement that sent

Hursit's curved blade clattering to the floor.

Without conscious thought, I took up the blade to strike at his wrist hanging limply from the bed. 'Thief! You stole my life. I know what Turks do to thieves!' I missed the offending hand to slice open the feather mattress. This angered me more, so I hacked at his hand until it fell. Hatred, incensed by flying gore, intoxicated me with a bloodlust. Only ever more urgent swings of the blade into his torso satisfied me. Now possessed by Satan, my frenzy only ended when, slippery with blood, the scimitar flew from my hand to spin across the stone floor. I fell, exhausted.

Despite the cold flagstones, I didn't move until a dog barked as it scratched on the other side of the door. I held my breath until a man called the dog away.

'Come here, he's too busy servicing another bitch to want to fuss you.'

In the first tinge of dawn the sounds of revelry still reached me, and as I used a chair to help me stand, sight of the horribly chopped carcass made me spew. The revolting smells of blood and guts smothered and disgusted me. I removed the gory jacket that covered me and flung it over the hated head. Shivering, I grabbed Hursit's outdoor cloak to wrap around me.

Adrenalin-fuelled anger obviously prevented rational thought as I punched through a glass window. It shattered to slice open a dangerous cut in my wrist. My backwards reel of agony sent me to rest against the bed. As my blood gushed, I decided I didn't want them to find two bodies on the bed. A piece of the slashed sheet served to wrap my wrist, and I took a draught of *raki* to lessen the pain. Why I didn't use the scimitar to smash the glass in the first place I'll never know. Breathing heavily from exertion and pain, I used the blade to knock out the remaining glass, regardless of the resulting noise.

Once on the veranda I limped towards the building I hoped was the stable. I found several horses saddled up, as if always kept ready for action. I used a mounting block next to a huge beast to climb on, and expected shouts of alarm as I urged the horse outside. Distant sounds of revelry continued, and with no sign of anyone to challenge me, I rode through the arch. Drained of all energy, I lolled over the horse's neck, a signal it took to mean gallop. I've no memory of falling from the horse; the next I knew you were tending me, Thea.

*

'That's it, Thea, I've told all.'

Thea rose, and returned holding the boots left by Jorgiakis. With a sob, she said, 'You'll need these.'

By noon the next day, Rodanthe was ready to leave. Her rucksack and saddlebag had been packed and repacked to fend off the moment of departure. After the two women had hugged for the final time, Rodanthe said, 'Will you keep that long gun for me, Thea? I'll collect it if I ever pass this way again.'

'Of course I'll keep it for you. Find a man to love, and bring him here to collect it as a fantastic wedding gift.'

With shouts of goodbye ringing in her ears, Rodanthe set off. To her left a deep chasm rose up to towering peaks of stark bare rock. Cloaked in the early March scent of anemones, broom, hollyhocks, and poppies, the ancient path made her wish she had a stick to clear it. Thea's advice was to discover where Kazanis made his home, and once in front of the famous man beg asylum. It wasn't a robust plan, yet Rodanthe had no other.

Over her left shoulder she carried the leather saddlebag, complete with tinderbox and rations. On her other shoulder, two silver blades intended as a dowry and a moth eaten blanket swung in her rucksack. Her own treasured knife nestled in Hursit's cummerbund that kept his voluminous green britches around her slim waist, and a cut piece of cummerbund served as a turban. With her feet snug inside Jorgiakis's boots, she purposely trod on thistles, just because she could.

Rodanthe made her way up the track, hunched over against a fierce wind, chilled with distant snow, that whistled through the mountains and threatened to bowl her over the sheer ledge. Tears whipped up by the wind blinded her, and, distracted by calling voices, she stumbled. Of course, there were no voices, just gusting wind. While rubbing her ankle she glanced upwards to the far side of the drop, and saw a crest topped by the unmistakable round shape of Kastello. Thrilled, she realised home was the other side of the mountain. Her euphoria was short-lived; she might as well be on the moon.

After this, she trudged up the steep path with her eyes on her feet to avoid another fall, until mewing buzzards high above claimed her attention. These soaring birds weaved tantalising acrobatics, each keen to lock talons with a worthy mate. Focusing on their mesmerising upward spirals on late afternoon thermals, Rodanthe kept them in sight as wind directed them along the valley. She leant over the cliff edge and stood on tiptoe, before lifting her arms, ready to launch into the void.

'Hey, there's a jinnee under my skin. I think I can fly!' A flashing memory of brave Manos, cruelly tossed from a cliff, made her arms drop. The moment gone, she screamed like a banshee, 'I'll strike my own blow. Freedom or death!' The wind dropped to accentuate the echoing 'Death'.

Rodanthe scanned the cobalt sky, hoping to regain sight of the birds. Instead, she glimpsed a white cross apparently suspended in mid-air. Intrigued, she walked on until the church it topped came into view. With great difficulty, Rodanthe pushed open the door, shifting rubble lodged behind it. Once inside it was evident that the decrepit church was a popular roost for pigeons. A worn icon just inside the door declared the church dedicated to Saint John. Without a second thought, Rodanthe kissed the icon, then, as her eyes adjusted to the gloom, they filled with dismay at the desecration. She kicked the charred remains of a fallen lectern, once a beautifully carved centrepiece, and derived odd satisfaction as it crushed beneath her boots. An icon of the Panagia lay among the debris on the floor. Rodanthe dusted and kissed it, and then placed it by the damaged iconostasis. 'Oh, Panagia Mou, what have they done? Still, I suppose I'm lucky. The remains of this church affords better shelter than a night under the stars.

'Panagia, can you hear me? You suffered the pain of separation. How did you bear seeing your son die? God wasn't looking my way, and now I am an orphan. Yes, Papa lives, but to him I'm dead. Although he'll be distraught, he won't search. Who wants a Turk's leavings?

'Believe me, I'd never bow down. Lord Jesus, Son of the immaculate Panagia, Most Merciful God, I beg forgiveness. Papa would say I should have turned the other cheek. I beseech you, sustain my Papa, and give me courage to endure.'

'I hear you, Rodanthe. You are a tender girl. If you were a boy, with a lion heart like Manos, you would not brook insult. Manos stood up for what was right, no thought for the consequences. Cut your hair, fight as Manos.'

With first light, Rodanthe yawned and removed her turban to scratch at the itchy stubble resulting from Thea's ministrations. Her hand froze on her head as she remembered a night-time conversation.

'Panagia, did you really ask me to cut my hair?'

In that instant, it was as if her mama spoke. 'No, Rodanthe, not your beautiful tresses.' Uncertain, Rodanthe hefted her blade and felt tears prick, remembering the hours Mama had spent tending her hair. Twice a year, Mama had carefully washed it using herbal rinses, then teased out the knots with a wide toothed comb carved from goat horn, admonishing, 'Be still, Rodanthe! Every time you struggle it pulls more.' Most evenings, even after Rodanthe had returned from school as an adult, Mama had used her bristle hairbrush for a hundred strokes, a routine that relaxed them both for sleep.

'Is that what you propose, Panagia? Shall I bring further grief to Mama and shave my head?' In answer, wind whistled through holes in the roof to cause the dusty remnants of votive offerings to jangle on the iconostasis. 'Thank you, Panagia! A symbolic gift of my hair will do you honour.' Her hand trembled as she lifted the knife to her scalp, then she stopped. By raking her fingers through her hair, she removed twigs and knots. Once satisfied, she remade a tidy plait.

'Well, Panagia, I remember the first day I sat on my hair. Mama was delighted. Now, it's yours.' Rodanthe cut the braid close to her head, and then cautiously used the knife all over her crown. With a farewell kiss to the feminine symbol, she hung it on the iconostasis.

Driven by a new urgency, she removed her blouses and wound the turban cloth around her chest to flatten her breasts. 'Oh, Panagia, do you remember when Thea bound my chest? She commented that I'm slight. Will I pass as Manos?' She took a step back and stumbled over the charred lectern. 'Not a good start, Panagia.' Back on her feet, she brushed her hands against the wall to clean them, and then stared at the sooty marks. With a hollow laugh, she stooped, picked up a lump of the blackened wood, then scrawled on the wall:

> A girl came in, kissed the braid, her votive humble,
> A boy went out, so now all bloody Turks must tremble.

A lad can stride up a mountain so much faster than a fearful girl can. At the top of the next slope, he waved down at the church.

'Goodbye, Rodanthe!'

PART 2

SPANOMANOLIS

1

KAZANIS

Papa? How can this be? I'd recognise that cough anywhere. Papa, can you hear me? They thought me a Turk!

The giant was angry. He had been born angry, tearing with his oversized hands at the umbilical cord suffocating him. Since then, not a day had passed without a flash of burning anger. Today he was angry that his sworn enemy had dared to restock his pigpen in early March, thinking it would pass unnoticed.

He adjusted the dead pig across his enormous shoulders, and with another angry thought turned to shout at the two men trudging after him.

'Bloody hell, that malaca made us steal pigs during the Lent fast. He's put my eternal soul at risk, the bastard.'

One of his companions couldn't bear to think his effort wasted, so said, 'Surely Pappas Stavros will arrange preservation of the meat for distribution after Easter.'

The third man, a slight wiry fellow who bore a hooded falcon on his shoulder, joked, 'Or, you can just wear pig collars for the rest of Lent!' As quick to laugh as he was to rage, the huge man gave a bellowing guffaw.

'Let's go, I smell snow. By the time we get back to Marmaketo, we'll want nothing more strenuous than to watch a pig roast.' With a sad shake of his head, he added, 'Will that malaca never learn?' His palikers knew better than to voice an opinion. The giant's cussing sounded as if the injury was recent, whereas in actual fact their victim's grandpa had upset their leader's grandpa. Both old men had died cursing the other, even though they'd forgotten the original reason for the vendetta.

As the odd trio neared a homestead, an excited boy ran towards them at full pelt, his shouts not making sense. 'Pa, come quick. Pappas Stavros brought a spy, a Turk. I helped Kostas lock him in with Pasiphae.'

When his pa told him to start again, the men listened in amazement, then ran after their leader as he strode off, shouting, 'A bloody Turk! Up here? Unbelievable! Kostas should've shot the bastard.'

A violent shrug sent the pig from the raging man's shoulders to land near the fire pit, then, without breaking his stride, he continued behind the house where he was astounded to see the Turk worming his way out from underneath the barn door. An enormous booted foot stomped on the Turk's exposed back to trap him as the breath was knocked from his lungs in an audible hiss. The giant's hands easily circled the dainty booted ankles as he dragged the Turk, who was still clutching two bags, out face down.

'So, Lord Turk thinks he can burrow away. What do you think, Son? Shall I stamp the remaining breath out of the bastard and be done with it?'

Petros didn't answer. He didn't want to antagonise his pa, so failed to admit that he'd been chatting to the stranger for most of the afternoon, and quite liked him. In the pause, the Turk lifted his head, as far as his awkward angle allowed, and said, 'I'm Christian. Kill me and Kazanis will never learn what I have to offer. Take me to him, and he'll reward you.'

The watching men pulled quizzical faces, while the huge

man hauled the Turk into a sitting position, saying, 'You're young to be a spy.'

Outraged, the captive screamed, 'Tell me, who is Emmanuel? I need to talk to him.'

With an elaborate wink to his companions, the colossal man said, 'Listen to that, Lord Turk seeks Emmanuel. Over to you, my fine palikers.'

A squat, rotund man stepped forward with a grin and reached out a hand, apparently encased in a fur glove, to haul the Turk upright before clasping him tight. Although the lad wriggled furiously, he only succeeded in squashing his face against the man's barrel chest to gain a smear of pig's blood for his trouble. His jubilant captor sang out a mantinade:

'Papa called me Emmanuel, his own name so fair,
Known as Trichomanolis you see, I'm hairy, and strong
    as a bear.'

Struggling furiously, the Turk yelled, 'I'm not afraid of you. I just fear dying without striking a blow against bastard Turks.'

Now the watching men knew it would only take seconds to squeeze the breath out of the Turk. When the youth's lips went blue and his thrashing stopped, Trichos dropped the barely conscious form. In celebration, the men cheered, slapped each other on the back, and passed around a *raki* flask. Trichos poured some into his victim's slack mouth.

'Here, this will set you right.'

Spluttering as he sat up, the Turk spat venom. 'Malacas! I need to meet the Emmanuel who can introduce me to Kazanis. Who is he?'

In answer, the falconer released the bird's hood and thrust her into the air. Relieved of his light burden, he then used both hands to haul the lad to his unsteady feet as he sang:

'My papa named me Falcon, so easy on his ear
But baptised me Emmanuel, so God's name I could fear.'

At a bellowed 'I'm the Emmanuel you seek' the lad cowered against his current captor's bird limed jacket. Without lowering his voice, the giant blared, 'I understand my cousin, Pappas Stavros, found you. Now he worries that he brought a Turk into our midst. If he's right, you'll soon wish you'd not strayed up here.'

Emmanuel knew he intimidated the lad. He proudly recognised he was the tallest, most ferocious man in Lassithi, and probably the whole of Crete. His bushy brows framed glaring black eyes, and no barber had ever sharpened a blade to cope with his matted moustache and beard. In fact, his beard was so thick it even housed a small knife tied on with a strip of leather, although why he needed this adornment bewildered most people. He carried enough arms to serve three men. Like other men, he caught his hair up in a traditional turban, but it failed to master the unruly mass that splayed out of gaps and holes. The negligible amount of his visible face had been burnt black in the sun, as had his forearms, and he looked like a Moor. Now he scowled ferociously, demanding answers.

'I need to know about you, Turk boy. My other cousin, Kostas, tells me that you claim to be an Emmanuel. Is that right?'

While the lad bit his lip and studied the ground, the two men looked to their leader for guidance, but then the lad surprised them all by flashing an audacious grin at the trio as he sang:

'I too am called Emmanuel, my grandpa's name in life,
But since a cruel slice, Spanomanolis can't trouble a wife!'

With a flash of enlightenment, the huge man guffawed. 'Fine, for now you'll be Spanos, unless I decide Mohammad suits you better. If so, you'll pray for death. I'll listen to what you have to say while we watch a pig roast. A swineherd of my acquaintance donated it. Follow me.'

The lad hung back to wait for Falcon, who scanned the sky. Unused to defiance, Emmanuel went to chivvy the lad, and then stopped to listen with interest. The lad took a deep breath, as if steeling himself.

'Have you met Pappas Stavros this afternoon?'

It took a few seconds for Falcon to register that the lad was talking to him, then, with his eyes still focused upwards, he said, 'Of course not. I'm no God botherer.'

The lad now known as Spanos faltered. 'Um, we need to talk.'

Instead of answering, Falcon cried, 'Come, my beauty!'

Falcon took a length of cord from his pocket and spun it in high loops, its weighted end providing momentum. A bird of prey swooped down to catch the twirling weight that Falcon whisked away just in time to thwart it. Not put off, it sped up high to make a second attempt. As it reached a point directly overhead, Falcon shouted, 'Haaaah!' and let go of the line. The bird dropped like a stone to clamp the lure in its talons before it hit the ground. Falcon congratulated the bird as he swapped the titbit of meat from the lure with a larger piece from his pocket. Only after he had set the lanner on his shoulder, as if it were the most natural thing in the world, did he turn to the astounded lad.

'Such a beautiful lanner falcon. Now, what do you want?'

'I'm sorry to bring bad news, Falcon. I found your

pa dead today. To be honest, at first I didn't even see a homestead behind the trees. The overwhelming stink made me investigate.'

Dumbstruck, Falcon stared.

Emmanuel said, 'Bloody hell, are you sure?'

'He must have been dead in his bed for more than a week. I'd already buried him by the time Pappas Stavros found me.' With tears in his eyes, Falcon stroked his lanner, still tearing at her meat. The lad turned to the huge man, Emmanuel. 'At first Pappas Stavros thought I'd killed Falcon's pa. I climbed down into the ravine to haul up the bloated corpse of a dog to prove they'd both been dead long before I happened upon them. I'd previously tipped the dog into the ravine for the vultures.'

As Falcon continued to stroke his lanner, Emmanuel awkwardly placed his arm around the man's vacant shoulder. 'Do you want me or Trichos to go back to the grave with you?'

'No, I need to be alone.'

'Wait, I've something for you.' A crushed fez fell to the ground as the lad produced a broken curved blade in an ivory handle from his saddlebag. 'I found this scimitar, which probably killed the dog. It must have some value. You could take it to a smith for repair.' Falcon stared at the stranger, Spanos, who added, 'The place was smashed up. I think your pa broke his leg, and he had a deep stab wound to his chest. I'm sorry.' Falcon remained speechless, so the lad continued. 'I picked this fez up in the hut of broken cages. It was on top of the largest cage. It was deliberate, as if they wanted to make it clear who'd done the damage. I stupidly wore it while I dug your papa's grave. It was seeing the fez, and my green britches, that made the pappas think me a Turk.'

'What about my birds?'

'All the cages were empty. Ugh, except for a maggoty

writhing mess that may once have been chicks.'

'They stole them all? My golden eagle was worth a fortune!'

Falcon bent for the lure, then turned towards to his home, and gave no response when the lad shouted, 'Falcon, be sure to dig beneath the rough cross that I placed on the grave.'

Satisfied that the charcoal beneath the pig glowed evenly, Trichos reached for the *raki* flask, and then stopped mid-pour as his outraged leader stomped towards him. Without preamble, the huge man jerked his thumb towards the strange lad, Spanos.

'He brings grave news. Falcon's pa is dead. Tell him.' Spanos did so. The news brought forth blasphemous outrage from Trichos that Emmanuel ignored, instead demanding of Spanos, 'So, if you're not a murderer, explain why you're here.'

'I understand why you mistrust me, and I admire Pappas Stavros for rendering me harmless. Believe me, I loathe bastard Turks. When I was a child, janissaries ransacked our home. Their depraved captain, may his soul rot in Hades, had no use for women, so had me cut. A few years later, he placed me as a wager in a card game. He lost. My ownership passed to an officer of higher rank. As he had no use for a gelding he gave me as a slave to Pasha Hursit's household.'

Both listeners winced and rubbed their crotches, as if checking their own vital parts were still there. Before Spanos could say more, another man joined the group. Emmanuel nodded an acknowledgment to Kostas, and then poked the lad in frustration.

'Get on with it.'

Spanos blushed under the stare of the newcomer, then swallowed hard before he continued. 'There was pandemonium in the pasha's compound. I worked in the kitchens so only heard about it second-hand. Apparently, the drunken guards failed to prevent a break in by a band of rebels. They killed the pasha to abduct his bride. A hard man from the west had recently arrived in Choumeriakos with additional troops. Within an hour of the news breaking he'd declared himself pasha, and then sent his forces out scouring the area.'

Kostas stood and drew a gun from his cummerbund, then pointed it at the lad. 'You tell us nothing new. Let me finish this, cousin. I'll take him behind the barn.'

Before anyone could answer, Spanos was on his feet to demand, 'Why would you execute me? Are you afraid I'll rush back to Choumeriakos to tell them I've found the band who stole the pasha's bride? Where is she, Kostas? What have you done with her?' As the pair glared at each other, the glow of the fire accentuated the anger in their eyes. Trichos reached for a weapon, and then relaxed as his leader took control.

'Sit, both of you. I wish one of us had killed the bastard pasha. Go on, Spanos.'

Spanos sat, glowering at Kostas who angrily righted his fallen seat then kept his pistol visible. Averting his eyes from Kostas, Spanos continued.

'I was sent to clear up the bloodbath in the bedchamber. When I saw the pasha's clothes strewn across a chair I couldn't resist trying them on. Filled with daring I ran to the stables, and took the only horse there. I was up on the mounting block and out of the gate before I stopped to think. I fell near a woodland chapel where a recluse named Theos found me, and he bound my broken ribs.'

'What nonsense! I should have shot you hours ago.'

'I'm not lying, Kostas. Look at me! No wonder Pappas Stavros thought me a Turk. My fine clothes belonged to the pasha himself. I expect the chief white eunuch grieved the disappearance of the clothing more than he did me. He'd certainly not have been brave enough to report me missing. It's as if I never existed.'

Kostas retorted, 'If that's true, it was weeks ago, so why appear now?'

'I must find Kazanis. If my hermit friend Theos hadn't mentioned fierce Captain Kazanis and his brave palikers I'd not have ventured up these mountains...' Spanos's voice trailed away as he swung to face Emmanuel. 'Oh, that pappas tricked me. You must be the Emmanuel called Kazanis.'

'I wondered how long it would take for you to realise!' The huge man extended a hand and rose to haul Spanos to his feet to shake hands,'I'm pleased our wiley pappas sent you here. Although Kostas certainly did the right thing to confine you, I'll take a gamble.' While Kostas looked sullen, Trichos sang out:

'W-w-well, w-w-what do you know, St-St-Stavros went
    and caught a sp-sp-spy,
And to await Kazanis's verdict, Kostas locked him in
    a sty!'

As Trichos drew breath for a second verse, Kazanis bawled, 'Petros! Where are you? Come here, you brat!' The boy appeared instantly; he'd hidden within earshot, anxious to know what was going on. 'Ah, there you are. Fetch the pappas, Zacharias, and Hannis. Tell them it will take hours for this pig to roast so we'll make it a party. When the pappas protests, tell him that I won't force pork down his throat. He deserves a drink if nothing else.'

Petros sped off, and waved to acknowledge his pa's final shouted instruction of 'Tell Zacharias to invite Anna.'

Satisfied that his afterthought would ensure a wider variety of food, Kazanis said, 'Clouds are dumping snow in the mountains, so you two rig up the hide canopy to protect the fire pit. Spanos, follow me.'

Papa, what a fabulous kitchen. Mama would have loved it.

Spanos halted in awe. 'Such a kitchen is beyond imagination. Is this huge alcove just for the loom?'

In a sad tone, at odds with his appearance, Kazanis said, 'Yes, a house for a family.' As if unsure what to do next, Spanos lingered by the disused loom, stroking the unfinished blanket until Kostas barged by to yell, 'Leave that, you're raising a dust storm.'

It was a long time since Kazanis had been so intrigued. He couldn't take his eyes off the lad, who now stared into the next alcove that housed a double bed, neatly covered with a fine wool blanket, two red pillows placed precisely in position.

'I guess that bed is for Kostas,' said Spanos. In a futile attempt to hide his blush, he knelt by the incongruous crib below the bed to adjust a rag doll resting beneath its lace cover. This earned him a painful tap on the shoulder and a sharp 'Move along, lad' from Kazanis.

At the fireplace, Spanos admired the assorted firearms adorning the chimneybreast. 'Panagia Mou, so many guns.'

'They belong to Kostas. Don't even think of touching them. Follow me, our store is through here.' Careful not to bump his head, Kazanis bent low to pass beneath the stone archway to a huge room containing wooden barrels of wine and *raki*, all decked with dusty spider webs. 'Make yourself useful and fill those flasks for the table.' This store, originally intended to house goats or sheep, now had two sets of wooden bunks and a dishevelled bed covered by reeking animal skins.

With a grin, Spanos guessed, 'So, this bed's yours?'

Scratching deep in his beard, Kazanis laughed. 'Yes, I'm a scruffy sod.'

Back in the kitchen, Kazanis instructed Spanos to sit by him as he raised a hand in welcome to a newcomer dressed in the local uniform of voluminous britches, their many folds tucked in boots, baggy blouses, embroidered waistcoat, and hooded jacket, all in faded black.

'Meet Zacharias. We'd not run this farm without him.'

'I'm pleased you've left my favourite cow, Pasiphae, in peace. Petros told me how you kept her and her bonny calf company.' Before more words were exchanged, a clean-shaven man entered, gaining a bellow from Kazanis.

'Handsome Hannis! Smooth cheeks enjoy more caresses, eh? Sit yourself down, your honeymoon is over.' With a wink, Kazanis gestured at Spanos and said, 'This malaca is my guest. You'll never believe it, stuttering Stavros caught him burying Falcon's pa. Stavros thought he was a bloody Turk, and tricked him into walking here by saying his Cousin Emmanuel might introduce him to Kazanis. Pure genius! Although I've still got reservations, we've agreed to call him Spanos and watch him eat pork.'

After briefly shaking hands with the lad, Hannis greeted Trichos who was tuning his lyre. 'Ah, a proper party. That's why I told my Marina to stay home!' With a final twang, Trichos played a familiar tune, and sang:

'S-S-Stavros t-t-thinks he caught a s-s-spy from the East,
New friend Spanos buried Falcon's pa, killed by a b-beast.'

Hearty laughter rang out as all except Kostas and Spanos banged on the table in appreciation. Kostas looked aghast at Spanos's acceptance and stalked out, leaving Spanos tentatively sipping *raki*. Kazanis brought Zacharias and

Hannis up to date, including proud boasts of how he had procured the pigs. With a lascivious wink, he said, 'Well, as I was in the mood for pig, I also paid a visit to Dirty Despinia.'

Spluttering his drink, Hannis said, 'My God, what desperation. You'll find yourself in a Turk's brothel next. Hey, they say if you use a girl right after a Turk, your dick will shrivel. Let us know if you test the theory!'

Raucous laughter again rang around the table as Kazanis slapped Hannis on the back. 'We don't all have a delicious new bride to warm our beds.'

Young Petros had lit a fire in the hearth and, oblivious to the ribald comments, said, 'Although our neighbour thought his pigs were safe, the one in our yard smells delicious!' After a large draught of *raki*, Kazanis noisily wiped his mouth and belched.

'Son, as long as I live, his pigs are my pigs!'

To no one in particular, Spanos said, 'I'm too hot by the fire. I'll sit over there on the floor.' Clumsily, Spanos stumbled against the crib to send it sliding along the floor with a clatter. Scarlet faced, the lad hiccoughed and said, 'Sorry, I'm not used to *raki*.' No one commented; instead all warily watched Kostas, who'd just re-entered the kitchen.

Kostas loathed me from the instant he saw me.

Blood drained from Kostas's face as he trapped Spanos against the wall and balled his fist to rest his knuckles against the lad's lips. His light touch amplified the menace. 'Touch my bed, or anything by it, and you die!' Then Kostas turned to the others. 'I'll see to the roast. I need air.'

Each man checked the liquid level in his glass, reluctant to break the ensuing silence, and even Kazanis was lost in thought. Spanos spoke timidly. 'Can I open the door? It will let the smell of slaughter out, I feel queasy.'

With a relieved blast of laughter, Kazanis said, 'Yes, open the door. You sound like an indignant housewife.' This brought hoots of mirth from the men that ceased abruptly as the door opened before Spanos reached it. A woman, laden with two heavy baskets, struggled in.

'Oh, Panagia Mou, this kitchen stinks like a slaughterhouse.' Bewildered by the hilarity her comment provoked, the woman emptied a selection of *mezes* from her basket on to the table, and then touched Zacharias lightly on the shoulder. 'I'll come back when my pies and potatoes are cooked.'

After an hour, Kazanis opened the door as if expecting someone on the threshold. 'Where's Stavros got to? Petros, did you tell him?'

'Yes, Pa. I doubt he'll come. He was in church praying for God's help to allay his grief. I wasn't aware he was that fond of Falcon's pa.'

Trichos commented, 'Perhaps he's asking God to forgive him for not getting the rascal to church in the past fifteen years!'

It was as if Spanos threw iced water over the laughter when he said, 'You've had no word of the atrocity at Adrianos?'

Kazanis barked, 'What about Adrianos?'

'Pappas Stavros told me about an appalling massacre while he escorted me to your homestead. He said that he'd visited Adrianos intending to conduct a wedding only to discover that Turks had taken the women and girls. Then he found decomposing men, stacked like a log pile. The top corpse wore a red fez on his arse. Babies and small boys hung from trees, like macabre fruits. I'm sure Pappas Stavros was on his way to tell you when he found me.'

The shocked voice of Kazanis would have chilled any

eavesdropping Turk. 'I'll kill the bastards. Those people were simple charcoal burners.'

After hot debate about how best to strike back, Kazanis asked, 'The fez, what does this tell us? It's unlikely that one would be left accidently at two places.' No one in the kitchen noticed Kostas and the pappas had entered, until a distinctive voice made them turn.

'It's that bl-bl-bloody new t-t-tax collector Omar. M-m-may God f-f-forgive my language.'

As the pappas spoke, Kostas steered him to the table. Although the cleric picked up a *raki*, he left it untouched to stutter, 'No one likes a taxman. This Omar that people have nicknamed Red Fez doesn't even leave folk enough to live on. We'll find it difficult to support the survivors.'

With a concerned arm around his cousin's shoulder, Kostas said, 'How did you bear it, Stavros?'

To subdued listeners, who totally ignored his stammer, he said, 'I didn't bear it alone. To start with, God helped me. Then six men, who'd been away hunting, returned. Without a word, they took the shovel from my exhausted hands and did what was needed. When I took my leave an old grandpa gave me his son's gun. He was heartbroken and said I should use the gun to defend myself as God has forsaken us. I could bring no comfort there.'

Through choking tears, Spanos asked, 'Did they go after the women?'

'N-n-no, th-th-they th-th-think of th-them as dead.' Stifling a sob in his throat, the pappas added, 'And they'll r-r-regret it, f-f-forever!'

White with fear, Petros asked, 'Will Turks come for us, Pa?'

'Don't be stupid, Son. No Turk will take me on, not with such a fine band of palikers. Even Spanos walked all this way because I'll not stomach interference from bloody Turks.'

'K-K-Kazanis, I don't want to fr-frighten your boy, but we've not seen the like of the one they call R-R-Red F-Fez.'

'Don't talk in riddles.'

Now the pappas stuttered even more to share what he knew. 'Before I went to Adrianos, I'd been to a hamlet called Limnes. There is quite a community of displaced Christians there. Several people commented that, although the previous tax collector was criminal, this Omar is the devil. They call him Red Fez because he always leaves such a token. It's a calculated way to increase fear. When I saw the lad wearing a fez I thought he was one of them. I was confused when he acted decently. Anyway, in the weeks since Omar gained office, he's made a bad situation worse. Two new inhabitants in Limnes, a woman called Maria and her simple son Jorgiakis, recently lived in Neapoli. This Maria said even Turks wonder what possessed the dead pasha to award such a coveted office to such a felon.' In the ensuing hush, the only sounds came from squabbling dogs. Pappas Stavros downed his drink with a single swallow, then continued, 'Just imagine how I trudged uphill and away from the remains of Adrianos. I felt sick, with nothing left to vomit. Those folk thought themselves safe in their hamlet at the foot of the gorge. One word ran through my mind with each step: why. Why did God allow such atrocities? Why did man become evil? Why do my words of comfort sound hollow? Why does God not reveal his purpose for me? Entering Falcon's homestead, I was astounded. Why was a Turk rummaging around? That last thought brought me out of my melancholy, and with sudden clarity I knew why God had put the gun in my hand.'

Kostas congratulated the pappas for taking a stand.

'No, I was mistaken. This lad is no Turk. Perhaps it's God's way of telling me not to jump to conclusions.'

Kazanis said, 'No, your thoughts were in the right direction. We can't leave such atrocities unavenged. I had two godsons in Adrianos.'

Papa, I caused that trouble. Omar's reward for delivering me to Hursit was to become the tax collector If I hadn't murdered my husband then I'm sure he would have revoked the appointment. Will God forgive me?

Spanos said, 'Our time has come. Believe me, Turks recognise the rebellion is gaining momentum. We must fight.'

'Brave words, lad,' said Kazanis. 'It will take grown men in a concerted effort. We'll do what we can. You can stay here with Petros.'

On his feet in a heartbeat, Spanos ran his gaze around the men, only avoiding eye contact with Kostas. 'If I wanted safety I'd have run to a monastery. Rebel forces are mobilising, under the motto "Freedom or death". That works for me. If I'm with you, Kazanis, I'll share my intelligence, and fight under your command to my death. If you don't want me I'll go west, to active rebel strongholds.'

Vast consumption of *raki* had reduced opportunity for careful deliberation, and the last comment from Spanos upset Trichos who seized the lad in another bear hug. 'Bloody Hell! What do you mean, active rebels in the west? We are active, damn you.' With the rough, hairy forearm crushed against his face, Spanos took the only defensive option available and bit down, hard. Surprised by the retaliation, Trichos released his grip just a little, allowing Spanos to drop down and dart backwards, leaving his captor clutching at air.

Kazanis bawled, 'Slippery as a fish. You're losing your grip, Trichos.'

In a flash, the lad darted to his rucksack near the fireplace to pull out a clothbound package. Any man might have felled Spanos had the scene not amused them, especially when the lad brandished a flat blade knife. His high-pitched yell invited Trichos to try to touch him again. From his seat, Kazanis quelled the trouble.

'Come here, lad. Let me heft that.'

Theatrically slashing the knife through the air, Spanos bragged, 'I stole another too, a *hançer* – we'd call it a dagger.'

The quarrel became history as Spanos rummaged to find the second knife which he passed to Petros, who stabbed an imaginary foe and exclaimed, 'Wow, this will do some damage.' His pa snatched it from him.

'Leave it alone, brat. It needs skilled hands.'

'Ha, you mean you want it, Kazanis,' said Hannis.

'No, I only take another man's arms in a fight.'

'What about the gun you took from Kostas on New Year's Eve? He sulked for a week!'

'That was cards, Hannis, that's different!'

Kostas and Spanos went to speak simultaneously. Spanos blushed and Kostas glared. Immediately, Kostas forgot what he'd wanted to say and headed outside. As Kostas slammed the door, Spanos turned to Kazanis.

'I've a head full of information but no experience with arms. I'll gladly trade a blade for tuition.' This prompted the pappas to roll up his slashed cassock sleeve to expose his bandaged arm.

'He h-had sk-skill to cut m-me.'

'I apologised! I thought you'd killed one man, and were after me.'

Kazanis slapped the pappas on his back and nearly knocked him from his chair. 'Well done, Stavros. I wish I'd seen it.'

Petros asked, 'Does it hurt, Pappas?'

'Not as much as my injured pride. I thought I'd die.'

Papa, what are you doing in this hell? I've a friend who is a pappas, I'll tell you of him. No, don't leave. Papa! Papa, it's Rodanthe. Come back!

The pappas was a timid man, so the listeners were surprised at the detail Spanos shared. 'I'd just buried the corpse in a shallow grave when a gunshot sent me speeding for cover behind a tree. I quelled the urge to run and carefully inched my way around the tree trunk, trying to judge where the shot had come from. Then, in a nightmare moment I felt a gun muzzle centre on my spine, so, with my back coated in ice-cold fear, I raised my hands. Nothing happened. My memory flashed back to childhood when we'd copied practising troops with our stick guns. In that moment, I realised my assailant hadn't had time to reload. I kicked a leg up behind me to land a booted heel in his groin. I spun round, snatched the broken scimitar from my cummerbund, and sliced the air. To my amazement it cut through his sleeve. My arm jerked, and I dropped the blade. That's when I saw the pappas. I was horrified and fell to my knees to beg forgiveness.'

All eyes turned to the pappas, who ruefully rubbed his crotch and stammered, 'In my anger over Adrianos I didn't think my actions through. That shot startled me so much I dropped the gun. After that I crept up behind the Turk, but the gun muzzle he felt was actually a stick.'

In admiration, Trichos said, 'Bravo, Pappas.'

'N-n-not brave, st-st-stupid.'

Indignantly, Spanos said, 'Imagine if I'd killed him for the sake of a stick!' Spanos faltered as Kostas returned to the kitchen, then he pointedly turned away to continue, 'I dusted off his fallen hat and passed it back. It's a shame that dent won't knock out. Even though he was hurt he continued to challenge me, and remember he thought me a murderer, so he's brave.'

'B-b-but you laughed at m-m-me. I can't hurt a f-fly.'

'I laughed because the way you replaced your hat reminded me of when I was a child, and I saw a prank played on our kardi. That proves I'm easily distracted. I need proper training.'

Kostas broke in, 'I think not. We've no need to worry about what mischief you'd wreak behind us.'

'Know this, Kostas, I've many wrongs to avenge. I've witnessed men executed for trying to feed their families, and seen girls dragged off to God knows what fate. I've walked through destroyed homes where those not killed were sold.' Now that Spanos stood directly in front of Kostas his passionate voice rose to a screech, and, red-faced in anger, Kostas shouted back.

'No more than any other among us!'

'Don't interrupt me, Kostas, I'll have my say. I held my mama's agonised gaze as she was raped and murdered. Believe me, all of you, I've escaped to avenge. God gave me one chance to flee, so I took it. I've seized my dignity back by refusing to stay a creature of the Turks.'

Mid-tirade, Spanos sped across the kitchen to the cloaks near the door. Then, shrouded by a hooded cloak and leaning on a stick, he walked towards his astounded audience. In a trembling, croaking voice, Spanos said, 'You're right, Kostas, I'm a spy, a master of disguise. Behold, I'm an old woman.' Next, he seized a tablecloth from the dresser and dropped the cloak to use the cloth as a veil. A demure feminine voice murmured, 'Welcome, My Lord. How may I serve you?'

Except for Kostas, the men enjoyed the pantomime. Hannis shouted, 'Careful, you sound so girlish there's more than one here who'll fancy a bit of that!' In response, Spanos whipped the veil away, and then rushed to his bag to seize the crumpled fez that he pushed on his head. In an arrogant pose, he addressed Kazanis imperiously.

Full of glee, Kazanis demanded, 'What did you say, Turk boy?'

'Leave my slaves alone, they're working for the glory of Allah, blessed be His name.' Irritated by the laughter, Kostas sensed he'd lost as Spanos pleaded directly to Kazanis. 'Use my skills to strengthen your band in different ways. If you think me a traitor, hang me as a criminal.'

In a far more kindly tone than his men were accustomed to, Kazanis said, 'You're small, hardly bigger than Petros. You can't run day into night across mountains. Our feast tonight is unusual, we frequently starve. You valiantly aim high, but you'll not bear our life.'

Spanos persevered. 'With God's help, I'll bear it.'

To the astonishment of all, the initiative passed to Pappas Stavros. 'W-w-with God at a m-man's side he c-can be a lion. H-here, you h-h-have this, Sp-Sp-Spanos. I pray God aids your aim and keeps you s-safe.' Lost for words, Spanos took the gun and reverently placed it in his cummerbund.

Kazanis declared, 'Well, palikers, we can't say no to another armed man, so for the time being little Spanomanolis stays.' Then Kazanis turned fierce eyes on Spanos to growl, 'If one word of concern about your actions reaches me, I'll kill you. Understood?' Not waiting for an answer, Kazanis thumped the table. 'We're palikers, all keen to strike a blow against bloody Turks, so if an untrained lad wants to face up to the challenge, we must help him raise his skills.'

Petros seized his chance. 'And me, Pa?' Before Kazanis could frame his objections, Kostas broke in.

'If you decide Petros joins us, of course I'll help keep him safe. Just don't force that other lad on us.'

Kazanis fumed, 'Enough! Watch his back as well as Petros. I've a hunch we'll not regret it. Trichos, lift the atmosphere with your lyre.'

'Bloody Turks, you'd better look out,
Now with palikers Petros and Spanos, we wield extra
    clout!'

After this, Trichos sang verse after verse of patriotic songs. Perhaps he thought the well loved tales of brave palikers fighting against Venetian rulers could lend guidance for the task ahead. Then he added a verse of his own:

'Thank you, Kazanis, your fists on the table stoke up my
    beat,
But come on, Hannis, so late on your feet.'

As if awaiting the invitation, Hannis leapt from his chair.

'I'll lead a patriotic dance, between table and door,
Come on all, let's take to the floor.'

For the next hour they exorcised demons with dance. The only time feet stopped moving was if a glass needed lifting. Each man took a turn to lead the dance, until Spanos protested, 'I can't. No call for such dancing in the harem kitchens.'

In a flash, Petros seized his chance. 'I'll take your turn.' As the beat increased, the boy leapt faster and higher until, with a flourish, he jumped to grip a pair of metal hooks set in a roof beam. He hung there, panting with exertion and enjoying applause as Anna returned.

'Petros, get down before you fall.'

'Anna! Did you see me dance?'

'I did indeed, you were grand. I expect the Turks in Constantinople heard you all!' Spanos rushed to help Anna, taking the basket that she handed over in amazement. He lifted the cover and sniffed appreciatively.

'I'm Spanos. These pies smell delicious. Sorry, I crumpled the tablecloth. I'll smooth it and help you set the food out.'

'Spanos, you're not a servant! Leave Anna to her tasks. Help me check the roast. No, not empty handed, bring a *raki* flask! For God's sake, I wonder if we've enough years to make a paliker of you!'

Satisfied the pork was crisping, Kazanis took a seat under the awning, passed Spanos a *raki*, and said, 'Tell me.'

'The seat of rebellion in Prevelli is destroyed.'

'My God, that's bad enough. What else?'

With a tremor in his voice, Spanos continued. 'Folk in Kritsa, a village east of these peaks, need help.'

'Bloody hell, no! We won't lift a finger to help them.'

'Well, in that case I've forgotten the rest.'

To underline his words, Spanos walked towards the house, ignoring the incensed shout of 'STOP! Don't you dare turn your back on me!' After a split second of hesitation, Spanos walked on, and failed to hit the ground when a shot rang out. Even though Kazanis knew it was a dramatic overhead blast, it didn't lessen his amazement over the lad's audacity. Startled palikers ran from the kitchen, guns drawn. When Kazanis roared, 'Stop that malaca,' his bemused men took uncertain steps forward. The plucky lad ignored the hostile line and turned to Kazanis.

'Shall we update everyone?'

Open-mouthed, Kazanis watched the lad stride indoors, then, struggling to regain his composure, he bawled, 'Slow, lads. You were slow.' He shook his head sadly. 'We must practise an emergency muster. Turks won't wait for you to sober up.' Of course, his men protested. Kazanis simply ignored their defensive pleas. 'Now, back inside, the news is so grim.'

Crisis point over, Kazanis shared the headlines, and then added, 'That's as much as I'd heard before I decided to test your readiness. Start with some background, lad.'

'The pasha's troops were in high spirits. He'd treated them to a splendid repast to celebrate his wedding to a bride he'd stolen from Kritsa.' Amidst jeering, Hannis sang out:

'Would you go to Kritsa for meat, or a wife?
The easy answer to that is no, not on your life!'

With hands on hips, sounding like a shrill housewife, Spanos demanded the reason why they took against Kritsa people. Young Petros spoke up for his new friend.

'Don't be cruel. The vendetta with Kritsa folk over ownership of Kathero has been going on for generations, and people in Kritsa need help now. After all, shepherds from both communities meet annually to trade prize rams to prevent inbreeding, so you can't dislike them that much.'

Spanos ignored the cheerfully remembered bargains that had got the better of the Kritsa men, and only rejoined the conversation when Kazanis yelled, 'Enough. These young ones are right. It is time to put history aside. We need to work together to seize the momentum. What else did you discover, Spanos?'

Subdued men sipped *raki* and listened. 'Consider my worthless position within the pasha's household. I was invisible. When I served food, those men thought no more of talking in front of me than they did their hunting dogs. Men splashed information around like cool water on a hot day. For example, I heard that last Good Friday, April 7 1821 by our calendar, Christian leaders in the south met to discuss their situation. Unbeknown to them they had a spy in their midst, and this despicable creature passed on information that weighty heads were to meet again the following week. This second meeting was to finalise the details for revolution.'

Unable to contain himself, Trichos said, 'I guess the spy went to the second meeting and reported everything back.'

'Yes, and what detail. They knew these rebels had a chancellery responsible for fundraising and procuring firearms. One man alone donated 400 kegs of black powder, and opened an armoury for donated weapons. This enabled them to send a boat to Malta to sell stock and buy weapons.'

Kazanis whistled through his moustache. 'And the bloody Turks knew when and where they landed.'

'Yes.' Above the angry murmurs, Spanos added, 'Is anyone aware of a secret organisation sponsored by men in Europe?'

After a pause, Kostas demanded, 'How can we answer yes if it is a secret organisation?' The ensuing laughter improved Kazanis's temper, as he had been annoyed not to have known of the organisation.

'Hurry up, lad, that pork calls me with each sizzle.'

'Sorry Kazanis. Boats from Malta beached at the foot of a river that runs down a steep gorge from the Prevelli Monastery on the south coast. While the boats were unloading, the abbot hosted a meeting with huge numbers of captains. Members of this secret organisation attended the meeting, so the Turks are aware of sponsors across Europe. Back in Prevelli, Turks landed boatloads of troops on the beach, seized the precious loads, and then rampaged up the ravine to destroy the monastery. They sounded affronted that many, including monks, escaped.'

Petros asked, 'Did any of the boats get away?'

'Some, but the captured men were tortured.'

A range of expletives bounced around the table, including 'Bastards', 'Bloody Turks', and 'God damn them'. Sensing the men's blood was up, Petros said, 'That's why Spanos says Kritsa people need help. This battle is beyond old hurts, it needs to be all Cretans against the devils.'

Thoroughly confused, Hannis said, 'I don't see a link between Kritsa and Prevelli.'

Close to tears, Spanos continued, 'There isn't one, except I learnt of it at the same time. The pasha stole a Kritsa woman as a bride. Six men broke in, killed the pasha, and took her off. The new pasha doesn't give a damn about his dead predecessor. He just wants to intimidate folk so that they are in no mood to resist.'

Full of contempt, Kostas asked, 'What do you intend? The woman will be in a brothel or convent by now, if she's not dead.'

Spanos flared, 'Well, brave Kostas, I hoped someone would go to Kritsa to find out what is going on. Folk might be suffering reprisals.'

White-faced, Kostas pulled a gun from his cummerbund and aimed at his antagonist's head. 'For all we know you're setting a trap.' The collective intake of breath left a silence that amplified the sound of cockroaches scratching in corners. Spanos glared at Kostas as the goading continued. 'You're sending us on a fool's errand, leaving an open door to let Turks on to Lassithi.'

Kazanis took control. 'Petros, get more *raki*. Spanos, sit down. Kostas, don't act a fool. We'll listen to what the lad says, weigh his words as we eat our pork, and then decide our action. Spanos, continue.' Although Kostas sat, he nursed both his gun and injured pride. Spanos remained on his feet to continue in his peculiar high-pitched voice.

'What does it matter if I die, or if a thousand Cretans die, as long as in the end we are free? For too long men have watched the horizon for the Russian fleet. They'll not come. The rebellion ranges from Macedonia to Crete, and with literally hundreds of islands in between Turks' forces are overstretched. Now is the time to act. To put it simply, they cannot spare the forces to crush us.' After he'd retaken his seat, Spanos quietly delivered the killer blow. 'We must move fast. The sultan has made a golden prize of Crete to his Egyptian allies.'

Instead of blazing at the news, the sheer impact made Kazanis thoughtful. He sat with his shaggy head bowed for so long it seemed as if the level of *raki* in his bloodstream had overtaken his capacity for thought, until he abruptly slapped Spanos on the back.

'Bloody hell, our Kostas is right. You're a spy! Thank God Stavros brought you here. Despite our rough reputation locally, the truth is we're not as organised as they are in the west. I'll make contact with other rebel captains and plan a way forward.'

Without waiting for comments, Kazanis opened the kitchen door to let in a freezing blast along with the delicious smell of the roast. He stared into the night, twisting his shaggy beard in turmoil, not even commenting on the light sprinkling of snow. When he returned to the table, he continued as if there'd been no break.

'If we go to Kritsa it leaves people vulnerable. Pappas Stavros leads feeding programmes in conjunction with the Kardiotissas Monastery, so where people have no access to food, we supply it.'

'What a wonderful strategy,' said Spanos.

'If the Turks realise we're no longer around they might ransack the monastery. Then, if they gain confidence, it puts the fifteen hamlets up here at risk.'

Trichos ventured a view. 'If we don't try the Turks will get here anyway.'

With a thoughtful nod, Kazanis said, 'Turks call us klephts, a more truthful label than rebels. We just irritate them, like fleas on a dog. If we're to meet the challenges that Spanos describes we must change! I'll sleep on it, and hope for clearer thoughts in the morning. Now, that wonderful pork needs carving, and Zacharias, you're the best man for that. Help him, Petros.'

Oh Papa, you're so thin. You'd have loved that pork, the crackling was delicious.

While Zacharias and Petros were outside, the kitchen table underwent a transformation. Spanos took the food keeping warm by the hearth to lay it out, and said, 'Anna's made a snail *pilaf* for the pappas. What a shame he's gone. Shall I set it out for anyone else who won't touch meat during Lent?'

Trichos answered, 'No, none of us has such scruples.'

Bewildered by the care Spanos took serving everyone, Kazanis eventually said, 'For goodness sake sit still, or I'll get Zacharias to take you home as a kitchen apprentice to Anna.'

Later, when Zacharias prepared to take his leave, Hannis rose to join him and, with a huge wink, said, 'I must get off to bed.'

After a ribald riposte, a disappointed Kazanis said, 'Shame, I fancied cards. Do you play *Diloti*, Spanos?'

We played cards, Papa. You'd disapprove for we wagered. Forgive me, Papa, I learnt to swear and cuss too!

'Oh yes, although I doubt I'll do well at this hour,' Spanos replied. Kostas initially declined the opportunity to play, and Petros wasn't invited. Trichos swiftly moved a small table to rest under a large oil lamp as he called to the departing Hannis.

'You get off then, but I'm keen to win my clay pipe back.'

'What, this one?' said Kazanis as he rummaged under his turban to remove a fragile pipe from his nest of hair.

'Mind you don't break it. I'm sure those little treasures will prove more popular than the bloody *narghiles* of the Turks. I've another to place on the table tonight, not that it's much good without some baccy.' These exchanges made Kostas rethink. With longing in his eyes, he picked up the pipe and gave it an imaginary puff.

'Count me in after all. I'll wager six rounds of ammunition for the winner's gun.'

As Spanos placed his broad bladed knife onto the table, Trichos said, 'That wager's too high for tonight's game. What about that knife in your waistband?'

'I'll die before I part with this one, and kill the bastard who tries to take it from me, whereas that blade is like a whore. It means nothing to me.'

Kazanis grinned and snatched up the blade. 'Well if it means nothing to you, lad, I'll welcome it in my collection. Now, our house rules are a table of four, and we play until the first man gets to thirty points. Then the two with the least points drop out, and the game continues. First one to fifty points wins all the wager items.'

With a nod, Spanos said, 'I've played those rules before.' He might have said more, but jingling from a bag held by Petros caught his attention. 'Are those coins?'

'These tokens have no value. Zacharias found them in a huge clay pot when he was ploughing years ago. We use them to count points instead of writing them down.' Petros didn't add that, like most men, he hadn't learnt to write words or numbers. 'I like to keep tally, but now I'm too tired so I'll leave the bag for you all to use.'

A curt 'Your lead' from Kostas started the game, and Spanos placed a card.

An hour later, Trichos cheered loudly on reaching thirty points. Kazanis was just one point behind, whereas Spanos and Kostas both languished far behind. Kostas shook his head.

'I'll bide my time until there's some baccy around before I win a pipe. Meanwhile, I'll take some air.'

Through his yawns, Spanos said, 'Pass me the bag, I'll tally.' The table hushed as both players concentrated. First Trichos built a good lead, then Kazanis overtook. The only sound was the clinking of coins as Spanos dipped in the bag.

Talos is the sun in our Cretan dialect, equivalent to Greek Helios. It also means cut down. Kazanis shines like the sun and hews Turks down. He loved me. Papa, can you hear me?

In a pause, Spanos said, 'I think these coins are very old. I'm sure that's an emblem of Talos. Have you heard of him? Legend has it he ran around Crete three times a night keeping it safe from enemies.'

This brought a booming laugh from Kazanis. 'How I'd love to move that fast. Your deal, Trichos.' Fortune favoured Trichos who won next points, so Spanos carefully added coins to the smaller stack to bring the two piles level.

'With forty-nine points each you don't need me for this hand. Goodnight, and good luck!'

2

PETROS

Christ said, 'Suffer the little children to come unto me.'
Please God, keep him safe. Have you met him, Papa? He's
a good boy.

Petros was a bad boy. Why else did his mama leave? Each
night he'd prayed, 'If I'm good, tomorrow please send
Mama back.' He was never good enough. When he turned
twelve last year, he made his final prayer.

'God, you're obviously busy, so I'll not trouble you
anymore. Although I'm old enough to care for myself,
please listen out for my mama, and if she ever asks, please
tell her I love her. Oh, and God, if you have any time left,
please stop Pa being angry. I didn't mean to make her leave.'

Although Petros realised he was awake he kept his eyes
closed, then inhaled again. Yes, he was sure it was there: a
long forgotten warm and musky smell. In the moments before
he fully woke, Petros put his arm around the sleeping form
next to him. 'Mama?' He felt a gentle hand brush hair from
his forehead as he came fully awake. 'Oh, it's you, Spanos.
I dreamt my mama was here.' As the room trembled under
an onslaught of snoring, Spanos put a finger to his lips to
indicate hush. With a grin, Petros signalled Spanos to follow
him, and led the way through the snowy yard to the privy.
Once between wooden dividers, they shivered and chatted.

'Great privy, Petros. When I paid a visit last evening,

I was impressed that you have separate compartments rather than a communal bench with several drops.'

'Yes, but don't use the third one. You might fall through!'

'Bet that one is for Kazanis.'

'Yes. If you visit at the same time as him, hold on to your seat. When he farts, the whole place shakes!'

'I bet it does.'

After many snorts of suppressed laughter from the next cubicle, Petros said, 'It's not that funny, Spanos.'

'Oh, but it is. At home, we kept a chipped *kazani* under the bed to pee in at night. So, next time your papa is angry with me, I'll think of our old *kazani*...'

'Of course, you've not heard the tale behind his nickname. His grandpa was born in Choumeriakos, and on the day of his baptism, Turks ransacked the church and smashed the font. Their resourceful pappas baptised Great Grandpa with a dunk in a *kazani* full of cold water. As the cleric lifted him, the screaming red-faced babe sent a plume of piss down the pappas. From that day the child was called Kazanis.'

'How did the name pass down to the grandson?'

'Stop giggling like a girl and I'll tell you. At Papa's baptism, Grandpa brought the *kazani*. His view was that, since everyone said the perpetually angry child was just like him, Papa should be baptised in the same pot. No sooner was the crying baby back with his mama than the pappas dropped the *kazani*, and Papa's grandpa dropped dead.'

'That's funny and sad. Do you and Kostas have nicknames?'

'Well, nicknames are earned, so I guess I just haven't done anything to deserve one yet. There's a story about Kostas. Like me, when Kostas was a boy he worked with Zacharias, and at that time Anna kept bees. As a treat, Anna gave him pieces of the honeycomb whenever she broke open a clay hive. One day he was playing with Anna's niece, a young girl called Maria, and he bragged that he knew where to find honeycomb. The only problem was he'd not actually seen Anna collect it, so he was unsure what to do. Anxious to make sure there were no bees in the hive, he rapped loudly on the top. The story goes that he ran, chased by a swarm, all the way to the lake underneath the Havga Gorge, and dived in fully clothed. From that day onwards Maria called him Honey, and before long so did everyone else.' Hearing the catch in his throat, Petros knew his voice wobbled. 'Kostas and Maria wed as soon as she was fifteen, and she even called him Honey when she said her vows. Of course, his nickname died with her.'

The mood broken, their chattering ceased while the pair concentrated on their morning business, until Spanos said, 'This place smells grim.'

'The six-bench privy at Kardiotissas Monastery is a sweet experience. It's over a chasm in the rocks that once served as a secret exit to evade Venetians. Best of all, the birds sing beneath your arse as your turd drops to infinity.'

'That sounds fabulous! I'd love to see it one day.'

Back in the kitchen, Petros enjoyed the responsibility of having a guest and bustled about finding breakfast, confident that Kostas was long gone from his berth. No matter how late Kostas turned in, the first grey streak of dawn always saw him off to spend the hour until sunrise running. The boy urged, 'Take some rusks, Spanos. It's a shame you and Kostas took an instant dislike to each other. He told me to lock you in the barn with Pasiphae because our pappas was scared you were a Turk.'

'He did the right thing. Sorry I screamed at you. I was frantic, thinking I'd swapped one form of prison for another.'

As Spanos spoke, the kitchen door opened and Falcon

struggled in. With his lanner on his shoulder, and a bulky bundle tied in a sheet clutched to his chest, the man became wedged for a moment then almost fell in.

'I've brought these clothes for you, Spanos, as thanks for dealing with my pa. He intended them as grave wear. I hope they fit.'

'That's so generous. I...'

Whatever Spanos might have said was lost as Kazanis burst into the kitchen. 'Ha, Falcon, just the man. How do you fancy a trek to Kritsa to find out what is going on?' Without waiting for an answer, Kazanis went on. 'I'm going down to Kardiotissas to round up would be palikers from those who farm the land around the monastery.'

'Not all men are as keen to battle as you, Kazanis.'

'Ha, if the men are reluctant I'll tell their wives we need to protect the miraculous icon of the Panagia Kera at Kardiotissas. They know that if the Turks sack the monastery, and steal the icon to prevent its spring procession, the resulting drought will mean there's nothing to farm anyway.'

'You think women will wipe their eyes and ask their men to pray beneath the icon for deliverance?'

'Exactly, Falcon. The fact that the stolen icon made its legendary way back from Constantinople will give them the heart that their men will return. I know you think it's all nonsense, but just wait, you'll see I'm right. I'll take Hannis with me, and then descend to the powder mill at the monastery of Saint George, the one near Vrachasi. As well as needing men for the mill, the monastery has huge dormitories to base recruits.' For emphasis, Kazanis banged Spanos across the shoulders, and growled, 'What do you think, Spanos? Does it sound like we'll be as organised as the western rebels?'

'Indeed! What about Kostas?'

'He'll lead a recruiting drive with Trichos. They can canvass the fifteen hamlets here on Lassithi before heading downhill to Krasi and other Christian villages. Men who want to strike a blow for freedom can rally at Vrachasi...'

Falcon interrupted, 'Do you want me to stay in Kritsa, or report back on what's going on?'

'Do what you think is right. If you send word to me it will only take us a few days to get men to Kritsa.'

'Pa, what about Spanos and me? Are we really palikers?'

It was obvious that Kazanis had forgotten how Petros and Spanos expected promotion. He was furiously scratching his beard, seeking inspiration, when Zacharias arrived.

'You're all up early. Petros, I need you to deliver seed potatoes to Kardiotissas.' It was the solution Kazanis needed.

'Both of you go. Show Spanos the revered icon and plant potatoes. Once Kostas completes his recruitment drive, he'll pass by the monastery to escort you to Vrachasi. There's no end to the need for labour in the powder mill, and you can take arms training with other volunteers. No, don't have other ideas. My mind is set. Ah, here's Trichos, finally awake to join us.'

Bleary eyed, Trichos slumped on to a chair at the table, and grunted at Petros who served him coffee, stolen when Kazanis raided the store of a hated Turk near Choumeriakos. The boy ignored Trichos's winces as he cheerily outlined his pa's plan. Meanwhile, Kazanis and Falcon stepped outside to finalise arrangements. Soon a shaggy head leaned into the kitchen.

'I'm off to rouse Hannis. Keep out of mischief, Petros, and look after Spanos. I'll see you both at the mill within a few weeks. I'll go via Kardiotissas to let the abbot know to expect you.'

Once Zacharias had readied two donkeys, he sent Petros to chivvy Spanos, who was donning his new outfit.

'You're so vain, Spanos. The last person I saw twirling like that was Anna when she made a new skirt.'

'No hint of Turk about me now, Petros. Look, I've put the green britches and fez in my bag as souvenirs. Feel this brand new cloak. Falcon's generous.'

'You stink of moth balls.'

'It will fade. Let's go, I'd like to see how Zacharias sets the bridles, and I'll stash my bags in a pannier.' They were almost at the stable when Petros stopped.

'You go on. I'll dash back for the cards and coin bag. We'll be stuck at the monastery for weeks, so if I stuff them in a pannier with your gear we can challenge the local boys.'

Petros and Spanos led their donkeys out of the yard via a snow-dusted path that zigzagged steeply downhill. A gap between stone houses gave a glimpse of the flooded plateau, now a broad silver lake shimmering in the morning sun, reflecting the snow blanketed mountains. As Petros was used to the wintery view, he was surprised when Spanos stopped.

'Oh Petros, this is wonderful. A mythical giant must have sculpted this mountain ring to guard the plateau. My grandpa told me about this place. He said it's very fertile once winter flooding subsides.'

'The way you turn your head to see all round the plateau makes you look like an owl.' To emphasise his point, Petros screeched like a frightened scops owl.

'Ouch, that was piercing! Look at those flumes plummeting down the Havga Canyon. Katharo must also be flooded. No wonder it's only used in summer.'

In confusion, Petros asked, 'Have you been to Katharo?'

'What? No, Grandpa must have told me. Well, I know you have oxen, but what about goats, or sheep?'

Petros didn't seem to realise Spanos had deliberately changed the subject, and, with a theatrical wink that he'd obviously learnt from his pa, said, 'Well, there's no point in keeping sheep when so many others do. It's impossible to keep tabs on them all, and one always strays our way when Pa fancies mutton!'

'My grandpa would get angry at that behaviour. Protecting sheep from Turks was hard enough, so he didn't need unscrupulous men ignoring another man's brand.'

Anxious that Spanos saw the fairness of it, Petros added, 'He only takes from people who deserve it. Never from family or kinsmen. Pa says it's hard to keep track of kin as so many ask him to be best man at their wedding or godfather to a son.'

'I'm not surprised! If I had sheep I'd soon bind him to me.' Perhaps Spanos realised his barb of criticism stung Petros for he changed the subject again. 'This is a pretty church.'

'It's dedicated to Saint John the Theologian. Pappas Stavros told me he fell in love with it as a child when he visited cousins to celebrate the Saint's Day on 8 May. That time, like every year, there was a miraculous re-flowering of the twigs previously used to cover the Easter epitaph. According to Zacharias, the real miracle is that it draws dispersed folk back, and he enjoys the way their gossip seasons a roast.'

'Where was Stavros visiting from?'

'He lived next to a bullying Turk in Choumeriakos, and my pa frequently stayed with Stavros. Eventually the adolescent Kazanis grew weary of the Turk's boasts and challenged him to a wrestling match. Satisfied with his win, my pa disappeared up the mountain. It wasn't over though. When Grandpa next took his mule to market, the humiliated Turk attacked him. While Grandpa lay dazed and bleeding, evil children scattered his apples, pears, and quinces, rendering them unsalable. Little savages even cut the ears and tail off his mule!

'Pa wanted revenge, so one cold night he went to Choumeriakos, hid until the Turk returned home, and then forced him to walk to Marmaketo at gunpoint. Imagine how angry my pa was when Grandpa refused to thrash the Turk. Apparently, he didn't want a feud to bring grief to the family for generations.'

'Did Kazanis tell you this?'

'No, Pappas Stavros told me. He said Pa felt let down, so I'm not surprised Pa didn't brag over that adventure.'

The testy male donkey raced ahead and ignored Petros, who was perhaps too wary of the beast since it had recently given him a nasty nip. To the boy's delight, Spanos expertly attached the jenny's reins to the jack's saddle, explaining it would serve to hold him back. While Spanos petted the animal to gain its confidence, Petros seized the opportunity to claim the placid jenny's saddle.

'Hey Spanos, now you're in the lead don't miss that track on the right. It skirts up and around Selina peak, then descends towards the monastery.'

'I was watching that man further along this track. From his gait I'd say he's exhausted.'

When Petros said, 'We're wary of strangers, let's see who he is', Spanos reached for his gun, and only relaxed when the figure came near enough for the boy to confirm that Zacharias traded with him. When the man drew near, Petros said, 'Zacharias is at our place.'

'I'm not after him today. It's your pa I need.'

'Sorry, you've wasted your time. Pa's gone to Kardiotissas. This is Spanos. He's new here.'

'Welcome, although your timing is poor. I met a man with a stab wound, but he was more worried about finding someone to get a letter to Kazanis than his gaping chest. My family are tending his last hours, so I promised to deliver this letter.'

'I'll not see Pa for weeks. What does it say?'

'No idea, I've no learning. Just keep it till you see him.'

Spanos asked, 'Who cut the man? What was the reason?'

'He rambled about Turks. That's why I'm anxious to get home. Take care.'

When the man was out of earshot, Petros said, 'Pappas Stavros can read. If we go back he'll tell us the message.'

When Spanos simply stated, 'I can read' the wide-eyed the boy handed over the scrap of paper torn from a precious book. Faltering over unfamiliar script, Spanos read aloud.

'My Brave Cousin, Captain of Lion Hearted Palikers,
I beseech you for aid. I'm sure you remember the vile hunchback, Bilalis, who you cursed and banned from the plateau for molesting his stepdaughters. I thought him dead.

Banished with other Christians from Choumeriakos, I took refuge among the hovels of Limnes where, to my dismay, I found myself living near him. I told others of his evil ways. In retaliation, he stole my daughter Irini. He has taken her to his brothel on the outskirts of Limnes.

Cousin, I beg you, pursue the hunchback. He's an abomination, purloining girls for those who wish to satisfy an urge to rape and slay. I took a blade in my chest trying to save Irini. Where I failed, please succeed.

God bless your endeavours, Giorgos.'

Choking on tears, Spanos said, 'If we hurry, there's a chance your pa might still be at Kardiotissas. If not I'll ask directions to the powder mill.'

Clouds blanketed the mountains with a fine drizzle that

slowly drenched Petros's wool cloak. Chilled to the bone, he was thoroughly miserable. He was lonely too, as Spanos had retreated into private thoughts, not even speaking when he frequently rested the donkeys on the steep uphill slog. Determined to endure without complaint, Petros huddled in his cloak until the rhythmic sway of his mount lulled him into a half sleep.

Gunshot woke Petros with a start, and in disbelief he realised the lead donkey had no rider. Another shot cut through the gloom, followed by the unusual sound of a horse's neigh. Instantly fearful, Petros dismounted, gripped the jack's bridle, and took cautious downhill steps through the grey pall of mist. A third shot caused the donkey to snicker in fear, and jerk its head so hard that it knocked Petros to the ground. As the jack strode away, a gruff voice came from above the prone boy.

'Hello, who is this?'

A fez wearer hauled Petros up, and ignored the boy's indignant squeal of pain and angry shouts to clasp him around his waist and drag him downhill. Through swirling mist, Petros glimpsed three stone shepherd huts, so he was nearer Kardiotissas Monastery than he'd thought. His captor called out, 'Hey, Bilalis, I've caught a boy out alone. You thought I'd wasted my shots.' About to deny he was alone, Petros clamped his mouth shut, realising Spanos may have good reason to hide.

A tiny hunchbacked man stepped out of a hut. 'Well, you didn't hit him, so that's a waste in my book. Who is it? Ah, the Kazanis brat. It's years since I've seen you. Who are you with?'

With a stutter to match that of Pappas Stavros, the boy answered, 'N-n-no one, b-but if I'm l-late they'll s-s-search.'

Deep in thought, the grotesque man stroked his straggly, thin beard while chewing and sucking on a wad of tobacco, then, turning his head slightly, he hawked a sticky mess that barely missed Petros. 'Who are you with, boy?' Desperate not to worsen the situation, Petros wondered how to answer. Distracted by seeing the donkeys at a water trough, he took a step towards them. Taking this as an affront, Bilalis swung a clenched fist into the boy's stomach. Shock and pain caused Petros to double over and fall to his knees. One of the dwarf's henchmen found this hilarious, so pushed the boy's face into Bilalis's stinking crotch.

'He's assumed a good position, he won't need much training!'

'I like your thinking, but I'll hold him to ransom first. Kazanis will pay a good price for his only boy, then we can run off with him and a hefty purse. I'll earn more when Omar sells the boy, he'll pay me commission.' Bilalis roughly lifted the boy's head with a filthy hand to demand, 'Where's your companion?'

'I complete errands on my own. I'm taking potatoes to the monastery. Pa is there with his palikers. Let me go.'

'Oh, I intend to take you to your pa. Hey, Ali, get this brat on a donkey. Tie him on. We don't want to lose our precious cargo. Wait! He's bound to have a knife tucked in his waist. Ah good, it has a distinctive horn handle made by Kazanis. I've always wanted one of those.'

In desperation, Petros flailed his limbs to make it difficult for this Ali to haul him to a donkey. Although the boy was ashamed that he couldn't prevent the rough oaf from manhandling him, he did take satisfaction from kicking up a steaming pile of droppings to make the brute swear. Five minutes into the steep downhill walk, the jack lowered his head, gave a disgruntled bray, and lifted his tail to drop another stinking pile. As the acrid odour stung his nose, Petros allowed a slight grin. Much more of this and Spanos would have no problem following them, if he tried.

This thought prompted the boy to recall the day Kostas had locked Spanos in the barn with Pasiphae. The stranger had sensed that Petros sat the other side of the locked door, and had called, 'Does this fine calf have a name?'

Unable to resist, Petros had answered, 'As soon as we knew Pasiphae was expecting, Zacharias said I could name her calf. I haven't thought of anything yet.'

Not sounding at all like a terrible Turk, the kind voice inside the barn had asked, 'What about her sire? What's the bull called?'

'It's old Minos. He belongs to Zacharias, who leads him round local farms on a strong rope fixed through a ring in his nose.'

The laughing voice had replied, 'Call the calf Ariadne!'

'Mmm, that's a pretty name. I've not heard it before.'

'It's a myth. Since I seem to have time to spare, I'll tell you. Minos, the legendary King of Crete, upset Poseidon, one of the gods. To wreak revenge, Poseidon sent a magnificent bull to bewitch the king's wife, Pasiphae, who subsequently gave birth to a terrible creature, half man and half bull, called Minotaur. This Minotaur was so vicious that Minos had a labyrinth built to house the beast. It took a dreadful annual sacrifice of seven youths and seven maidens from Athens to pacify it.

'The king of Athens had a son called Theseus, and one year Theseus told his pa that it was time to stop the ritual, so he volunteered to journey to Crete to kill the Minotaur. Understandably, the Athenian king was worried, and begged his sailors to journey back under white sails to signal success, or hoist black shrouds if the news was bad.

'Once on the island of Crete, Theseus fell in love with Ariadne, a daughter of Minos and Pasiphae. Of course, Ariadne trembled at the thought of the Minotaur devouring Theseus. Unable to talk him out of tackling the beast,

Ariadne gave Theseus an enormous ball of thread, urging him to unwind it as he went, then, if he became lost in the labyrinth, he'd be able to find his way back.

'When the day came for Theseus to face the creature, he unravelled the thread as he went into its lair, where he bravely faced the evil being with tenacity to strike a fatal blow. Triumphant, Theseus rewound the thread to find his way back, and this left King Minos with no option other than to agree that Ariadne could leave with him.'

A shouted 'Hey, what are you doing? Stay on that donkey!' ended Petros's reminisces.

'I'm just getting comfortable.' As soon as the man lost interest, Petros continued to pick a hole in the pannier until a seed potato fell through. Then, by kicking the pannier in time to the donkey's footsteps, he left a trail in the hope that Spanos would recognise the potatoes as markers.

After emerging from the pine-clad hillside, the path opened on to a wide grassy slope, and with relief Petros saw the monastery. Bilalis had ridden ahead on the horse. Now he waited under a stand of walnut trees, just a short gallop from the monastery's gatehouse.

'It's taken you an age to get here. Bring me the boy.'

Ali undid the rope bindings, then dragged Petros off his saddle and over to the horse, where he helped Bilalis to haul the boy up. Appalled at his fate, Petros sat in front of the evil man, shivering in terror as a rough rope was passed around his throat. Thinking fast, Petros continued his bluff that Kazanis was at the monastery.

'Papa, Kazanis. Help! Hel—'

His cry was cut short when Bilalis dropped from the horse, looped the rope over a stout overhead branch, and pulled. Although Petros sat as tall as he could in the horse's saddle, there wasn't enough slack to prevent the rope rasping. He expected a painful death.

The twisted man cackled, 'Stand up, Petros, it will ease the pressure. I'm passing the rope to Ali. You'll be safe if you keep steady.' As the boy struggled to stand, he clung to the rope above his head to ease the strain. From his elevated position, he saw an old crone among goats slowly making her way towards the monastery, leading a tethered ram. Petros had a fleeting thought that the cheerful goat bells were at odds with his predicament before he was distracted by a murmured conversation between Bilalis and his second man.

Bilalis's thug charged towards the woman. When the crone appeared deaf to yelled demands, the bully physically stopped her, and then roughly pushed her towards Bilalis. Unable to hurry, the herder shuffled through milling animals to reach Bilalis, who demanded she take a message to Kazanis.

'Eh, what did you say? You'll have to speak up.'

'Take my message to the monastery.'

'Eh? I'm just taking goats to the monastery.'

'Leave them. Go to the monastery. Tell Kazanis to come. He must pay a good sum if he wants his boy to live.'

'Eh, who do you want?'

'Kazanis, he's in the monastery.'

'There's a man called Kazanis at the monastery?'

The herder led her ram to the grazing donkeys, now tied to a tree, and Petros felt his hopes rise when he heard, 'Very well, let me tether my ram to this donkey's harness.'

From his perilous perch, Petros watched the gatehouse. In truth, he thought his pa such a hero he expected Kazanis to charge out, bristling guns and knives, to do battle. Eventually the boy spied the bent figure come into view, alone. Crestfallen, Petros's grip slackened, and the resulting jolt demonstrated how his life literally hung in the balance. Alert to the sudden movement, Ali yelled, 'Steady, boy, you're worth more alive. I'll tie the rope on this branch. If it stays taut, you'll have a better grip as long as the horse stands still. Now, I'll wait with the others, and you can hope my mare enjoys her rest.'

The terrified boy saw the monastery gate open. His hopes rose as a group of monks hovered indecisively, and then plummeted when they returned to the sanctuary. In his despair, Petros didn't spot a solitary monk race away. Instead, he saw the herdswoman shuffling back. Eventually she reached the odd group, where she ignored the men and aimed for the tethered animals. Without bothering to stand, Bilalis shouted, 'Did Kazanis give you a purse?'

'Eh? I'm having trouble with my ram.'

Now exhausted, Petros found it impossible to keep his balance. Each wobbly movement caused the rope to cut deeper into his bleeding neck. To ease the strain he placed the fingers of one hand inside the noose, and then pulled hard on the rope with his other hand to reduce the tension. Immediately Petros noticed a shift of weight, and seized a slim chance of escape. He shinned up the rope, hand over hand, until he hung precariously over the branch, then reached for the small knife hidden in the headband of his sheepskin cap, placed there to mimic his pa.

Under the tree, the men focused on the woman as she walked from the tethered animals towards Bilalis, with her hand outstretched.

'Take these coins and release the boy.'

Bilalis took the coins, and then quizzically bit one. 'Who gave you these worthless coins?'

'Kazanis. He said these Talos coins are fit for thieves.' In that instant, the crone flung a handful of coins at the man and sprang forward. Bilalis felt a blade at his throat. His men backed off. Frightened by the commotion, the horse bolted. Then, with an adrenalin-fuelled scream of exhilaration, Petros leapt. The boy swung on the rope like a pendulum to knock Ali and his crony to the ground. In those seconds, the woman dragged Bilalis backwards.

Crouched where he fell in a heap, Petros saw the crone whisper in the dwarf's ear, and was amazed to hear Bilalis respond by instructing his men to strip. They hesitated. The woman's blade drew a line of blood across her captive's throat. His shriek convinced them. Shivering with cold and fear, they pathetically begged for mercy.

Spanos threw back his cowl. 'Mercy? I've shown more than you deserve. Run after your horse, and don't halt until Neapoli.' They fled, and despite his pain Petros cheered until he saw Spanos dragging the tiny man backwards.

'I've broken my arm, Spanos, I can't help.' A shove from Spanos sent Bilalis sprawling, and when he found his feet he faced Spanos's gun.

'Let me go. I've got money.'

'Strip and go. I need to attend my friend.'

Bilalis fled.

Despite his painful arm, Petros was happy to ride behind his hero. 'We've proven to have lion hearts, Spanos. Now even Kostas will have to accept us as palikers!'

3

KOSTAS

Bless Kostas, Papa, I loved him the moment I saw him.

An enduring pall of grief consumed Kostas. He knew he was despicable. Other men stood by him and said 'You can't chase ghosts.' He knew he should have tried.

First light the next morning found Kostas and Trichos jogging to Kardiotissas, confident that their recruitment campaign had been a success. Many men had promised to join Kazanis once they'd completed spring planting. Now the duo looked forward to a meal at the monastery, so were perplexed to find the monastery gate shut and unattended. Eventually, their frantic banging brought a response from a novice who'd scrambled up the inside of the stout wall to a high vantage point. Once they'd satisfied the vigilant monk they weren't Turks, he clambered down to open the gate. Before the monk could give any explanation, Kazanis sped up from the other direction and fell to the ground, exhausted.

In shock, Kostas exclaimed, 'Kazanis! Why are you here?'

'Bastard Turks. They've hung my boy!'

Kostas dropped to his cousin's side. 'How? I'll kill the culprit, I promise. Oh, and what about Spanos? They were together.' For six years Kostas had hidden his emotions.

Now his voice cracked. 'Which way did the bastards go?'

In an awed voice, the novice assured them, 'Don't worry, your Spanos is amazing. He sent the Turks off stark naked!' Confused, Kostas fell back to his knees as jubilant monks overwhelmed them all, until the abbot's commanding voice broke through.

'Your boy lives, Kazanis. Follow me.'

With a great roar of delight, Kazanis hugged his son, drowning the boy's squeals of pain and the ominous creak of the bed as he sat. When Kostas saw Spanos on a stool by the bed he couldn't trust his emotions, so chose to lean against the wall just outside the room to listen.

'Once I knew Kazanis wasn't at the monastery, I hoped for a chance to reach for my gun, even though it was empty. Those bullies felt so superior they didn't even rise when I returned. They moved once Bilalis felt my knife at his scrawny throat!'

I knew I'd kill him another day. I'd promised Mama.

'Did you find my potato trail, Spanos?'

'Yes, the first one I trod on made such a crunch. Then when I stepped on another I realised they were from your pannier. What a fantastic idea to set a trail.'

'Like Ariadne's thread?'

'Well it worked until goats ate the potatoes. Their shepherd was amazed at my offer to swap my new cloak for his threadbare one, plus the pleasure of herding his goats to the monastery.'

Outside the infirmary door, Kostas listened as Spanos and Petros vied to answer the furious questions that Kazanis fired at them. Hearing their tale unfold, Kostas was amazed at their escape, and overcome with remorse that he'd not been around to save them. Kazanis turned the conversation in a different direction with his next question.

'So, when did you tell my son of Ariadne's thread, Spanos?'

'Ah, he is a kind boy. He took pity on me when Kostas quite rightly had me locked in the barn.'

'Pa, when Spanos told me the myth, I was disappointed it had such a happy ending. I'm delighted now!'

Overcome with unaccustomed emotions, Kazanis gave Spanos a happy punch to his arm, sending him reeling. Rubbing his bruised arm, Spanos righted his stool, and said, 'The next part of the story was sad.

'As Theseus and Ariadne sailed back to Athens, they stopped on the beautiful island of Naxos, and while Ariadne slept another god, Dionysus, appeared to her in a dream. This Dionysus commanded her to stay on Naxos to marry him. Theseus was distraught, and sailed away as fast as he could, so fast that he forgot to tell the sailors to hoist white sails. The Athenian king kept watch for his son's return, so was the first person to spy black sails on the horizon. Overcome with grief at this sign of his son's death, the king jumped off the cliff.'

A gruff voiced Kazanis said, 'I understand that. Grief plays havoc with the strongest of men.' In the ensuing hush, Kostas heard a barely audible Petros.

'Mama used to tell me stories, when I was small.' Like a moth drawn to a flame, Kostas peeked around the doorframe, and as he did Spanos beamed a smile of delight that hit him like a punch. With a gasp, Kostas stepped back out of sight, collapsed to his haunches, and then strained to catch the soft, almost feminine tone.

'I miss my mama desperately, Petros. I cry for her daily.'

'I was bad, Spanos. Mama had a baby girl, and then left.' Kostas heard the pained intake of breath from beneath the huge shaggy beard of Kazanis, and knew his own matched it.

'Oh Petros, that's sad. Many women die giving birth. It can't have been your fault.'

Petros whispered his reply, as if to reduce its dreadfulness. 'She chose to leave. She went back to her own mama on that island you talked about, Naxos.'

'There must have been overwhelming reasons, for she'd have been distraught to leave you.' Drawn again by an irresistible force, Kostas stepped into the sickroom, and then froze at the sight of Spanos silently begging Kazanis to tell his boy the truth. Kazanis gave Kostas a slight cautionary shake of his head, then turned to his child.

'Petros, you're the finest son a man could have. Women think differently to men. She left me, not you. Your mama saw Turks kill Kostas's wife and daughter, so she fled with your baby sister. I forbade her to take you. We couldn't keep our women safe, so she had good reason to leave. Now, thanks to Spanos, I can say that I love you. My dread is that I can't ensure your safety.'

'Oh Petros, did you hear that? How happy I'd have been to hear my papa say he loved me. Although I'm sure he did, I'd give anything to have heard him say so.'

Kazanis leant across to place his hand on Spanos's shoulder, and, sounding even gruffer, said, 'From today, Spanos, I have two sons, and I love you both.' When Kostas saw Spanos leap up to draw Kazanis into a hug, he realised he had no right to be there.

Late that afternoon, Kostas stood outside of the monastery with Trichos, impatiently waiting for Kazanis. He eagerly anticipated a night in the local village of Krasi, so famous for its wine. At last, Kazanis stomped out and shouted back over his shoulder, 'Keep my boys safe, Abbot. When Petros is well, send them to Zacharias in Marmaketo, out of harm's way.' With an odd sensation of loss, Kostas shrugged and set off.

After their descent to Krasi, the three men made for the huge Venetian-built water cisterns, where in summer the area benefited from a shady canopy of vast plane trees. Even without leaves, the colossal trees provided shelter as someone had draped sewn goatskins from branch to branch to create a snug marquee over a brushed dirt floor, studded with braziers that issued a cheerful glow. Certain of a warm welcome, the Marmaketo men accepted prime positions and copious jugs of wine. Hours later, villagers set off home, where many spent a last night with their family before following Kazanis on the quest to expel Turks. Before the Marmaketo men settled to sleep, Kostas paced the perimeter of the awning to check security. His hackles rose as dogs barked.

Kostas drew a gun. 'State your business, or I'll shoot.'

A frightened voice came out of the dark. 'It's Petros, with Spanos.'

A rush of pleasure caught Kostas by surprise. 'How? Why?' Kostas couldn't hide his amazement at Petros's garbled explanation that with all the excitement over his escape from Bilalis both he and Spanos had forgotton that they had a message for Kazanis. When Kostas shouted for Kazanis the boy could hardly contain his excitement and he ran forward to share his news.

'Pa, Spanos was amazing. The abbot was reluctant to let us leave, so Spanos told him that if the gate didn't open he'd take the drop under the privy.'

'Then Petros said he'd follow me, and if he fell and broke his neck, his pa would hold the abbot responsible. Poor abbot had no choice. Once we were mounted he wished us God speed.'

Disappointed that Kazanis laughed to condone the escapade, Kostas sneered, 'What message compelled you?'

In deference to the mystical power of a written message,

silence fell as Spanos unfolded the paper. In the ensuing hush, all present regarded Spanos with new respect. Once Kazanis had digested the news, he said, 'Those are snow laden clouds blanketing the moon. Although I'd toss you into a fray, I'll not lose a man to a snowdrift. We'll move in the morning.'

Slowly Kostas realised he was awake, and then he lay under his woollen cloak, desperate not to spoil the magic. Warm tantalising breath on the back of his neck made him gasp, and transferring heat released butterflies of joy in his stomach. Confused and filled with self-loathing, Kostas wracked his brain for the foundation of this turmoil. True, he didn't long for a woman, and thought that was out of respect for Maria. Now he felt sheer joy that Spanos had curled up against his back, probably seeking comfort in the cold pre-dawn. Tormented, and scared of breaking the spell, Kostas held his breath as the blazing heat of arousal surged through his core. Then the magic evaporated; he realised it was the odd creature's fault for venturing to Lassithi. As if scalded, Kostas jumped up to yell at the sleeping forms around him.

'Get up! You've overslept. Move, Spanos. It's not winter now, whatever this late snow thinks.' With a yell of bravado, Kostas pulled off his sheepskin cap and ran to plunge his face into a cistern. Then he dried his face on his cap and strode into bushes.

By the time Petros and Spanos found space at the cistern, the men had dispersed. Busy chatting, they didn't notice Kostas. Spanos used a finger to trace an inscription above the cistern.

'Look at this. Thinking, Knowledge, and Beauty once met together under the many leaves of Krasi plane trees.'

'I've no idea what it means, Spanos. The cisterns are ancient, although not as old as these huge trees. I've been told they were seedlings at the time of Christ.'

'Well, fancy you two having time to chat. For some strange reason Kazanis insists you come along. I'd hoped he'd send you both to Zacharias in Marmaketo.'

Even Kostas, fit as he was, found the pace over rough terrain in the face of a freezing gale gruelling, so he was surprised that the two youngest palikers voiced no complaint. He also conceded that having panniers to stow gear was useful, although he'd been annoyed that Spanos was tetchy about 'his' pannier, until he recognised he felt the same about 'his' bed at the house. Much later, sitting on a ridge near the hamlet of Vrisses above the plain and lakes, Kostas studied the terrain. One of the Krasi men had traded a pipe with a pouch of tobacco for twenty shots. Now, as he savoured a satisfying puff of smoke, he thought the extortionate cost worth it.

'Ah Kostas, I thought I smelt baccy. Will you fill my bowl?'

'What's your exchange, Kazanis?'

'Petros and Trichos will be back from a nearby monastery soon. They went to trade for supper. Will that do?'

With a nod towards the contents of a small leather pouch, Kostas added, 'You'll have to owe me something else. I've made three shots for Spanos. He was lucky once to pretend his gun was loaded, but I thought it best not to tempt fate. Where is he anyway?'

'Some devil got into him. He set off to the local monastery with Petros, then rushed back to ask if it was the Hanging Monastery. I said yes, and he ran off. Bloody odd.'

To hide his concern for the lad, Kostas changed the subject. 'Shall we go to Limnes tonight?'

Intent on watching his fragrant smoke spiral away, Kazanis said, 'Probably. I'm keen to get back to those mustering at the powder mill.'

Exhaling smoke, Kostas said, 'It can't be hard to close a brothel. I'll go with Trichos.'

With obvious relief, Kazanis clapped his cousin across the shoulder. 'I dashed off when the monk came to tell me about Petros, so yes, I'll leave you to it.'

Intent on their conversation, neither man realised Spanos was near. 'I'll go with Kostas.'

In shock, they looked down the barrel of a modern flintlock gun, and in unison exclaimed, 'Where did you get that?'

'I stole it when I fled, then hid it with the person who tended me. I recognised this area so went to reclaim it. Take the gun for your collection, Kostas. I'll not do it justice.'

Shock drained Kostas's face, then his eyes gleamed with joy. I wish you could have seen it, Thea. It was originally your idea to give the gun to the man I love.

A revolting smell from a midden heap wafted over the palikers as they crept near lakeside hovels. Kostas wrinkled his nose in disgust, and led the way with pistols drawn. As the palikers approached a remote windowless dwelling, they disturbed two tethered dogs. Frantic barks sent the band into trees as an unkempt man appeared in his squalid doorway to yell, 'Quiet!'

Trichos muttered, 'Damn, go back to bed.' The hidden men held their breath as the man looked around, shrugged, and then hunkered down to soothe his dogs.

'You'll have to get used to a succession of customers to the bawdy house. Omar's already built a steady business. I wonder how Omar smuggled you here. When they discovered the grim remains of Hursit, half-eaten by a dog, the new pasha ordered a cull. I heard that a dog carried the severed hand to them. I bet the bastards choked on their *narghiles*!

225

Rumour has it that troops ran into Hursit's bedroom and tripped over his spilt entrails. No sign of his bride though. A band of twenty rebels had spirited her away, and then stoned her to death for sleeping with a Turk.' Eventually this one sided conversation calmed the dogs, so the man went inside.

Papa, I did it in my rage, after he was dead. He'd stolen my life. Will God forgive me? It was justice of a Turk for a Turk.

A tatty curtain at the brothel's unglazed window allowed Kostas to view five naked men lounging on sofas around a table littered with food. Their hats, discarded among the debris, labelled them janissaries. Three rough Turks hunched over a card table at the back of the room. A lilting lyre gave out an incongruous tune, usually enjoyed at weddings, evidence there was at least one other man. Sad faced women with lank unbound hair served in a desultory fashion, apparently deaf to ribald comments.

'Come, sweet Elli, sit on my lap to dance your jig.'

'You're for me tonight, Irini. See my stallion rear!'

'Lower your head down here, Anna, I'm ready.'

'Kostas, you slovenly creature, make the beds.' In shock, Kostas had reeled backwards before he realised it was not his name the bastard called. This allowed Spanos to take his place briefly. In whispers, Kostas shared his view that those inside were certainly not on their guard, although arms, including a mean *yataghan*, littered the table and floor.

Trichos asked, 'What's our plan?'

'Take them by surprise, literally with their britches down.'

'What of the girls?'

'Well, Spanos, they're already dead to their families, and if that's the price to save others...'

Spanos grabbed Kostas's arm, and hissed, 'We must get them out.'

Annoyed at the challenge, Kostas pushed Spanos to the ground, then hunkered over him to demand, 'Tell me if you've a better idea, you malaca.'

'I'll bluff my way in, as if I'm a senior officer.'

'Don't be ridiculous, you'll get us all killed.'

Petros spoke up. 'Let him try. I live thanks to his resourcefulness.' Disloyally, Trichos sided with Petros.

'Spanos will probably die in seconds. I'll only agree if Petros goes up to that wooded ridge before we start.'

Crouched at the window, Kostas signalled Trichos to go beside the flimsy door. He'd given Spanos a second gun, and both were primed for their single shot. There was no more he could do. With rising nausea, Kostas grasped his guns in clammy hands and inwardly fumed at the delay.

Moonlight across the muddy yard illuminated Spanos settling the crumpled fez on his head before he adjusted the voluminous green britches he'd taken from his pannier. Next, he clasped his young squire, talked earnestly, and pointed away. With his nod of comprehension, Petros earned an embrace from Spanos, and then, with just one glance back, he rode for the ridge. Fervently signing the cross, Spanos strode towards the brothel. At the same time Kostas looked up, as if beseeching the starry heavens, murmuring, 'God, keep this fool safe.'

About to rap on the door with his gun, Spanos dropped his hand and whispered, 'The scum playing cards are mine.' After a deep breath, Spanos threw the door open.

'Allah adına, neyin kötü buraya?' Despite the stunned hush, an icy chill enveloped Kostas.

'Ignorant peasants, in the name of Allah, what goes here?'

From his vantage point, Kostas saw janissaries scrabble for their clothes, while shocked card players remained seated. With great authority, Spanos stamped his foot and pointed to the door. His menacingly calm voice demanded, 'Whores out.'

They'd judged that the janissaries would quickly regain their wits, so Kostas yelled, 'Do you want us now?'

'Not yet, Lieutenant, I'll give them one last chance. I've a squad of twenty outside. Walk out unarmed and they will arrest you. If they come in, only bodies will leave. The choice is yours. First, I want those women out. Now!' In a huddle, the women made for the door. As they drew level, Trichos shouted, 'Run up the western ridge. A friend awaits you.'

On later reflection, Kostas couldn't remember what came first: the scream of his name or the gunshot. Either way, he sprang through the window to enter the fray. Brave janissaries they might have been, but as naked men they fell quickly. In a pause for breath, a savage sight distracted Kostas. Wielding a *yataghan*, Spanos hysterically hacked at the head of a small corpse. Horrified, Kostas leapt over two crumpled bodies, one still with cards in his hand. Desperate to halt Spanos he failed to notice an injured man crawl to reach a gun. Kostas slipped in gore, fell, and knocked Spanos from his feet. The bloody *yataghan* clattered across the floor.

Kostas screamed, 'Enough, Spanos.'

Held in a personal nightmare, Spanos stared at Kostas with blind eyes, his blood-smeared face appalling. Instead of accepting Kostas's proffered hand, Spanos curled up, and through ragged breath wailed, 'I shot Omar, but he lives.'

Resigned to the fact that Spanos wasn't going to move, Kostas bent to lift the lad, then horrendous pain engulfed his flank, even before the gunshot registered. He dropped

Spanos, snatched up the *yataghan*, and turned on his assailant. Trichos beat him to it and slit the janissary's throat.

'Bastard! Sorry, Kostas, I didn't realise he still had life in him.'

'Bloody Turk, I'll not enjoy a morning run for weeks! Give chase, Spanos thinks he shot another.'

Unable to ignore the burning pain deep in his innards, Kostas carried Spanos towards the agreed muster point, without noticing how the lad clutched a ghoulish trophy. At the point Kostas recognised he couldn't haul Spanos much further, he heard the screech of a startled scops owl just within the tree cover. Confident it was a signal from Petros he lowered Spanos, then dropped beside him, too exhausted to move even when he heard footsteps running behind him.

'Bastard got away. Are you...'

Trichos's voice trailed away. At the same time, Petros ran out from the tree line to cry, 'Oh my God, is Spanos dead?'

'No, the gore comes from a villain. He's in shock. So am I. He killed two with a single shot! One stood to face him, gun drawn, and with no hesitation Spanos shot him. The body fell to knock into the musician who'd swapped his lyre for a pistol. The unlucky minstrel fell backwards, knocked his head on a table, and that was that. Dead. I was busy with the janissaries so was unaware of other action. The next time I saw Spanos he was hacking away at a dwarf with a *yataghan*.'

Petros pointed to the severed head gripped by Spanos like a macabre prize, and squealed, 'Filthy bastard!' Unable to avert his horrified gaze, Petros explained his acquaintance with Bilalis. Throughout this account, Spanos sat alone, not participating in the buzz of victory.

In need of respite, Kostas took time to check and reload all the guns. He was midway through his task when he caught sight of Petros caring for the passive Spanos. Even though Petros had to cope with his own broken arm, he tipped water on a length of white cloth then wiped his friend's face. Petros looked relieved to see Kostas walk towards him.

'Help me, Kostas, I can't get Spanos to let go of that.'

Kostas bent to help, and asked, 'What's the cloth?'

'It's out of his pannier. When Falcon gave Spanos an outfit of clothes, a sheet formed the bundle that wrapped them. It's all cut into neat lengths now, and this is one of them.' When Kostas stooped to prise the lad's fingers open, he had to grit his teeth on his own involuntary cry of pain, and shut his ears to the eerie wail of distress from the lad.

'Let it go, Spanos, you did well. Kazanis will be proud of you.'

In a flash of lucidity, Spanos asked Petros, 'Are the girls safe?'

'Only two reached me. They agreed to go to the chapel you described, and, like you said, I told them that if the Panagia's icon is visible they should say, "Goldfinch begs sanctuary for her friends".'

With a shrug, Kostas said, 'So, now they're not our concern. Pass me some cloth, I'll dress my wound.'

By the next nightfall, Kostas lay in an infirmary overflowing with men injured in a powder explosion. Despite the chaos, word of their arrival at the mill reached Hannis, who sought Kostas and provided details of the horrific accident where eight men and five boys had died. Now the dead, maimed, and injured were in the mortuary, infirmary, refectory, or dormitory, depending on the scale of their injuries, and several men remained trapped beneath the fractured church tower.

Instinctively, Kostas rose from his bed to assist, and

then fell to the flagstones, overwhelmed by such agony that the next he knew he was praying for death on the surgeon's table. Now he watched Kazanis walk towards him, with so many guns and blades strapped across his huge body they sounded like clinking pans on a tinker.

'How long will you lounge about?'

'A week or two. I swear that surgeon was a butcher before he took his holy vows!'

'Sounds like you nearly met the Hades ferryman.'

'My surgeon told me if he closed me up with fragments of cloth inside me, I'd burn in fever and die in days. Believe me, at times that felt preferable! What's your news?'

'Petros is on the mend, unlike Spanos who hardly utters a word. I thought he'd approve of new palikers using Bilalis's head for target practice, but nothing, not a flicker. He's the hero of the hour. The men already sing a mantinade. Listen.'

'S-S-Stavros caught a spy, a bloody Turk,
Now in Christian clothes for Kazanis he'll work
Kostas our peacock, with feathers so fine,
Took lions to Limnes, Turks had to resign
Our cub paliker the upper hand gained,
Then with one shot, two heads Spanos claimed
Dropping his *yataghan* a felon hit the floor,
That ugly brute Bilalis suffers headaches no more!'

With a shrug, Kostas said, 'Spanos is not well in the head. Where would we be if we agonised over every dead Turk?'

'A live one causes his grief. He feels responsible that Omar fled, and now he's vowed to kill him, or die trying.'

Instantly Kostas recognised a need to keep Spanos safe, and, struggling to sound offhand, said, 'Can the lad stay here? I understand you're heading to Kritsa.'

'Yes. My message, via Falcon, is from Alexomanolis,

Kritsa's leader. Battles have depleted their numbers, and villagers are losing confidence, especially since their pappas disappeared. We'll give them a boost while they regroup. Both my boys will stay here. God knows, the mill needs extra help after that blast.' A painful spasm left Kostas breathless, so Kazanis proffered a *raki* flask.

Retaking his flask, Kazanis gulped a draught, belched, and continued. 'It seems Spanos was right about Egyptian troops. I've intelligence that the mercenary, Hassan Pasha, landed in the west with a strength we can't imagine.'

'Let's humble them,' said Kostas struggling to rise.

Kazanis shoved the invalid to his pillow. 'Stay and get fit. Despite the blast, Hannis has production and transportation of black powder under control. More volunteers arrive daily, so I need you to turn them from farmhands to fighters. No, don't argue! Anyway, here's the surgeon with your potion.'

4

Mediterranean Queen

By summer I had a settled routine, and mainly worked alone. It was for the best. Oh Papa, how I longed for Kostas.

Exhausted from a long coastal run, Kostas slumped under the feathery fronds of a tamarisk tree to enjoy welcome relief from fierce August sun and the pain in his side. Then, lulled by the music of squawking cicadas, a brisk hot wind, and waves breaking on the shore, he succumbed to sleep. It was past noon when a strong gust brought a branch crashing down. Kostas jumped up, instantly alert, then, realising his narrow escape, he kicked the bough aside and strode to the shore. Even shielding his eyes against the sun's glare didn't help him scan the horizon, for the hot gale had whipped waves high to reduce visibility. He recognised the need to find someone who knew about boats, so he continued along the coast, splashing barefoot in foaming surf as he went.

By the time Kostas reached a finger of rocks protecting a narrow harbour, searing heat made a swim attractive. He tentatively reached under his blouses to feel the scar along his flank and judged himself fit. He'd started to remove clothes when a shrill cry stopped him, and an iridescent turquoise spear flashed past. No, it wasn't the halcyon's cry. Another shriek followed, then 'Got your eye, you bastard.' It was only then that Kostas noticed a floating keg, fighting angry waves as it tried to wrench free from its rope tether. Two stones in quick succession ricocheted off the keg.

'Stop! You'll hit me...'

A shocked gasp, then an excited 'Is that Kostas?'

'Spanos! Why are you here?'

Suffused in sudden joy, Kostas reached down to help Spanos. 'It's lovely to see you, Kostas. I've learnt to swim, if that's not too grand a name for my feeble splashes. Even the harbour's too rough for me today, though, so I'm practising with my catapult. It trains my eye, especially in such wind.'

'No, lad, I mean why are you in Sisi?'

'Those two men over there, by the old carob store, are unloading kegs of black powder from my string of donkeys. I'm a drover now. Trekking down the mountain suits me much better than the choking mix of saltpetre, charcoal, and sulphur at the mill.'

'So you've been to Sisi often?'

'Although I've lost count of the number of trips, I still get a thrill when my path through the ravine suddenly gives way to the broad expanse of the sea. When I first arrived, I stood on the cliff edge wondering how to descend to the skinny cleft-shaped harbour. While I dithered, the lead jack took the initiative and followed his usual route down.'

'Do you know the Sisi village captain?'

'It's Spiros. His wife, Poppi, will make you welcome as long as you eat fish.'

'Is Sisi a large village?'

'No, just a hamlet clustered around a church. Apart from our black powder, they despatch carobs annually, and their harbour berths three fishing boats. How did you get here?'

'Along the cliffs from Milatos. They have a proper harbour, not like this rock gap. Could a larger boat use it?'

'I've only seen small boats, and even that looks risky

234

when waves run high. I doubt they'll put out today. I only swim where there's an anchored boat in the harbour, then I cling on when I tire. Other lads tumble into the water stark naked, their bodies gleaming in the sun like burnished bronze. Although they tease me for wearing clothes, they'd be horrified if I stripped!'

Intended as a joke, that last comment from Spanos made Kostas uncomfortable. Instead of responding, he looked away to continue.

'How those breakers crash! I'm certain they'd dash a boat onto the rocks. I must find Spiros.'

'That's Spiros and his brother unloading my drove. I'm sure they'll be glad of a chat once they've finished. Meanwhile, what news do you have?'

Instead of answering, Kostas watched a crab scuttle across the rocks, then asked, 'Do you know that Kazanis led a force to assist Kritsa?'

'Yes, he briefly visited the mill to replenish his powder stock. I understand the Turks fled, so you can imagine how the *raki* flowed.'

Kostas continued talking to disguise his rising discomfort. 'Have you met Kazanis since?'

'I've not seen him for months. Do you know where he is?'

'Yes, he's ranging the eastern province, harrying Turks to create an illusion of a greater numbers of rebels. Your idea of offering Talos coins to evil Bilalis inspired Kazanis. He emptied the clay urn at Marmaketo, and now leaves a Talos as ironic payment whenever a Turk is relieved of stock.'

'That's fantastic! What of Trichos?'

'After the mill explosion we moved our training base above Vrisses. Now Trichos leads new palikers on skirmishes to test their resolve. Today he's enjoying the feast day with his family in Milatos. I'll meet him later.' Reluctant to make eye contact with Spanos, Kostas concentrated on the crab until a wave washed it away in millions of tiny white bubbles.

'How are you, Kostas? Why are you here?'

Loath to admit his internal wound had still not fully healed, Kostas snapped, 'You'd best get back to work.'

A deep flush rose up Spanos's neck. 'I was just going.'

After he'd clambered along the rocky outcrop, Kostas anticipated the thrilling rush of a dive until a huge wave drenched him. He reluctantly recognised Spanos was right: the harbour promised a safer swim. He might have used the harbour if the wretched lad wasn't there. The sight of his nemesis jumping to touch whipping palm fronds distracted Kostas so much that he was oblivious to a towering surge.

Washed from his feet, Kostas spluttered to the surface and, despite his frenzied splashing, made slow progress pulling against the current. His relief at reaching the slippery rocks evaporated when his second step caused a boulder to fall away and wedge his foot. Relentless swell almost wrenched his leg from his body, and then dashed him against unforgiving rock. Between each deluge, the primeval urge to survive gave Kostas energy to cough up swallowed brine and snatch burning breaths. Eventually exhausted, he relaxed in the water's warm embrace and smiled at his ma's call.

'Hang on, Kostas.'

He gurgled a reply as tons of crashing water washed her away to be replaced by his Maria's croon.

'Don't die, Kostas.'

Next came a screamed 'Take my hand.' As he reached through the spray for the outstretched hand, he recognised Spanos's anguished face the very second the lad was swept away.

Air trapped in Spanos's blouses ballooned to keep him afloat, and the next wave washed him towards Kostas. With renewed energy, Kostas reached to grab Spanos. With great resolve he thrust the lad clear of the next crest, and hissed, 'Go! My foot's jammed.' Horror drained all remaining colour from Spanos's face as he sped away.

Semiconscious now, Kostas imagined a gunshot, and then dreamt Spanos ran back through the spray with an oar. After a snatched breath, Spanos went under. Almost immediately, he bobbed up. He still clutched the spar as he choked on brine, and two surges passed before Spanos plunged again. In agony, Kostas rode successive waves as each cruelly tugged at him, until searing pain in his foot rendered him unconscious.

Spears of sunlight flickered through Kostas's eyelashes to send spasms of torture through his head, matched by those in his mashed foot. Unable to fight nausea, Kostas spewed. A calloused hand wiped the mess away, then turned him to his side. Dimly, Kostas heard, 'Rest now. I'm trying to get this one back from Hades.' These words span around until something registered, and Kostas dragged his body to kneel. A wet, bedraggled man pumped Spanos's back to force water out of his mouth. Relieved to see Kostas move, this stranger said, 'I'm exhausted. I'll turn him, you blow air into him.' Without a word, Kostas passed breath after breath into the slack mouth, until a kind voice stirred him.

'Come away. We did our best.'

Distraught now, Kostas stared at Spanos in disbelief, then thumped the lad's chest as he screamed, 'Don't you dare die!' All hope spent, he collapsed over the body.

With his crushing weight warming me there was nowhere else I'd rather be. I kissed him.

At a light touch on his cheek, Kostas whispered, 'He lives.'
In full sun, Kostas lay like a lizard to relish the heat

through his soaked clothes. Then he remembered how his saviour had sped off with Spanos over his shoulder, and his blood ran cold. Soon afterwards, footsteps scrunched towards him. He chose not to rouse, perhaps to delay the bad news.

'My brother sent me to tell you Spanos survived. Just imagine how the women fuss over him! Now, let's get you to them.'

With supreme effort, Kostas grasped the proffered hand. As he tried to stand flames of agony shot up his leg. Unable to bear weight on his foot, Kostas fell, then gagged on the stink of fish, sweat, and black powder as the man hauled him up.

'Argh, that malaca lamed me. Every bone in my foot feels broken. Try again. I need to thank your brother.'

'Then you'll thank the wrong person. Spanos levered your foot free with an oar before the current took him out. Spiros thought he'd hauled his corpse ashore, so it's no surprise that Spanos declares he'll never swim again.'

When Kostas fainted, his bearer dispensed with finesse to drag him along.

Poppi had hoped to complete her ministrations before Kostas regained consciousness; instead, he revived with a jerk of pain.

'Sorry, Kostas, your broken bones rub each other like pebbles in surf. You need more skill than mine. Here, take a *raki* and I'll do my best.'

As Kostas clenched his teeth and looked away, he saw Spanos sprawled on a nearby nest of fishing nets. With a smile of relief, Spanos croaked, 'My drink is warm milk and honey to ease my raw gullet. You stick to *raki*, and when Poppi's finished with you we'll set off for the mill. The monastery hospitalier can set your foot. Apart from bruises, and this dreadful throat, I'm fine.'

Clearly disappointed, Poppi said, 'That means you'll miss the feast.'

Quick as a flash, Kostas demanded, 'Is that why there are no guards here?'

Spiros answered, 'Everyone else is busy with preparations at the church for this evening's celebrations. We intended to join them once we'd set the donkeys to graze. Spanos's gunshot brought us to you. If not for his quick thinking you'd both be dead.'

'But the black powder, why no guards?'

'We fish in the evening, tend crops in the morning, unload donkeys, and maintain a guard overnight. Quite simply, we needed a break.'

Keen for conciliation, Spanos kissed Poppi and shook hands with Spiros. 'He's grateful. We both are. We know we'd be dead without you. Enjoy your Panagia feast this evening.' Shamed, Kostas gave terse thanks, then sat brooding until he reached a decision.

'Spiros, can you help Spanos to get me mounted? We need to leave.'

'Of course. Then, as you say, we should guard the kegs. I'll get the women to bring the feast to us at the store.'

Once out of earshot of everyone else, Kostas turned to Spiros. 'I came to Sisi from Kazanis with a message for Bouboulina. Now I need you to pass it on. Our forces haven't contained the Egyptian bastard Hassan Pasha, he holds the west. Even though our palikers culled six hundred of his bastard troops, we hear he plans to assault Lassithi.'

'Your grain stores will be full, that must be their aim.'

'I fear you're right. We'll place marksmen on narrow mountain passes to keep them at bay. At least I can shoot sitting!'

Unable to keep quiet, Spanos asked, 'Then what?'

'Only God knows. It depends on the force from Egypt.'

Spiros whistled through the gap in his teeth. 'Panagia Mou! What message shall I pass on?'

'Urge Bouboulina to spread the word. We need guns, cannon, and boatloads of men. If Egypt gains control of Crete, even rebels on the mainland will kiss goodbye to hopes of independence. Go back to maintain guard, Spiros. Leave me with the lad.'

As Spiros left, Spanos asked, 'Who's Bouboulina?'

'Unbelievably, she is the brave captain of a fleet of boats that ferries men, guns, and money around the Mediterranean islands. I ask you, how do men stomach that?' Irrationally, Kostas found the lad's wide-eyed amazement annoying, so he snapped, 'What are you up to? We need to go.'

'Sorry, these panniers are still full. Spiros must have overlooked them in the panic of rescuing us. I'll just empty this one to make room for your legs.'

Unused to riding, Kostas jogged and swayed in discomfort, surprised at the way Spanos expertly rode or led his donkey depending on the terrain. They made good progress across the sweep and up the track into the gorge, not speaking for nearly two hours until Kostas said, 'Do we have any water, Spanos? I'm parched.'

'Yes, of course. Give me a minute.'

'Why use the ravine? The track from the coast is easier.'

'The last drover was killed on the open track to that place you mentioned earlier, Milatos. A mounted brigade of janissaries saw his string from a distance and ran them down for sport. It seems the janissaries didn't even realise what he carried, because the load of black powder exploded when they shot the animals. When the news reached Hannis at the mill, he asked me if I wanted to try my hand as drover. I think Petros had told him I was good with donkeys. At the same time, they decided to make the switch from storing kegs in Milatos to Sisi. After Hannis had explained the possible routes, I thought it unlikely Turks would risk horses over these rough boulders. I love the colour and scents of flowers, while songbirds cheer me, and it makes no difference to the donkeys.'

'I'll die of thirst before gangrene bites my foot.'

'Sorry, I can't remember which pannier holds the water. Perhaps I should have taken unloaded beasts. These two are my favourites, so I trust them to get you back quickly. Ah, here's the water. It's not much so drink it all. I'll refill at Selinari spring at the top of the pass.' As he waited for Kostas to empty the water skin, Spanos took a lingering view towards the coast. When he turned back, Kostas was struggling to reach a gun.

'What's the matter, Kostas?'

'High up on the rim of the gorge, do you notice anything?'

'Sorry, I was looking out to sea. I think I glimpsed a boat. Point out where you want me to look.'

'I'm sure I saw a flash, beneath those circling vultures. There, it flashed again. Can you still see a boat?' With his eyes fixed on the ridge, Kostas scanned for movement while Spanos stared out to sea, until they simultaneously shouted, 'There!'

'Damn! If that's the Mediterranean Queen, I'm afraid the flash I saw was sunlight reflecting off a Turk's spyglass.'

'Panagia Mou! Kostas, I know of this. When I lived in the barracks, the men discussed the Mediterranean Queen.'

'Why didn't you tell us?'

'It made no sense.'

'I doubt we can face down God knows how many Turks.'

'What if we block their path to slow them?'

'How? What are you thinking of?'

'At Selinari there is a spring, right where our path emerges from the ravine to join the track to Sisi that Turks will use. This pannier still holds a keg of powder, and my jack has paced this ravine for so long he expects a rest at the spring. I'll give him his head to deliver an explosive surprise.'

Doubtful of success, Kostas reluctantly agreed.

'This fat skein is black match. Do you know it?' With an annoyed shrug, Kostas accepted that Spanos held the initiative. 'It's a slow-burning fuse made from lengths of cotton, saturated with a solution of black powder then dried. Boys steal odd bits to use as firecrackers. Our Petros and his friend were caught throwing some under the refectory table during a Sunday Grace, and were punished by a meal without meat.'

Unable to resist a smile, Kostas skewered the reel of black match on to the long barrel of his prized gun to create a spindle. After Spanos had fixed the free end of the fuse into the keg, he removed his belongings from the lead donkey's pannier. Then, fussing the donkey in farewell, Spanos walked alongside it to make sure the fuse unfurled freely. When the length was spent, Kostas shouted 'Halt!' then used his tinderbox to light the fuse. As Kostas jumped backwards, Spanos slapped the donkey to send him on his way. When the lad sprinted back to Kostas, he found him rubbing his hand.

'Sorry, Kostas, I should have emphasised it gives off plenty of side-spit. Those sparks will certainly spur the donkey! Move up, I'll sit behind you.'

A muffled boom signalled the jack had reached his end. Initially disappointed, they were relieved as an unexpected retort reverberated through the ravine a good minute later to set their ears ringing. Terrified by boulders raining down, the usually placid jenny bolted, ignoring the violent headwind.

Bouboulina's angry face matched the tempest, and her twisted, lank hair snaked out behind her like a mythical Fury as the wind tore away her screamed instructions. Although able to pull an oar as strongly as the eight exhausted men flanking each side of the open vessel, Bouboulina was wrestling with the tiller. Valiantly straining against furious breakers and peering through grey spray, she wasn't confident that she'd actually seen the tiny harbour entrance.

With all her weight against the resistant helm, she gambled on the next surge to shoot her through the gap. Certain there was no second chance, Bouboulina just closed her eyes and trusted God. The difference was immediate. Oars smoothly pushed tons of water, the rudder responded, and she had control. Without constant drenching from beating waves, the oarsmen felt the heat of the sun and slumped forward, spent. Although she shared their fatigue, Bouboulina yelled, 'Don't slack, men, muster for us. I can smell their *raki*! Together now, pull.'

As soon as she judged it safe, Bouboulina leapt to the quayside, passed her bow rope to Spiros, then ran to catch her caique's stern rope. Even before the vessel was secure, the deck hatch opened and her crew formed a chain to pass out wooden crates streaming water. As the first crate hit the wharf, the Sisi men bowled kegs towards the boat where Bouboulina had orchestrated two lines; the first swung crates to shore, and the other lifted kegs on deck. Within minutes, women appeared carrying baskets of food. Gulping *raki*, Bouboulina said, 'Panagia Mou, I never thought to taste this holy water again. What a storm!'

Poppi poured her another. 'We certainly came out in a sweat of fear for you, and now this fickle wind's dropping.'

Spiros overheard the women, and commented, 'The August *meltimi* doesn't usually blow this late in the day.'

Although Bouboulina nodded, she said, 'Tell Kazanis to identify another harbour, I'll not risk this one again. Those waves nearly beat our oars. Only God knows how we missed being smashed on those rocks.'

'Well I thank the Panagia,' said Poppi. 'If it weren't for her feast our boats would have put out, and I shudder to think what would have happened. Excuse me, I'll fetch more food.'

As Poppi turned, she faced the far ridge. 'Oh Panagia Mou, the hills are aflame!' A raging inferno was consuming the pine forest west of Selinari to blanket the mountain with black smoke. At first glance, Spiros thought there was a second seat of fire, then, as his stomach gave a sickening lurch, he realised the nearer smoke line was dust from charging horses.

'Bloody hell, Turks are heading this way.'

With practised discipline, the crew stowed the crates and kegs still on deck, then battened hatches. Women wailed, collected children, and assembled under palm trees, while their men rushed to shoulder arms. As the first Turk hurtled into sight, Spiros swung his gun to take aim. Then he lowered it again and gawped, for he'd never witnessed a galloping donkey.

Kostas yelled, 'Turks are near. Take to your boats.'

Bouboulina recognised Kostas from previous trading missions, and shouted, 'I can't leave the harbour in this headwind. I'm a sitting duck.'

With more confidence than he felt, Spiros called, 'Take the risk. Loosen your sails. This time of day often brings a fierce wind off the mountains. It generate gusts towards the sea, and they help us leave the harbour to fish.'

Tearful women herded excited children on to fishing boats or the caique, so failed to notice Spiros and his brother hug their pa. When the elderly man reached Kostas, he paused to shake his hand, and then continued his brave walk to the store.

'Come aboard, Kostas, before it's too late.'

'No, you set off, Bouboulina. I'll try to get word to Kazanis.'

Spanos ran to the store to return with two fresh donkeys. He hung his bags from a wooden saddle, then reached for Kostas. 'Here, slide across. You don't need to dismount.'

In the harbour, the caique and three tiny fishing boats, now free of their moorings, bobbed aimlessly as the perverse wind ceased. To show good faith, Spiros set his tiny sail, and above the caique's deck men climbed to unfurl their sails, then rushed down to take up their oars. Although Spanos and Kostas had just set off, frantic shouts from Spiros halted them.

'Bouboulina! Wait, I have a message.' From his boat nearest the dock, Spiros flailed his arms in a futile attempt to attract Bouboulina, and sadly made an irresistible target for the first janissaries to reach the harbour.

Instinctively, Kostas urged his donkey under the palms, and expected Spanos to do the same. Instead, the lad dismounted and leapt into the water. Kostas felt his heart lurch. It seemed the stupid lad was going to try to save Spiros. With a surge of relief, Kostas saw Spanos head for the caique. He'd obviously realised he had more chance at sea, and Bouboulina stood ready to haul the swimmer. From his hiding place, Kostas saw the forward party of janissaries range along the harbour, and guessed he'd take at least two bastards before they saw him.

A relieved Kostas saw the Queen move swiftly under the rhythmic dip and rise of her oars, whereas men in the smaller boats paddled desperately with bare hands. In a rush, the janissaries made for the narrow harbour mouth where the Queen would be a sitting target. Kostas broke cover to ride to the opposite eastern side. At the same time, a vast flock of birds, swooping in unison to create dense swirling shapes, distracted Bouboulina. With an instinctive glance towards the mountains to see if there were more, she saw billowing smoke heading towards the coast.

With her faith confirmed she grasped the tiller firmly, then shrieked, 'Thanks be to God! The wind blows, lads. Brace, brace for the wind.' Almost at once, a gust hit the flaccid sheets with a violent crack to shock them taut and thrust the caique forward. A second blast sped the boat almost out of range of the musket volley on the far side, and Kostas was relieved when only one body splashed over the side. In less time than it took their adversaries to reload, two of the small craft, with sails billowing, made out to sea. The third fishing boat became the janissaries' target, and Spiros's boy tried to untangle the sail. He died in seconds, then the frail craft smashed onto rocks. Overwhelmed by frustrated brutes, the petrified screams from the boat were mercifully short-lived. With most craft free and the janissaries out of range, Kostas had just decided it best to flee when he heard, 'Wait! Kostas, please wait! I'm exhausted.'

Astounded to see the sodden Spanos desperately scrabbling up the rocks, Kostas pulled his donkey to a halt. 'My God. Why did you come back?'

'I only swam out to deliver Kazanis's message to Bouboulina.'

'Now I know you're mad Spanos. Get up here. I'll take the coast path to Milatos, it's too treacherous for janissaries to follow on horseback.'

Explosions from the keg store drowned out whatever else Kostas might have said, and the ground shook far more than any earthquake they'd known. Overawed at the old man's courage, neither rider found words to comment.

5

FREEDOM OR DEATH

Poor Kostas suffered distress from his injured foot, while I thanked God for time alone with him.

Although it had been his choice to ride on a hot late-September morning, Kostas cursed his pain. The surgeon at Saint George's Monastery admitted he'd never dealt with such a damaged foot, then prayed for inspiration. As a result he bound the mashed foot in mud soaked bandages, and once they'd set hard he wrapped them in protective goatskins. Frustrated at his lost independence, Kostas had made the wooden crutches now bound to the flank of the last donkey in the string. With a groan he realised it hadn't been a good idea to join Spanos on this trip to deliver black powder to Kardiotissas. Now, after four uncomfortable hours without conversation, Kostas needed to pass water. He felt awkward, so opted for an innocuous, 'You seem to relish the task of drover.'

'I love to be free from the claustrophobic monastery, and have you to myself.'

'There's no need for sarcasm, I'd not choose your company either. I can't make you out. You don't drink, and spend hours practising your aim or on your knees at prayer with the monks – when you're not crying like a girl, of course.'

Spanos adroitly avoided the barbs. 'I'll rest the drove

here in the shade and help you down. Wait, I'll untie your crutches.'

Just as Kostas hobbled out from trees, Spanos emerged from bushes on the far side of the glade. Kostas paused, mesmerised, to watch the lad poke a stray strand of hair under his turban, a gesture that emphasised his long neck. Next, Spanos ran his hands sinuously to smooth his clothes, and then smiled as he spotted Kostas. Unwelcome lust made Kostas angry.

'You've been ages! Help me on this wretched animal.'

A profuse blush flooded the lad's cheeks. 'Sorry, Kostas. Here, take a draught of *raki* for your pain.'

They fell quiet, each wrapped in their own thoughts. Kostas worried that his foot would render him useless. He overlooked the fact that he'd only narrowly escaped death, and complained, 'If I'm lame I'll probably be sent to Marmaketo as an invalid for Zacharias to tend, after he's finished with the other animals.'

'I'm truly sorry, Kostas. I couldn't find another way to release your foot. Panagia Mou! Do you think that revolting smell is from the monastery?'

I never forget the stench of the Faneromenis massacre, Papa. I knew what awfulness to expect.

Alert on a rock ledge above the wooded approach to the smouldering remains of Kardiotissas Monastery, Falcon warily watched two figures on a shared donkey. With dainty, sure footsteps, the first donkey led the drove up the steep path, and by instinctively choosing the shade it dragged its riders through undergrowth and knocked them against rocks. When Falcon heard 'Spanos, control this bloody animal' he flew down from his rocky perch to land nimbly on the path, greeting his comrades with, 'Not quite the password I'd hoped for!'

Any pleasure the pair felt at meeting Falcon evaporated as he shared the dire news that Kardiotissas was a shell. At the monastery's remains, Trichos and his gang were shovelling devastation. A neat line of six charred and broken bodies lay under mulberry trees. With an upwards circling gesture of his hairy hand, Trichos signalled his despair.

Casting sickened eyes over the debris, Kostas asked, 'All monks?'

'Yes. The abbot rescued their precious icon and led the brothers out via the treacherous escape. Three plunged to oblivion. We met ten of them near the plateau and sent them on to Marmaketo to raise the alarm. They told us they'd left six volunteers to hold the bastards off as long as possible. We've one Turk though. What have you done to your leg, Kostas?'

'Our Spanos saw fit to crush my foot.'

If Trichos expected further explanation none came, so he said, 'You two head for Lassithi. Tell Kazanis these Turks lost their zeal after torching the monastery.'

Grimly, Kostas shared his view that the raid would signal that Lassithi was accessible, and predicted that Kazanis would set snipers on passes. With relief, he added, 'At least I can still shoot!'

About to leave, Kostas called, 'Trichos, where's the Turk you caught?'

'Over there, in full sun. I'm enjoying his groans.'

Spanos was off his jack and at the man's side in an instant. It made Kostas's blood boil to see the lad pour water into the wretch's mouth, and then exchange words in his foul tongue. Enraged, Kostas shouted, 'What are you doing, Spanos? For God's sake, come here and...'

Then he stopped, his mouth agape. Spanos shot the man through the temple, then calmly walked back to say, 'These weren't locals. That Turk was with an Arab expeditionary force, so they've no idea the fertile plateau is near. It was sick sport.'

Kostas couldn't believe his eyes. 'Spanos, you shot him, now you're in tears. I'll never understand you!'

We mountain snipers spent the autumn preventing Turks from scaling Lassithi. With modesty, I'll admit to a good tally.

Petros was bored. His excursions between mountain passes used to be exciting. Then, the men wedged in their craggy eyries were pleased to see him, or rather his baskets of tasty fare sent by women. Now he lounged half asleep under a tree until, at his pa's roar, he raced to the kitchen to learn that his errand was to find Spanos and Anna. Certain it was the only way he'd learn about the bloodied stranger in the armchair, Petros ran.

Soon an out of breath Spanos elbowed his way through the crush. Perhaps only Kostas noticed the lad's face blanch at the sight of the visitor. When Kazanis judged enough inquisitive men had squeezed into the kitchen, he boomed, 'You've not shot a fez for weeks, and this wretched Tinker knows why. Now, Tinker, tell them the news before you faint again.'

'The Egyptian bastard, Hassan Pasha, landed in the west, then led sixteen thousand men on a march of destruction to Ierapetra to await reinforcements.'

To quell the immediate clamour, Kazanis bellowed, 'True, they have munitions we only dream of, but we are fired by the quest for freedom.' With a wave of a blood-smeared parchment, Kazanis added, 'Tinker's risked much to bring this message. Read it, Spanos.'

The letter shook in the lad's hand, drawing a caustic comment from Kostas. 'It seems our brave Spanos is queasy over a drop of blood!'

Spittle bubbled at Tinker's lips as he struggled to ask, 'Have we met, lad?'

Without looking up from the letter, Spanos mumbled, 'I've never had coin to buy from a tinker.'

There was no time for further discussion as Anna arrived, and Kazanis warned her, 'That's gunshot in his chest. He came through what's left of Adrianos, and, as you can see, they didn't wait to check if he was friend or foe. Now, Spanos, read.'

'Brothers, heed our plea. Fierce battles near Kritsa forced Hassan Pasha and his mercenaries to retreat. If the bastards had faced us for one more hour, they would now be in Lassithi. Aid us to save your folk, for the bastards will return.

'A brave Queen evaded the Turk's fleet, based at the island fortress of Spinalonga, to deliver powder and arms to our nearest port at Agios Nikolaos. We carried the loads to our munitions cache, and now need help to wield them, so we long to count the palikers of Captain Kazanis among us again. Tinker will lead you to our muster. Godspeed, Alexomanolis.'

In the immediate hush, each man thought first of his family, and then of battle. Spanos split the silence with a shrill cry of 'Freedom or death.' Men took up the refrain until it bounced off the mountains.

The next morning Kazanis stood with his tot of *raki* paused midway to his open mouth. 'Dead? What do you mean, Zacharias? How can Tinker be dead? I've sent runners to rally forces. Women have stirred, baked, and wrapped all night. Across the yard, a workshop full of nimble fingered boys pack shots and quake in fear of not meeting Kostas's high standard. How dare he be dead?'

Those sitting mute around the table wondered who'd venture an opinion. It was Falcon.

'I'll lead. I'll go via Adrianos and pick up more hands. Tinker found to his cost at least one of them has a gun! Then I'll scramble up the far side of the ravine, pass under Kastello Mound, and then head for the klephts' lair at the head of Kritsa Gorge. I'll lay a trail of stone cairns for you all to follow.'

Loath to stir Kazanis further, Zacharias spoke directly to Falcon. 'You'll need to amend that plan. Before Tinker died he told me the klepht camp is empty.' Clatter distracted everyone as Spanos fell from his seat. He gave a swift apology as he righted his stool, then kept his crimson face down as Falcon spoke.

'That alters things. My intended contact was a klepht. Now I suggest we halt at their base, and I'll scout for the rebel lair. Will that do, Kazanis?'

'Yes. Now, listen all. Falcon and I will take thirty men with Spanos to lead the first drove. Kostas, ride beside Spanos with your guns primed. Petros, stay close to them. Each of you around this table will lead a platoon of thirty men, with a drove loaded until the beasts' bellies trail the ground. Zacharias, you guide women, children, and older folk further up the mountains.'

Oh Papa, there was no trace of klepht folk or their livestock. In their absence, more than mice had consumed their stored cheese, rusks, and raki!

Once Falcon was sure the last of his group had made it over the precipice, he crept downhill. Even without Tinker's warning, he knew ill lay ahead as not one dog barked in alarm. Those at the front of the group heeded Kazanis's gestures to fan out, and stealthily make their way forward. Keen for a place at the heart of the action, Kostas showed his frustration when Spanos held the drove back, and said, 'If it's clear, we'll go forward. If not, then we'll save all we carry. The contents of our panniers means life to many, and I've promised Falcon to keep his lanner safe.' On cue, the bird beat its wings against its cage bound to a pannier, startled by the arrival of breathless Petros.

'It's safe, and Pa's happy. He's found a huge barrel of *raki*!'

Klepht meadows filled as platoons arrived to set up camp, and it was near midnight when Trichos slumped on the ground, grateful for a proffered *raki* flask. 'Thank God for miracle water. It's a great camp, Kazanis. Is it near Alexomanolis?'

'Well, Falcon has just returned to answer that question.'

'I've seen hundreds of enemy campfires in the fields below Kritsa. No sign of Alexomanolis, though. The places I searched were deserted. I'll go again in daylight.'

None realised Spanos sat nearby until he spoke. 'Can I go with Falcon? I think we'll find a secret plateau, invisible from Kritsa. It has room to muster and is easy to defend.'

A *raki* fuelled jibe from Kostas rang out. 'Spanos will tell us next that he used to live in Kritsa!'

Kazanis couldn't stomach the way Kostas goaded the lad, so stated, 'I've accepted Spanos is a mystery, and have reason to thank God for it. He goes with Falcon!'

A forward party of six went with Kazanis, including Spanos who led a donkey for Kostas. With additional height advantage, Kostas was the first to see through the trees to the sheer drop below. 'My God! Kazanis, the Christian forces of Crete and beyond are down there.' Where the trees thinned, the group stood in a line to peer down. Only the donkey seemed unimpressed. Kazanis had an awed note in his voice as he turned to Spanos.

'You've done it again, Son! I'm just pleased the guard didn't accompany us for he'd laugh at our wonder. This hole even has a flock to feed a multitude.'

Falcon enjoyed his leader's reaction, and took shared credit to add, 'We'd almost given up when guards stopped us at gunpoint. I admitted we'd no knowledge of the password, so hoped Tinker's letter would act as our pass. Of course, the guards couldn't read the damned thing. Then Spanos astounded me and addressed one of them by name.' Falcon mimicked the lad's high voice. 'I once knew your family, Yannis. Your aunt is Roula, and her youngest grandson another Yannis. Please get word to Alexomanolis that Kazanis awaits.' A galloping horse ended Kazanis's appreciative laugh as Alexomanolis arrived to welcome his guests.

Sitting companionably over a *raki*, Alexomanolis updated his visitors that the last time Hassan Pasha had marched his Egyptians at Kritsa it was after delivering barbaric slaughter through unprotected villages. Alexomanolis explained, 'Our resistance must have amazed them, for they reacted as if our puny force was a multitude. They pulled back to Kalo Chorio to await reinforcements.'

Spanos piped, 'Shame it's not summer. Mosquitoes would see them off!'

With a nod, Alexomanolis turned to Spanos. 'Ah, you know this area. The bastards razed Kroustas to the ground to give them easy access to Kritsa. My intelligence source told me they await cavalry, more infantry, and cannon from Egypt. Sadly, I've heard no more. Where are you from, lad?'

'Sorry, I shouldn't have interrupted. Please carry on.'

'Of course. Come, Kazanis, I'll take you to meet the other captains. We have men from Crete, Greece, and beyond, so our strength totals over 3,000. Best not to think how many Turks and Arabs are against us!'

The next morning, Alexomanolis took Kazanis, Falcon, Spanos, and a mounted Kostas to look down on enemy forces. 'This ridge is virtually invisible to them at this time of day. We've made an exit at the back of our bowl to meet them where the rocks create a funnel below Lato. I wish I knew why they delay, it's hard to contain our force.'

'I'll find out,' volunteered Spanos.

As usual, Kostas was first to cast scorn. 'What a joker you are! Will you just bowl down the street?'

'Yes. I'll adopt their garb and go an hour before dusk.'

Kazanis looked dubious. 'Why take such risk?'

'In the hope I can return with key intelligence, of course. Will you come with me, Falcon? As an ardent falconer I'd be bound to have a slave to tend my lanner.'

Papa, I was scared as I led through Kritsa. I hoped you'd pass by to save me. Kind Falcon ignored my tears.

As the pair walked along dirty, forlorn alleyways, the lanner on Falcon's soiled shoulder was content to digest her crop of food. Most of the abandoned homes they passed had doors that swung on broken hinges or lay in pieces on the ground. Behind one of the few intact doors, a toddler's whine gave scant evidence of inhabitants. At a nearby spring, Spanos washed away his tears, set his fez at a jaunty angle, fluffed out his wide green britches, adjusted the weapons tucked in his cummerbund, and gave Falcon a grin.

'Don't react to anything I say unless I specifically ask. Walk behind as my slave. Oh, and pass me your broken scimitar.'

Kritsa was eerily quiet, and remnants of silk curtains

fluttered like pennants from broken harem windows. Bold Spanos strode downhill to lead Falcon behind deserted Turk homes and down to a forge by the riverbed. All around were makeshift huts, tents, and campfires, surrounded by bedrolls, men, and horses. At the forge, the fetid smell of too many animals and people in close confines threatened to overwhelm Falcon as he followed his 'lord' past a long queue of men and horses. At the first anvil, Spanos's shouted demands were no match for the clang of metal and the steaming hiss of molten ore meeting water. In exasperation, Spanos took a bellows boy by the ear and led him to a relatively quiet area, where he wielded the broken scimitar and spoke as a Turk.

'I want this mended within the hour. Tell your smith.'

Wide white eyes gleamed fearfully from the young dust-blackened face. 'We don't know your tongue, Lord.'

With a wide sweep of his arm, Spanos continued his rant. 'Surely someone here can speak like a human!' When it looked like the boy would run, Spanos caught his wrist and passed it to Falcon, who squeezed, hard. When the boy whimpered, 'If he breaks my wrist I'll earn no bread', Spanos indicated Falcon should increase the boy's pain.

'I'll have my man snap off your hand to feed his bird. How quickly can I have my scimitar?'

'Believe me, Lord, I don't know what you want. We local Turks, speak local.'

An annoyed smith lumbered towards Falcon. 'What's his sin? If he needs a thrash, I'll do it.'

Spanos answered for Falcon. 'I need this mended.'

'You come here in your fancy clothes uttering garbage, and expect Allah to interpret for you. Go to the west field for the Arabs, or the east field for the highborn Turks. Piss off and let the lad work!'

Although certain Falcon wouldn't understand, Spanos barked at him, 'Let the lad go.' When Falcon took the instruction to mean grip tighter, the boy's squeal proved too much for the smith, who snatched him clear and kicked him in the direction of his bellows, all unremarked by the crowd.

With his haughty head high, Spanos stalked off, quickly followed by Falcon, who muttered, 'What was that about?'

'I guessed they'd not understand me and inadvertently let me know where those who might can be found. I wonder if Arabs speak like Turks.' Above them, the first stars pricked the greying sky as the muezzin called and all around fell to their prayers. In panic, Spanos hissed, 'Hide in those bushes. Even the basest Muslim knows how to pray, we risk exposure.'

Sitting close to Spanos, Falcon heard heavy breaths, and realised that, no matter how terrified Spanos was, he wouldn't make such din. Cautiously, Falcon pushed the bushes aside to see dark dragons with great peaked backs, issuing foul plumes of steam from their mouths with each roar.

'Panagia Mou! What evil beasts are these?' As Falcon leant forward to better view the beasts, he knocked the lanner off his shoulder, and she flew up with a loud 'Kak-kak'. Torn between the need to hide and his wish to retrieve the bird, Falcon crept out making a soothing 'Kak-kak'. Too late, Falcon realised his folly.

From nests against the huge beasts, four men rose to walk towards them. Spanos sprang forward, his gun visible. 'Halt! Come closer and we'll kill you!' The men stopped mid-stride, cowered, and spoke unintelligibly. Their movement and cries disturbed the dragons. One broke in half to reveal another steaming head at the end of a long neck. Part of the beast hissed and groaned as it struggled to rise.

'Camels! Falcon, these are camels. I never dreamed to see such creatures. I'll try to calm these men before they bring trouble.' With a great show, Spanos put his gun away as he said, 'No problem, I was mistaken.'

'They don't understand you, Spanos. Let me try.'

Quick thinking Falcon offered his tobacco pouch, and then grinned as anticipation replaced fear on the camel herders' faces. One beast moved towards the group as far as its tether would allow, its hump lolling to one side. With the lanner safely back on Falcon's shoulder, the interlopers took this distraction as a signal to leave.

To Falcon's amazement, the two Christians were invisible in the crowd. He felt fearful though, and kept his eyes down as Spanos wove through the dark maze of resting platoons, wrestling men, roasting meat, bleating sheep, stinking middens, and tents of raucous laughter. On passing hundreds of heavily guarded horses corralled in old sheep pens, Spanos feigned disinterest and walked beyond the noise and stink to approach a solitary round silk tent that glowed like a giant lamp from many dancing wicks within. Like a moth drawn to the flame, Spanos went closer. When the lad halted in front of the guards, Falcon, a dutiful slave, dropped to his knees, grateful to fuss the lanner while he endured Spanos's exchange in the unintelligible tongue.

'Peace be upon you, brothers. Allah be praised, I've found you. I beseech you, tell the esteemed Mohammed Osman that the falconer is here as he requested.'

'And upon you be peace. You seek incorrectly. None with that name rests here.'

'My instructions were precise, and it wouldn't be the first time a high born hid their true station to lower the price.'

'Wait then. It might take a while, I'll not interrupt.'

With a swift cup of his hand to his ear, Spanos signalled to Falcon that he could overhear the conversation within the tent.

'...Now the cannon have arrived by camel, we needn't wait. Spinalonga fortress cries out for cannon, too many infidel boats scurry pass.'

'A bey from Kritsa will bring a guide. He was hard to find

as local cowards with means fled to Megalo Kastro months ago. Low folk, mainly converts, ran to the mountains, frightened of retribution from infidels. Men with heart joined our ranks, although most have never stepped from their village.'

When two men emerged from the darkness, Falcon expected a frightened reaction from Spanos. Instead, the lad stepped aside and continued to pick his nails with a dagger. The man in uniform accepted the guards' salute before he marched into the tent, followed by the scruffy one.

After many flowery greetings, it was obvious that the senior man had settled with refreshments, while shadows on the tent side panel showed the other remained near the door flap by the guard who'd entered on the falconer's behalf. Still picking his nails, Spanos edged forward to listen.

'This filthy wretch is your chosen one?'

'Allah will strike me down if I mislead you, Hassan Pasha. This convert, Omar, knows the area, and has no love for infidels. I'll translate as best I can.'

At the sound of his own dialect, Falcon inched closer to hear the traitor's answers. 'The track you've already identified leads to cobbled steps to Lakonia. From there you'll gain easy access to the barracks at Neapoli, the coast at Elounda, and Spinalonga beyond...'

'...Yes, Lord, there's a track to Lassithi. Once you've gained control of mountain passes, there's a steep track to the coast and the main route to Megalo Kastro. Your only problem will be the saddle between hills nearby. My suggestion is to set Kritsa aflame to divert rebels who will want to rescue their families...'

'...No, cannon carriage will not travel the route to Lakonia...'

'...Ah, a purse of silver, much appreciated. What? Oh, if that is your wish, then of course I'll join your infantry.

This night? As Allah wills, My Lord.'

Before the Judas had finished speaking, Spanos bent to adjust his boots, not looking up as the disgruntled villain walked out. There was a pause while the men inside seemed to assure themselves that their visitor had left before their conversation resumed.

'What a foul oaf. I don't trust him not to double cross us. Put him in the thick of action.'

'We might need to wait a day. Apparently, it's so long since the camels ate that their flabby humps won't bear weight. I've instructed their keepers to feed them all night.'

'It's just a small matter of breaching the hilltop – how hard can that be? We've 5,000 infantry lodged on the plain. Hassan Pasha, will you lead the cavalry?'

'Of course. I suggest you set cannon on that flat area we identified yesterday. You blast a gap in their defences, and I'll sweep through with my 1,000 men. The infantry will follow us to ensure no infidel breathes, and this will guarantee your cannon safe passage. Scourge Kritsa just before dawn the morning after next. Darkness will ensure the conflagration distracts their forces.'

At that point, the lanner fluffed her feathers and called a loud 'Kak-kak', giving the guard inside the tent a cue to speak. 'Excuse me, Lord. A man outside craves audience with Mohammed Osman. He bears a falcon.'

When the tent flap opened, Falcon watched Spanos stand tall, place his blade inside his cummerbund, and greet two armed men. 'Allah be praised, I hope to have found the esteemed Mohammed Osman.'

'Be off, you seek in the wrong quarter.'

'These were my directions.' A third man emerged, clad in a metal studded leather overcoat with his head swathed in an elaborate white silk turban. Bold Spanos bowed, and said, 'Am I greeting Mohammed Osman?'

At a barked 'Don't you recognise Hassan Pasha when he stands before you?' Spanos dropped to prostrate himself in obeisance.

'My Lord, thanks be to Allah that I can claim to have seen your face. I'm not worthy. I'll go.'

'You may stand. Why do you seek this man?'

'I've a lanner he wishes to buy. I must have lost my way.'

'I may be interested in such a bird.'

'Then stop your ears, My Lord, I need to use the heathen tongue. Step forward, Falcon, and don't utter a word. Let the bastard admire your lanner.' As if on cue, the bird spread her wings. Later, when Falcon ruefully recounted the tale of his lost lanner, he expressed admiration for the cool-headed way Spanos played on Arabic passion for falconry.

Once dismissed by Hassan Pasha, the pair dashed through blackness until they were out of danger, where Spanos hunched over to spew. After roughly wiping his mouth, Spanos said, 'I thought our scam over. Thank God Hassan Pasha can speak as a Turk!'

'And knows a prize lanner! Shall we head back?'

'We'll follow this riverbed to the foot of Kritsa Gorge. Best keep to the edge so the oleander gives us cover, no need to take risks.'

They'd not crunched far when Falcon cleared his throat. 'I'm not good with words, Spanos, and I should have said this before. Thank you for what you did for my pa. I dug up the gold coin you buried beneath the stick cross. Wherever did you find it?'

'It was clasped in his hand. I'm so sorry.'

'The first time I visited Kritsa I sent it to Faneromenis. I knew the abbot would see Pa's Napoleon well spent.'

You once told me you were one of them, Papa, and I'm sure you donated gold Napoleons. Where did they come from?

Uncomfortable talking about his generosity, Falcon shrugged and walked on. They'd only trudged a few more steps when Spanos pulled up. 'Return to the camels. The herders trust you. Show them the nearest riverbed, and get them to feed oleander to the camels.'

'Would they fall for it? They might know it is poisonous.'

'And they might not. Someone once told me Napoleon lost horses to oleander in a country called Spain. You'd not get among Turks' horses, so just try with the camels.'

As Kostas hobbled to the plank table set under trees, he was relieved to see Kazanis had Spanos at his elbow. He'd felt sick all the while Spanos was away; now he couldn't bear the way Spanos and Falcon regaled everyone with their clandestine stunt. Kostas had to admit their intelligence was impressive, so wasn't surprised that Alexomanolis raised his glass to them as he summarised, 'So, now we know they have cannon for Spinalonga carried by huge beasts. There's no doubt that the pass at Lato is key to deny them access to the breadbaskets of Laconia and Lassithi. We must seize this opportunity to turn them back.'

A voice, heavily accented from the mainland, stated, 'Just tell me where to place my men. There's twenty of us sworn to freedom or death!' That sentiment echoed around the table before Alexomanolis could continue. Although he hoped the camels would die poisoned, he planned for their advance. He explained how the relatively flat area had many walls, previously used to pen animals, and explained how he wanted to set snipers behind those walls to prevent assembly of the cannon at all costs. For the first time that morning, Kostas spoke.

'I'll lead the snipers.'

Next, Alexomanolis used flasks and cups on the table to illustrate the natural funnel formed by rocks and trees. 'This terrain will make it easier to pick off cavalry. Along each side, we need men with a fair shot who can also face up to a fight. Where the ground allows, use pickaxes to dig trenches either side of the natural funnel. Make them the length of a coffin and twice as wide. If four men work together, two can shoot while the others reload, and as long as they set a good rhythm they won't shoot each other!'

A man stood, saying, 'I know these slopes so I'll lead, and where the ground's too rocky to dig, we'll stack stones for cover.'

'Choose patient men. You must wait until the cavalry is trapped.'

'I understand, Alexomanolis.'

'Good. That leaves our rearguard. We need brutes who can swing an axe and crush skulls to stand the force of oncoming infantry. This is your quarter, Kazanis.'

'Why label me your thug? I'll have to put down my delicate embroidery!' His quip brought so much banter that Alexomanolis had to wait before issuing his next instruction to one of the oldest men present.

'Here's a job for you, Grandpa. Take those too infirm to fight and build a hell's gate of black powder at the crest. If all else fails, detonate to prevent the bastards reaching Laconia.'

Another old timer said, 'What about the plan to set Kritsa aflame? I could slip in tonight and get word that women should take children up the herd path to Kathero. Thank God there's no way horses can use that route.'

'Good thinking! Only the grandmothers, girls, and babies though. Bring the others to join our muster as errand boys and nurses to aid the surgeon. He's set up hospital at the ruined church, and even as we speak he sits with a local deacon, butcher, and blacksmith to await customers.' All fell silent, uncertain of their next move, until Kazanis stood.

'I took the liberty of bringing a *raki* cask. Let's drink to freedom or death!'

Papa, I'd never imagined such horror. I took my place before dawn, when the flaming glow of Kritsa illuminated the Kastello facade above until daylight weakly broke through dismal grey clouds. Slow, torturous hours passed, to bring leaden limbs and sick fear. Hairs on my neck bristled as the roll of drums signalled Turks' advance, and I steadied my gun. Fuelled by hate, I aimed, shot, reloaded, and aimed again. Men shriek inhumanly as they fall. The stench of torn bodies and black powder was dreadful beyond imagination. We stood on the threshold of Hades.

A collective gasp ran along the rebel lines as infantry forces swarmed instead of the expected cannon. Indiscriminate shots while the enemy was out of range set off a cacophony. When the first rank of attackers caught a crop of shots, the Christians cheered until they recognised their impact was no more than a wasp sting. From their allocated position on the left flank, Falcon and Spanos established a steady rhythm to send many to their paradise. One time, while Spanos crouched to reload, Falcon saw camels flanked by artillery men led by officers wearing eye-catching plumes on metal helmets. Sickened, he dropped to shout in the lad's ear, 'Well-fed camels advance. Follow me. We'll pick them off from the side.' They scurried towards a cluster of trees, parallel to a point the beasts would pass.

'How near should we let them get, Falcon?'

'Wait for my shout, then aim for the lead beast. I'll take the second, and we'll both go for the third.' Confident in his partner, Falcon leant on a rock to sight his gun. Before either could shoot, the lead camel roared, reared, and fell. Hardly daring to believe the writhing, screaming mass of camels and artillerymen in front of them, Falcon punched the air.

'It worked, Spanos! They must be ruminants, like goats. They needed time to chew their cud to release the oleander poison. Those artillerymen are vulnerable now. Shoot before they realise our hide.' A spray of blood and bone splinters signalled their accuracy. They'd each managed two shots before the last six artillerymen escaped the wreckage to run towards them, sabres drawn.

'There'll be no time to reload, Spanos. Shoot when you're certain you'll hit a bastard. Then draw your blade and be ruthless. Don't leave this earth cheaply.'

From his position on higher ground, Kostas realised his snipers had virtually wiped out the advance hoard, so signalled the remains of his force down towards the fallen camels. Hampered by fallen bodies and slimy viscera, the Christians screamed like banshees to fuel their downhill rush. Once Falcon saw how this reserve force would overwhelm the remains of the cannon crew, he called, 'Fall back, Spanos. We'll join those awaiting the cavalry.' Above them, Kostas recognised his inability to join the downhill charge, so he despondently limped up to join the entrenched men.

Even grey drizzle didn't smother the rising dust cloud that heralded a thousand mounted Arabs, their height emphasised by tin helmets covered in coiled lengths of silk. Bold surcoats hid wicked curved blades for use if lances didn't tame the foe at arms' length. Soon a wall of horses, clad in bright quilts, enveloped the heap of camels and fallen men, and then advanced several lengths to halt in precise formation.

Falcon whispered, 'Those bastards finished off our advance party. Now they'll race up as if their path isn't strewn with dead rag-heads.' His prophetic words signalled the charge.

Hidden Christians shuddered at enemy screams of

exhilaration and vibrations from drumming hooves. Aware of his own gut churning fear, Falcon encouraged Spanos.

'Hold steady, lad.'

Gunfire signalled the trap sprung. Broken riders died among a melee of flailing equine legs. Their leader, Hassan Pasha, galloped forward unscathed. A few lengths later, he realised his predicament and reined sharply. He screamed for his unhorsed men to fight on, then wheeled his horse around to lead those still mounted back to regroup.

This turmoil gave Christians scant respite before fallen cavalrymen surged towards rebel guns. Those in the closest trenches had no time to reload, so resorted to hand-to-hand combat, a poor match for sabres and armoured shields. Men from the next stretch joined Spanos and Falcon as they raced from their burrows to aid their comrades. All bawled, 'Freedom or death'. Enraged palikers fought like demons to gain the advantage, until a single boom demanded momentary stunned silence. Propelled in a high arc, a cannonball, designed to pierce a ship's hull, hit a rock, then ricocheted into a tight knit group to shatter bodies.

Spanos screamed, 'Kill those at the cannon.' He didn't even check backup followed.

Two injured gunners had assembled enough of one cannon to discharge a random shot. They were frantically stuffing black powder for a second attempt when Spanos and another rebel shot them. When Falcon caught up, he yelled, 'Fall back. The bastards have sent more infantry.'

As the afternoon waned, Alexomanolis climbed rocks to use spyglasses looted from a cadaver. Rebels still held the key slope, littered with ghastly remains. When he realised Hassan Pasha had signalled a full withdrawal, he knew it would take time before the Christian force sensed the benefit.

Among those still embroiled, Falcon had lost his guns so slashed and stabbed with steel. He abandoned his weapon in each new corpse while it twitched, then snatched the blade it no longer needed. Another Turk rushed at Falcon. He heard a whoosh of air as he ducked under a sabre slash. Still low, Falcon swung his current scimitar to sever ligaments at the back of his attacker's knee. Allah ignored the wretch's anguished plea as he crumpled.

With no time to claim a weapon, Falcon took a split second opportunity to tumble along blood sodden ground to bowl his next antagonist over. He sprang up to land a brutal boot on his victim's larynx. Unable to breathe, the stricken Turk clutched his throat, so Falcon kicked the man's exposed soft underbelly to rupture his liver. Without pause, Falcon snatched up a discarded blade to face his next attacker.

A Turk thrust a killer strike at Falcon's chest, but inexplicably dropped his arm before he made contact. Through his confusion Falcon realised that a shot from Spanos had blasted half his attacker's neck away. A dramatic crimson spurt drenched the ground as the brute fell. Falcon managed a quick 'Thanks, Spanos!' as he turned to face his next tormentor. He swung his most recently acquired *yataghan* to slice the arm raised against him. Now another bastard reached for Falcon with a lance. In desperation, Falcon leapt away to slip awkwardly in a bloody pool. His attacker drew his arm for a fatal plunge, and then froze, abject terror written across his face.

Falcon heard a screeched 'Omar! Don't you recognise your sweet cousin?' The coward fled, Spanos at his heels. By the time Falcon caught up, the terrified Turk had backed against a tree.

'Spare me!'

A controlled, calm voice said, 'I've waited over long for this, Omar.' As a merciless silver knife flashed to gouge his eye, Omar's agonised screams blended with the cacophony, just one more death in the chaos. For several heartbeats,

Spanos stared at the sprawled body. Then, with a diabolical shriek, he seized Omar's *yataghan*. Even in the midst of battle, the spray of gristle, hair, and blood revolted Falcon. Oblivious to events around him, Spanos retrieved Omar's fez to plonk it on the grisly head, now impaled on steel. With hysterical screams, Spanos waved his grotesque trophy.

'Omar is dead. I did it for my mama. Ha, ha, Omar is dead.'

Incensed by the gory sight, Turks rushed forward. Falcon fended two away, and yelled, 'Drop it, Spanos. Take up your arms.' Dazed, Spanos turned to meet an attacker. Too slow to parry, he fell from a stab to his stomach.

'Falcon! Take my prize head. Don't let a Turk win it.' Yet another oaf set about Falcon. Too late, Falcon struck at the knife aimed at him, then slipped in a river of blood to lie concussed, an easy target for a sabre. Spanos's last shot hit Falcon's attacker in the temple at close range, sending a fountain of blood and brains over his fallen friend. As Falcon wiped gore from his face, he saw Spanos spin and fall, shot in the flank.

Mathaios sprawled in agony among cannon ball fragments and broken bodies. He stared uncomprehendingly at the tattered remnants of his left hand. Through his torture, some instinct prompted him to clasp the mess with his other hand to stem the pulsing blood. He shuffled uphill until, by some miracle, he fell by a bucket boy who heard his mumbled plea for water. As he reached for the cup, a stray shot hit his upper arm. Mathaios heard his own exclamation of 'God help me' with surprise. Full of hate, he'd not invoked God's mercy for months. Despite this, God sent a saviour. He vaguely recognised her.

'This hell is no place for women.'

'Shush, save your breath.' Like other brawny women,

Roula ran bravely behind the battle line to rescue men who made it that far. At the decrepit church, she ignored the overworked surgeon to rush to the splattered workspace where a butcher and blacksmith delivered 'chop and stop' among carnage that stank worse than a dozen midsummer privies.

When the horror began, Petros had watched other boys for signs of fear, desperate not to show his. Scared witless when shots whizzed close, he'd messed his britches. It no longer mattered. What was a bit of shit when all he could hear, see, taste, and smell was slaughter? Now, without stamina for another step, Petros rested his wooden bucket to sit, hypnotised by the ripple effect on the water caused by constant earth tremors. He'd just realised the persistent smog had an orange tinge to signal dusk when he heard the over familiar plea for water. Insensate to gore, the boy didn't flinch at the mangled mess that was once a hand.

'Use your other hand, Grandpa. Be quick, we're not in the safe area yet.' A startled look struck the man's face as a stray shot sank into his arm, and he fell forward with a tortured 'God help me.' A body collector appeared at just the right time, so Petros wearily picked up his pail and trudged off.

Roula dropped her burden on the grisly bench. 'No need to chop, a bastard's done the job.' God watched over Mathaios, for he was unconscious before the red-hot iron sizzled.

Task complete, the blacksmith instructed, 'Bind the stump loosely. If he makes twenty days that wound won't kill him.'

Roula lifted the unconscious man and gave a hollow laugh. 'Ha! I can't imagine any of us finding out.'

A ragged cleric noticed Roula's search for a berth, so offered, 'Rest him here...Oh, God be praised, it's the pappas!

Can you hear me, Mathaios? I'm your deacon. I'll see if there's any pain relief.' On the deacon's return, he lifted a cup of opiate syrup for Mathaios, and said, 'Once this takes effect you can bless those on the verge of death.'

In panic, Mathaios said, 'I can't. I've lost my faith.'

His deacon gently urged, 'Don't deny men that comfort. I'll help you.'

At the next broken body, the weary surgeon cut blood-drenched blouses away, then jumped back as if scalded. Apoplectic, the surgeon yelled, 'Who brought this girl? Take her out, she can't stay here.'

Perplexed that the surgeon moved on, Falcon strode over to remonstrate. 'Hey, you can't ignore him, he's one of Kazanis's finest...Oh, Panagia Mou!'

Already with his next patient, the surgeon instructed, 'Get that poor maid to the women. They'll wash and shroud her decently. Look, there's Kritsa's deacon, he'll pray for her.' Shocked into obedience, Falcon covered the girl with his mired waistcoat, and reverently carried her out. Totally bemused, he passed his precious load into the care of tutting women. Then, he flew.

An unmistakable roar stopped Petros in his tracks. The appalling events he'd witnessed all day didn't numb him to the fierce hand-to-hand fight in front of him; he knew how quickly men died. His pa faced a giant Moor, who slashed a knife towards his opponent's chin. Kazanis ducked under the thrust and hopped aside. The Moor cleverly reached for a javelin that had stuck in the ground. With the advantage of extended reach, he lunged. Kazanis swiped the point aside with a bellow. As he staunched his slashed hand against his chest, a sinister chortle signalled the Moor's killer strike. Then a wooden bucket flew in from his blindside to shatter his kneecap. This Moor survived through two anguished screams before Kazanis impaled him with his own pole.

'That was a fine throw, Son.'

'Pa, you're hurt. Let me tend you.'

'It's not so bad. I've had worse gouges from a goat horn. Is there any water?'

'Not a dribble, I'll fetch more.'

'No, I'll walk with you. There's another day for battle tomorrow.' Petros was still relishing his pa's arm around his shoulder when Falcon flew at them.

'Kazanis, I've dreadful news of Spanos. Such a terrible wound, and...'

Petros ran.

Mathaios kept enthralled eyes on Rodanthe's beautiful face, and tenderly stroked her bloodied cheek as he thanked his deacon for fetching him to her side. Through tears of anguish and joy, he said, 'Such a gift God has given me. Dear child, what have you been through?'

'I'll leave you to watch over her, Mathaios...Oh, who is this?'

A distressed boy hurtled in and slammed down with an anguished shout, 'Spanos, stay with me!'

Outraged women tried to stop the colossal man who barged through to tower awkwardly above the wretched trio.

'Will he live?'

Without looking up, Rodanthe's papa answered, 'Ah, you must be Kazanis. Your son told me of you. She'll not live. God's gift to me was to kiss her again.'

Petros disagreed. 'Spanos might live, she said my name.'

Resigned to fate, Mathaios shook his head. 'Rodanthe's uttering odd fevered phrases.'

Kazanis gently lifted his son. 'Leave them, this time is special.'

Left alone, Mathaios felt sure Rodanthe heard him. 'Could you not have sent word? Ah, you probably felt it best to stay hidden. You could have no suitor.'

You think me sullied? I'm pure, Papa. I kept my honour and my faith.

'I fell in love with you the moment I saw your rosebud lips. No matter what your nonsense, I always melted at your smile. God will forgive me, he always does, but, my child, can you? I stole your life. If I'd followed your godfather's wishes, you'd have life in front of you.'

With a gasp of disbelief, he heard Rodanthe speak coherently. 'What do you mean, forgive you? I love you, Papa.'

'Too late I understand why pride is the deadly sin from which all others derive. My decision cost your life. An old friend, a wealthy Russian priest, lodged with us when you were born. Like me, he instantly fell in love with you, and stood as your godfather. He gave you an amazing baptismal gift of one hundred gold Napoleons. Of course, I said it was a fortune beyond our needs and suggested three. The saintly man insisted. Oh, how I regret not telling your mama. It felt right to use the money for the benefit of many. I cheated you of life.'

There is Mama full of smiles as she beckons me. Oh Mama, please wait, here is Kostas.

An indignant woman grumbled, 'Yet another man approaches her deathbed. Perhaps she was a favourite whore. His face is like thunder.'

Despite his limp, Kostas towered over the rough berth to rant, 'You evil malaca! Such games you played on my mind. You devil! You imposter, you…'

'Kostas, is it? Rodanthe says your name frequently. I think she heeds us.'

The tirade froze, then came a whispered 'Really?' Standing awkwardly above the comatose figure, Kostas mumbled, 'Um, er, thank you for saving my life, Spanos. I should have said so before. You were brave and quick thinking, and I…' He stared at the sun-tanned face that haunted his nights. Even through blood and grime, it was blatantly obvious. How had he been so blind? Suffocated by overwhelming grief, Kostas dropped to her side.

He stroked her spiky hair, and then tenderly kissed the cherished mouth. 'I love you, Spanos.'

Grateful for this last chance, Mathaios bent to kiss his daughter. 'Goodbye, my precious Rodanthe. I love you.'

KRITSOTOPOULA NOTES

My Cretan odyssey began in 2001 with the purchase of a small house in the backstreets of Kritsa, a village that nestles in the foothills of the Dikti Mountains in the Lassithi Prefecture. Keen to learn more about our new 'home', we toured the village with Hilary Dawson, who still works at local estate agent, Crete Homes, as she shared an insight into local customs and stories, including that of a female rebel named Rodanthe. I remember peering into Rodanthe's long abandoned family home, with its distinctive cross carved into the door lintel, as Hilary shared the history. Despite the many gift shops in Kritsa, and the daily influx of summer visitors, it seemed strange that no written account of Rodanthe's story was available.

In May 2009, a wonderful monument to celebrate the bravery of local rebels in their fight for freedom was unveiled at the battle site where Rodanthe had died. It is near Lato, three kilometres from Kritsa. The English sculptor of the exquisite relief, carved in local stone, is Nigel Ratcliffe, who lives and works in Kritsa. Nigel took inspiration from an epic poem called 'Kritsotopoula (Girl of Kritsa)', published in 1909, by Michael Diallinas from Neapoli, Crete. I'm indebted to Nigel for sharing his translation of this poem to provide me with much finer detail than I could manage, and for his wise feedback and encouragement on my early drafts.

Another Diallinas poem describes the exploits of a rebel leader from Marmaketo, Emmanuel Rovithis, known as Captain Kazanis, and nicknamed Talos for his ability to cover ground at speed. When the early rebellion ended in

1829, Kazanis left Crete to work, and die, on the island of Naxos.

The people of Kritsa are so proud of their special rebel that they named the main road through the village Kritsotopoula Street, and it leads right to her front door! Descendants of Rodanthe's family still live in Kritsa. One of them, Aimilios, provided Nigel with outside space below his butcher's shop to work on the sculpture. This allowed villagers to watch a large chunk of rock slowly become the wonderful sculpture that brings the story to life. Another descendant, Nikos, inherited Rodanthe's house, that now houses a museum enabling local people and visitors alike to learn the village history and the legend of Kritsotopoula.

On the second Sunday in May each year, villagers hold an annual remembrance service dedicated to the memory of Rodanthe and her brave companions at the Lato memorial, with a brass band, prayers from the pappas, and a moving wreath laying ceremony, all followed by *raki* and *mezes*.

It was while I watched Nigel work on his sculpture that I researched more about Rodanthe's life and times, and realised I wanted to tell her story. The many gaps and inconsistencies that I discovered gave plenty of room for my imagination, and I hope Kritsa folk will accept that my tale is a tribute to their legend.

It would be satisfying to have an epilogue that confirmed Rodanthe's death was part of the final battle to gain freedom from Ottoman oppression. However, Crete didn't gain freedom until ninety years after the rest of Greece. A plaque in Chania harbour, Western Crete, eloquently describes their eventual relief – *Turkish Occupation of Crete, 1660 – 1913, 267 Years, 7 Months, 7 Days of Agony.*

Rodanthe, her papa, Kazanis, Kostas, Daskalogiannis, Bouboulina, Alexomanolis, and Lord Byron certainly all contributed to the rebellion, and many of the events I've described are a matter of historical record, but, of course, the way I've portrayed them is fictional.

Remains of pygmy hippopotamus and other fossils are available to see at Giannis Siganos's taverna on Katharo.

With the exception of Megalo Kastro (Large Castle), which is modern day Heraklion, I chose to use place names that are in use today. All monasteries mentioned exist with the names I used, but these days Kardiotissas is signposted Panagia Kera. I wanted to avoid confusion with the wonderful church of that name on the approach to Kritsa.

ACKNOWLEDGEMENTS

I now understand why so many books give thanks to the people who contribute their time and expertise during the development of a story, and I want to acknowledge the huge contribution of my husband Alan, who literally drew blood for Rodanthe! Other people to thank are:

Nigel Ratcliffe, telephone 0030 694884270

Hilary Dawson of www.crete-homes.com

Phil Dawson, an exceptional walk guide, phil72051@hotmail.com

Manolis Farsaris from Moutsounas Cafe at Zenia, on the road to Lassithi, who inspired me with tales of his grandpa, who died aged 106 years, and his sister Maria, who gifted me a copy of *Ροδανθη* (*Rodanthe*) by Aimilios Massaros.

Manolis from Skapanis Taverna, Lassithi, who, when I was searching for information about Kazanis, pointed me to Babis Dermitzakis, hdermi.blogspot.com

Irene and Aristidis from Aristidis Cafe in the centre of Kritsa.

Nikos from 'NIKITAKIS' museum copy, gift and bookshop.

Beryl Darby www.beryldarbybooks.com

Lynne McDonald of Eklektos Books, Elounda www.facebook.com/EklektosBooks?fref=ts

Michelle Bowen, an objective reviewer, who has not been to Crete (yet).

Colin Stratton for information about sailing and winds.

The team at SilverWood Books.

The internet provided a rich source of information, although many sites have duplicate text so giving due credit is difficult. Without doubt, www.explorecrete.com proved my most consistent resource to supplement my visits to various museums in Crete.

Finally, thank you for reading this novel. You can find background information and news of further books at kritsayvonne.com, or you can follow me on Twitter @kritsayvonne, or email me at kritsayvonne@talktalk.net. I'd love to hear from you!

Lightning Source UK Ltd.
Milton Keynes UK
UKOW02f2057181016

285584UK00001B/22/P